# WHEN ANGELS FEAR

POLLY J. MORDANT

Sigilhouse

TO MY DEAR HUSBAND
MALCOLM. MY INSPIRATION.

*WHEN ANGELS FEAR*

## 1

## ESCAPE

Emma swiped away the tears before they had time to form.

She scrawked back her wiry red hair, clipping as much as would go into its usual unruly twist. Though her heart was breaking, this small act of determination somehow lessened the enormity of her leaving. She nearly made it out the door, until the urge to take one final look overwhelmed her. Rays of early morning autumn sun, filtering through the fanlights in the bay window, shed achingly familiar shadows everywhere.

Her home. This was her beautiful home, and she was being forced to leave it.

Hand nervously fingering her pendant, she looked around the room one last time. Emma desperately wanted to take more with her, cram the car with cushions, lamps, the odd side table. But there wasn't time, so it all had to stay.

Still she lingered, eyes resting on her mobile which lay on the table by the sofa. The phone brought on a surge of memories and this time, she couldn't help but cry. She fought an impulse to pick it up and throw it at the wall. No. She'd meant it as a two-fingered goodbye note. It needed to stay. He'd get the message.

Hardening her resolve, focusing only upon the journey ahead, Emma checked through her new denim shoulder bag, splotched now, with stains of tears. She had all she needed for now - purse, a few toiletries and underwear, her work laptop. She could buy the rest later.

With no more delay, she grabbed her car keys and left.

Once outside, she scoured the street for movement. Barely past dawn, it seemed deserted. The cold breeze slapped her face, shocking her with the actuality of her leaving. And made it all the more terrifying. She still could go back …

Twenty minutes later she was heading southbound on the motorway.

Driving through endless ranks of rush-hour lorries, she brooded back and forth over the long mental checklist that had evolved during months of anxious planning.

Her schemes included the little jeep that now carried her into unknown territory. Secretly swapping it with her knackered old Ford had been the act that brought her to the point of no return. If he'd found out what she'd done, the consequences wouldn't bear thinking about. But he who knew everything, had seemingly suspected nothing. She'd parked it in plain sight two doors down, ready for the off.

After an hour of driving, her stomach in constant churn, Emma passed a motorway services sign. No way had she been able to eat before leaving, but as she approached the turn-off, she wondered whether a coffee and a bite would settle her nerves. Though sorely tempted, she drove on. Simply changing a car could not guarantee escape. If he'd twigged, he'd be using it as a longer leash, letting her go so far before reeling her back in. No, she couldn't afford to stop. She needed more miles; needed to check no one followed.

To hell with nerves.

She mirrored for the umpteenth time, changed lanes again, then again; lost herself amidst the heavy commuter traffic.

A good hour passed before she felt able to relax her death-grip on the steering wheel. The easing of rush hour had extended her rear view, making it easier to check for a familiar car. So far, so good.

She turned on the radio. The reception was awful and talk programmes got lost under the carriageway rumble but jabbing the presets eventually landed her on something which suited: soft jazz, amenable and anodyne. Just like she used to be.

Before.

Onwards she drove, eyes darting between the mirror and the road ahead, praying she'd made it.

A city-dweller all her life, Emma had chosen a village destination as refuge. She'd gone for total reinvention, since all her past choices had been disastrous. She wanted to cut herself off and bury herself in the mundane. Not too remote—she worried about phone signals and getting help if she needed it. Let's face it, even a plumbing problem could turn into a crisis. She needed disconnection, not isolation.

Flammark fitted the bill exactly. The parish website boasted shops around a central square, a few cafes, a church, a post office and even a small community library. A further attraction, the craggy heights of Seely Tor, guarded the village.

Emma had been drawn to Flammark's quirky name and, crucially, found a six-month rental opposite the church with the option to extend if necessary. The timing couldn't have been more perfect. Thank God for the internet. Earthviews, street-views and digital maps were all essential tools for the mature runaway.

Apart from safety and shelter, blending in and finding work were top priorities. 'Incomer' nonsense didn't faze her but being too easily identified as a stranger did. The last thing she wanted was to attract unwanted and dangerous attention.

The next burning issue concerned money. She didn't have much in the way of a stash. Thankfully, Flammark's proximity to two much larger centres killed two birds. It acted as a commuter village, sandwiched between Ledbridge to the south, which housed an industrial complex, and Sandmarsh, a small cathedral town twenty miles north. Strangers wouldn't be unusual on its streets, and if no jobs came up locally, there'd be no need to look too far afield to find work.

As far as she could see, there were no significant disadvantages to the place. Nothing to prevent her making an appointment with the estate agents to arrange the let. She'd decent credit references, but so desperate had she been to secure the property, Emma had emailed them about some 'urgent business in Sandmarsh' and how she needed an 'immediate let' and 'would six months cash-rent in advance speed things up?' They'd snapped up the offer, hence her cash flow problems.

Emma arrived mid-afternoon. At first, she found it a bit of a faff to park the jeep, it being market day. She circled the village a few times before finding a space but didn't mind as it orientated her. First impressions? No problems blending in, on this day at least. The market was crowded.

She sat a while, in no hurry to get out of the car, since leaving it meant facing a future that was no longer theoretical. Her accelerator foot ached, though, having been been jammed in the same position for over five hours, so eventually she peeled herself out and stomped out the cramp. Arching her back, she circled her shoulders. Her legs felt unsteady, but she couldn't tell whether it was from the strain of the journey, or relief that she'd arrived. Probably both. She leant on the jeep for a few minutes, hoping her knees wouldn't buckle.

Deep breaths helped. Not only did they calm her, they detected curry, its smell emerging from miasma of mouth-watering odours which came from a convoy of catering vans. God, was she famished!

Soon other senses kicked in as she viewed the tented stalls which lined the cobbled square, stacked high with linens, fruit and veg, books and all sorts. Clothes hung from rails, plant-sales lined pavements and barkers shouted their wares from the back of wagons. Presiding over everything, in the centre of the square, rose a pretty clock tower. Kids were congregating on its steps, shouting, joshing with each other, playing idiot. People haggled, gossiped, laughed all around her. In all her speculations about Flammark, she hadn't imagined it a noisy place.

She couldn't rely on the safety of the car park forever, and it certainly wouldn't feed her, so she joined the throngs to find something to eat. A bad move. Almost immediately they made her head spin, and she began pin-balling about, bumping against shoppers, getting pushed back and stared at. Ears thrumming, she tried for equilibrium but panic set in as she drowned in the sound of her heartbeats.

What a shit show!

Somehow, Emma managed to struggle into an empty side street to lean against a wall. Bent forward, hands on thighs, she waited for the dizziness to go away. She'd made a terrible, terrible mistake coming here. He'd been right all along about her. She was weak and pathetic, and wrong. Stupid to think she could make decent choices and cope on her own.

*Eat, Emma. Eat. You're just hungry. Not thinking straight.*

Her thoughts made her look up. Opposite to where she rested stood a quaint café, revelling in the name *Food for Thought*.

She sighed. Should she go back home or push forward? Both options made her heartsick. But she needn't make that decision now, for another pressed her much more urgently. She needed a wee.

Emma opened the door to the café and entered. Despite the panic attack, she caught herself smiling at a stupidly normal sound: the tinkly overhead bell. Then, somehow, this simple, basic reaction turned into the last straw, as sensual and emotional overload overwhelmed her yet again. She welled up and, head down, stumbled to a seat at the back of the café where she buried her face deep in the folds of a laminated menu.

Fighting sobs with little choking coughs as she fought to control herself in this very public place—so much for blending in—Emma glimpsed a tiny packet of tissues slowly appear from behind the menu, followed by, "Why don't you pop to the loo, dear, and take a moment?"

She peeped over the menu to see the friendly face of a middle-aged woman leaning towards her from the next table. "You look like you've come a long way. Wiped out, too, I should think. I'll order a sweet tea, shall I? For when you get back?"

Overcome by the kindness of the stranger, Emma struggled, "Th-thanks. No ... yes, I—"

"You go along now, dear. The Ladies is just through there."

Following the woman's finger, Emma nodded and made her second escape of the day. After using the loo, she held onto the sink and retched out more tears before blowing her nose and washing her face with a paper towel. Three deep breaths later, she felt ready enough to run the gauntlet of the prying eyes she knew must be waiting for her.

But nobody had seemed to notice anything, or if they had, they weren't looking at her now. There was no sign of the friendly stranger, but a large mug of steaming tea rested on her table instead. She drank it deeply and gratefully.

"What can I get you, today?" a pale and harried-looking young waitress asked as she advanced with a tiny pad, pen to the ready. "The fish is all gone, but we've got everything else."

Emma trialled her voice with small talk before making any monumental decisions. "Busy in here..." she managed, lamely.

"Always the same on market day. They come from all over. It'll be dead tomorrow."

Emma nodded and returned to her new friend, the laminated menu. "I'll try the lasagne, and can I swap this for a large cup of coffee, please, while I'm waiting?"

The tea had revived her enough to relax a bit and take in the easy atmosphere. Not that difficult, now the panic had subsided. White painted walls, a few chocolate-box pictures, some with prices on—local artists perhaps. What's not to like?

The food hit the spot. Emma felt tempted to order cake but decided against it—knowing it to be a malingering tactic and she really should get moving. With a sigh, she waved the waitress over for the bill, paid and with a nod and a thank you, left the cafe.

Emma found the estate agents easily enough. She knew roughly where to find it from the internet. The crowds had eased, so the part of her brain that kicked off earlier decided to behave. She gave her name at the reception desk and the girl smiled and turned her head to loudly announce her arrival to an open door at the back of the office. A tall, suited young man came in from the back with a serious, but welcoming smile, "Miss Blake? Welcome to Flammark. I'm Michael Parker. Please come through. Everything's ready for you."

"Thanks," said Emma. She coughed away the nervous tick in the back of her throat and cursed herself for not making eye contact. He must think she had something to hide. "You said the owner was okay with the arrangement?"

"Absolutely. He didn't take much persuading to make this into a cash transaction. The house has been available for a few months now. It usually goes without much trouble, but not this time for some reason, so the Force is with you! Are you expecting to stay beyond the six months?"

Emma stiffened. Eyes locked-on. "Why?"

"It's just ... I'm sure we'll be able to extend the contract should we need to. Especially if it's on the same cash basis."

"I'll have to see. I don't know what my plans are."

Parker, seeming to sense the iciness that had edged into her voice, got down to business. He produced the lease agreement which Emma pretended to read before signing. She did the deed and paid up a painful amount of money for the rent. Needlessly too, since he'd said there'd been no interest in the property. The first screw-up of her new life. If she didn't get a job soon...

The mini ordeal over, Emma forced a smile. Parker seemed to take it as a cue to indulge in chit-chat. But she would have none of it, so he took her back to reception and handed her what she'd been dreaming of for months.

A new set of keys.

## 2

# CLEARVIEW

Emma rolled up in front of her new home. It had a name.

*Clearview*.

She looked at the simple but substantial two bedroomed stone cottage. Detached and pretty, it didn't quite fit the 'roses around the door' cliché but got near enough. The lawned garden boasted plenty of shrubbery, mingling with the last blooms of autumn. A brass house-plate on one of the double gates declared its name loud and proud. Emma thought it unremarkable and unimaginative, considering its setting. Seeing the house in situ, something more romantic might have been better. A Honeysuckle or Rose Cottage maybe. Heavens, Miss Marple herself might have lived here.

Emma opened the gates and reversed into the driveway. For the second time that day, she got out of the car to examine strange surroundings. This time no crowds, no smells, just the oxygen of a beautiful space. She breathed it in and silently rejoiced. Maybe coming here hadn't been such a stupid idea after all.

Keys to the ready, she unlocked the cottage door. It opened straight into paradise.

Usually, interiors look deceptively large in estate agent literature. Not so in this case. In wonder, she stepped over the threshold to gaze at the low beamed ceiling, wide shelved alcoves, and cute iron-latched doors.

Emma loved the three-seater sofa, shabby-chic and complete with throws and scatter cushions, a long, pine coffee table resting in front. She also liked the over-sized and mismatched comfy chair next to the hearth, with its side-table and pottery lamp. No need to have brought hers with her, after all. The fireplace was open, the chimney breast bricked to the ceiling. Back in the day, it would have sported spits or cauldrons. It had no mantle. Instead, another oak beam had been set into the brickwork. *Clearview* clearly had some age to it. Nineteenth century? Eighteenth?

A door to her right led her into the next room. Smaller but still a considerable size, it had probably been meant as a dining room. Now it contained a large, red leather Chester-field sofa. It sported another fireplace, but this was fronted by a gas fire—the only ugly thing in the cottage so far. She could use the room as her study—she'd never had one before. Emma ran her fingers over the small oak desk in front of the window. She always wondered if she had a book in her. Maybe she'd find out, in a room like this.

From this second sitting room, she stepped through into a simple kitchen that ran the full length of the ground floor—another door at the far end no doubt leading back into the living room. There was a Belfast sink, wooden worktop—upon which rested a coffee maker, kettle, and a big jar of cooking implements. Fitted oak cupboards lined the walls.

The whole place might have been made for her.

A sheet of paper rested on the long refectory table enti-tled, 'Welcome to Clearview.' She glanced over its introduction to the house, appreciating the attempt at hospitality. The landlord had even made sure coffee and tea bags were stocked in a cupboard, biscuits 'in the tin on the side' and 'milk in the fridge.' Nice.

Upstairs, she chose the prettiest of the two bedrooms and switched on its light. Evening had begun to draw in. It was yet another lovely room, but exhaustion had started to take too much toll for Emma to appreciate it fully. Her heart sank as she looked at the bare mattress. She hadn't even thought about bedding. Something else she'll have to fork out for tomorrow. She shrugged off her shoulder bag and emptied its contents onto the bed, taking possession of the house by putting away the tragically few things she'd brought with her.

Being reminded of what she'd left behind, flattened her mood. As Emma closed the drawer of the small dressing table, perfectly centred in front of the chintzy window, an image in its mirror of someone she barely recognised startled her. God, what a bloody mess. Leaning in, she scraped something crusty off her chin which looked a lot like snot, missed the first time from all that crying in the café loo. Horrified, she realised it must have been there when she talked to Michael Parker. Her pale, freckled face seemed whiter in the artificial light, lending her green eyes a dazed sort of transparency. Her hair, having long ago escaped its clip, corkscrewed everywhere. She looked like a spent firework.

Moments later, she dragged herself down to the living room. Looking out of the window, she suddenly understood the reasoning behind the house's name. Clearview. There being no wall at the end of the garden, she could see the small pavement and narrow road that fronted the house. Beyond that lay a green; a great swathe of mown grass at least a hundred and fifty yards square. The structure that stood opposite the cottage and across the space, was according to the internet, Flammark Church. The direct alignment seemed to forge a palpable connection between the two buildings, and the church loured as it rested, now darkly silhouetted, in front of the setting autumn sun.

Absent-mindedly tugging at her pendant, she studied the building. She couldn't make out many features, only that it had no tower or spire, just an odd sort of chimney. What would a church want with a chimney? It seemed to be divided into three sections, one slightly lower than the next —for what purpose she couldn't begin to guess—and their gables were topped off with some sort of decoration. She was too far away to make out any details, but the shape intrigued her. She'd never seen a church like it.

Peering at the round-arched and mullioned windows, she couldn't tell if they were stained or not, since they were inset within the darkened brickwork of the silhouette. From her vantage point, they lay satin-black within the facade, their glassy surface barely perceptible from their brick surrounds. The church had real presence. It drew her in, made her lean forward. Oddly, the more she stared, the larger—no, wait— the *closer* it became. Obviously, some sort of optical illusion. Emma would never claim to be of a superstitious frame of mind—not a magical thinker—but without doubt there was a compelling quality to it.

Emma gave herself an internal shake. She mustn't lose it again, not now.

Crossing her arms, she rubbed them to offset the sudden chill. Having not yet sussed out the central heating, she used the matches left on the hearth to set light to the paper and kindling which peeped out from under the logs in the fireplace. Watching the flames take hold for a while, feeling their incipient warmth, Emma started to relax and ventured into the kitchen to make a mug of coffee.

Once back in the living room, made cosy by the flickering

fire, Emma stared at the church again, almost lost from sight as it gave itself to the night. Drinking from her mug, warmer now, a wave of tiredness enveloped her. Legs still aching from the long drive, she yawned. In the nick of time she managed to place her cup on the coffee table before dropping down on the sofa, returning her gaze to the window; letting the calm in, mulling over the day. Her eyelids began to droop and her head nodded as she relaxed. Dozed. Without any real consciousness of doing so, she lay back, curled up her legs and let the soft cushions embrace her into deep exhausted sleep, whilst the church watched her back.

## DISCOVERY

*E*mma … Emma …

*Not here. He comes back early, just for her, and what thanks does he get for his trouble?*

*He sniffs the air. The place stinks of emptiness.*

*Where is she?*

*A friend? No. Unless she lied, she has no friends anymore. Have you been lying to me, Emma…?*

*He sees her phone. Breaths shortening, he picks it up.*

*Understands.*

*Licking his lips, he relishes the memory of the night he'd found her with it, talking about him to one of those so-called-fucking friends. But he'd shown her. Upstairs, bent over the bed. He feels his erection grow at the thought of it; rubs himself as he remembers the moment when he inserted himself into her for the first time in this way; how he'd put his hand over her mouth as he rode, suppressing her terrified screams.*

*Bitch.*

*Just wait till he finds her. He taught her a lesson once, he'll fuck her senseless again.*

*And again.*

*His nostrils flare as he inhales deeply.*

*Nothing.*

*Head to one side, he listens. Not a scintilla of noise. He tastes the air.*

*Gone.*

## ❦ 4 ❦

### GABBY

Climbing the walls after two nights of insomnia, Emma perched on the sofa, laptop open in search for work. The only proper sleep she'd had since arriving had been on her first night, in front of a roaring fire. She'd woken long after it had died, cold and headachy. Beds not made up, she'd had to huddle under a sofa throw; fretted until dawn.

After a return trip to the village yesterday, having eked out what was left of her savings on basic bed linens, clothes and groceries, she'd come back with little to do but worry. Her mistake had been to think she needed a few days to settle in and calm down. Take stock of her new home. After moving idly from room to room, tweaking cushions and jumping at every sound, she felt more nervy than ever. Even the odd aimless walk didn't help, since she couldn't stop glancing over her shoulder.

Now she faced destitution. Needlessly handing over too much of her stash in advanced rent was stupid. When Michael Parker had told her there had been little interest in the cottage, she could have kicked herself. There was only enough money to last till the end of the month.

Occupation. In every sense of the word, that's what she needed now.

Emma had brought her work laptop with her. There would no doubt be spyware in the one she used at home. She'd found a tracker on the phone he'd given her, the one she'd left for him to find. Though the mobile had been a birthday present, he'd always considered it his, since he made her turn it over to him every night to check her messages and calls. Her stomach lurched at the memory of his what-have-you-got-to-hide expression if she tried to protest.

The memory made her jumpy. For the umpteenth time, she left the sofa and peered out of the window, checking the lock on the front door again before sitting back down.

As he'd had no access to this laptop Emma felt confident about its privacy, and she tapped in the wifi code lifted off the *Welcome to Clearview* sheet before starting a search for local job listings. Nothing around Flammark. She'd have to try Ledbridge or Sandmarsh.

A few hours later definite progress had been made, three employment agencies and a few offices were now in possession of her uploaded CV. Though not particularly confident anything would come of her efforts, at least she'd tried and, more importantly, had been able to forget herself—and him—for a while.

She looked up. Movement outside the window.

That optical illusion again. The church, north facing, dark against the light, appeared nearer than before. And something else. She squinted, leaned forward to be sure. Someone, some woman, stood in front of it, waving urgently. Although Emma knew the church lay a good hundred yards away, she had no doubt the figure waved to her. To Emma.

Trap.

Instantly, her tongue felt like flannel. Hand flying up to her pendant, she struggled to swallow. So soon? How could he have found her so soon? And who had he used to lure her out?

Immediately—how easy it was to fall back—the room began to spin. Emma gripped an arm of the sofa, hyperventilating, trying to control the panic attack growing inside her knotted stomach as she waited for the fist to bang at her door.

But no sound came.

Eventually, panic subsiding, her brain began to work again. It told her the waving woman could have nothing to do with the man she'd left behind. Even if he had found her— God forbid she hadn't covered her tracks well enough—no way could he have procured someone that quickly to help him entice her out of the house. And anyway, why would he? Involving others had never been his style.

Despite the return of common sense, Emma remained rooted to the spot, fixating on the figure, who still waved, still beckoned. The woman might need help! Try as she might she couldn't move, overwhelmed by the primitive part of her brain which told her to stay put.

Then it came. Thudding at the door. Loud, incessant, demanding, so ear-splitting she imagined the whole of Flammark would share her terror. She pressed her hands to her ears, keening at the sound, wanting it to stop and for him to go away.

It did for a few seconds. Then, started again.

"Hello? Are you there?"

Emma held her breath, nonplussed. At the sound of the voice coming through the door, she dropped her hands, though not her anxiety . On high alert, she glanced at the window. The woman wasn't there. Had she run over the green that quickly? In her panic, had Emma momentarily lost track of time?

Seconds passed, then came a few more thuds. "Hello? I can call back later if it isn't convenient?"

Slowly, Emma's brain began to resume normal service. She wiped her sweaty hands down the front of her jeans and managed to get to the door. Before unlocking it she swallowed hard and her wavering voice managed, "Who is it?"

"My name is Gabby, one of your neighbours. I've just popped over to say hello."

Relief flooded over her so violently, she had to take yet another moment. The voice didn't sound upset or in the throes of crisis. Eventually, she fumbled at the lock and opened the door. Facing her was a rag-tag bunch of hand-picked flowers, and behind that, the face of a freckled, middle-aged woman with a large biscuit tin perilously balanced in the palm of her spare hand. But not *the* woman. Not the one waving from the church. No urgency here. Instead a face beaming with smiles, and dimples and friendliness.

And Emma knew her.

"Hello," said the visitor cheerily. She gave a double-take. "Oh! It's you! Remember me? In the café? Well, what a coincidence! Really, really nice to meet you again. I live down the road there, in the end terrace. The vicar said the house had been let. I've been keeping an eye on it for him while it's been empty, so I thought I'd give it a few days before bobbing over with some flowers. You know, for a bit of welcome."

Emma, still in recovery, took a breath to clear her head. She looked over Gabby's shoulder to the dark facade of the church, restored, thank God, to its usual size and quite deserted. "Oh ... Gabby ... so kind of you. I'm Emma."

"Nice to meet you properly, Emma. Can I come in?"

Gabby, clearly having imagined she'd been invited, tripped

slightly over the threshold as she slipped past Emma to enter the cottage. "I'm so sorry about the noise. My hands were full and I couldn't get to the knocker so I had to use my boots. Don't worry, there's no mud or anything on them. It's been a very dry autumn altogether, hasn't it? Oh, dearie, you look really pale. Did I give you a bit of a shock? I'm so sorry if I did."

Gabby's northern accent reminded her of home, its flat vowels a comfort. Only first impressions, but her chatty visitor seemed to have no edge. Friendly. A bit clumsy, maybe, but that felt a comfort too.

Emma still hovered near the open door but tried to make up for her earlier lack of welcome. "A shock? Not really, it just took me a little while to come downstairs. I'd … been taking a nap."

"Good idea, dearie. You looked terrible at the café. I said to myself, Gabby, what that girl needs is rest."

Emma, not quite knowing what else to do, nodded politely at the well-meant insult. Give the church one last quizzical glance, she shut and re-locked the door before following Gabby to the kitchen. A heavy, dank smell emanated from the flowers, triggering a memory of her father, Josiah. Were they dahlias? Her Mum hated them; said they were full of earwigs. Dad's favourite flower, though. He was never allowed them in the house.

Gabby was a fussy thing. A short figure, she bustled about, taking control of the kitchen and although Emma, in another universe, may have objected, in this one she quite liked it. As she watched her visitor's familiarity, rifling through the cupboards for crockery, she'd bet anything Gabby had written the welcome sheet.

"Oh, sorry. You must think I'm really, really rude. It's just that I usually look after the cottage—it was me that did this …"

Gabby pointing at the sheet as she rummaged, paused at Emma's knowing smile. Or maybe it was because she'd only just realized she was encroaching on someone else's space. "Is it all right if I carry on?

"Go ahead." Emma even managed a wider grin. Gabby clearly had inveigling down to a fine art. "Feel free."

After the kettle boiled and sitting at the table, Emma took proper measure of her visitor, now cupping a mug of hot tea in both hands, trying to keep the wayward locks of her shoulder-length, dirty-blond hair out of it.

"So pleased the vicar finally got a tenant," said Gabby. "He doesn't usually have to wait long, but this time was a bit of a stretch."

"Yes, the agent said as much. I didn't know the house belonged to the church."

"Oh, you met Michael, then? Lovely lad. Been here forever. No. It actually belongs to William, that's the vicar. He grew up here and after his parents died, managed to get a curacy in Sandmarsh before becoming priest-in-charge at Flammark. There's a big vicarage at the other side of the church. Well, I say vicarage. It's so bloomin' large they turned it into a training centre for clergy. They hold conferences there and stuff. William's in charge of that too. It didn't make any sense for him to live here."

Gabby must be close to William. Her ample bosom swelled with pride. "He's rushed off his feet, poor lamb. His last curate didn't do so well, and they've never found the right person to replace him." She took another gulp of tea. "So, where have you come from then, dearie? Travelled far?"

"No, not really … have you lived here long?"

"Off and on. I have lots of family here and there and, being on my own, often stay with them. I've known William for ages—and his parents. They passed when he was eighteen; that's when he went in for vicaring. We did wonder if it was the right thing for him to do at the time, but—" Gabby paused for breath while she scratched her armpit, leaving Emma to wonder if she was going to be treated to her landlord's entire life story.

"... but that's by the by. William's having a bit of a time at the moment though, poor love. So much going wrong. One or two of our parishioners have come down with something and the heating's off in the church. Hardly anyone turned up this Sunday. It's never been this bad."

She shook her head, changed the subject. "So, what about you? Are you settling in all right?"

"Yes," Emma lied, then realising she had a lapse in hospitality to make up for, said, "I really like the house."

The two of them continued chatting about this and that, getting friendly. Gabby, obviously an inveterate gossiper, tried her very best to wheedle information. Where did Emma get that pretty pendant? Was she expecting to stay long? Did she have a job lined up? Emma had been out of the habit of social intercourse for too long. She found it utterly exhausting.

Still, it felt good—normal—to have a personal conversation and make a friend, though she couldn't bring herself to be as forthcoming as Gabby might have wanted. Nonetheless, she warmed to her neighbour, and not just because she'd been thoughtful enough to welcome her. She'd rescued Emma in the café, allowed her to find equilibrium in that terrible fight or flight moment, and for this she felt a huge debt of gratitude. Somehow, though she hadn't understood the game, Gabby seemed to know the score.

During a rare lull in the conversation, Emma remembered the frantic waving she saw from the window. "Gabby, is there anything going on in the church at the moment?" Trying not to appear paranoid—to herself as much as anyone—she racked her brain for an example and dug out, "Flower arrangers?"

Gabby thought for a moment. "We do have flower arrangers, part of the W.I., but not today. They're Wednesdays. Cleaners is Thursdays, so no. Why do you ask?"

"Oh, no reason, really. Just thought I saw someone at the church before you ... knocked."

Gabby grinned at the implied tease of her thudding boots. "Did you now? I wonder who that was then? What did they look like?"

"To be honest, I'm not really sure. I got the impression of long dark hair, an ankle-length skirt, maybe a dark overcoat, but she stood too far away so I could be wrong. Definitely in a state, though. She was waving like mad in my direction."

Gabby exclaimed, "Haha, so you weren't napping after all!" Then, a solemn expression clouding her face, she said, "You thought *I* was her, didn't you? No wonder you looked flustered." She fell uncharacteristically quiet. "I don't know anyone who'd be in the church at this time. Could have been a visitor, I suppose, but why would she have been waving over here?"

Out of the blue, her face suddenly becoming more serious, she made a move to go. "I'm sorry, Emma, but I'd best be on my way. I'll pop over to the church on my way back and see what's what, so don't give it another moment's thought. I'm sure it's nothing." But something about Gabby's demeanor told Emma otherwise and by the time they'd got to the door, her hand had started tugging at her necklace again as she anxiously turned its key.

"Very wise, locking up," Gabby remarked. "You never know what's out there do you?"

"No. No, you don't."

Emma waved Gabby on her way, expecting her to walk over the green. But at the end of the path she turned, presumably to go home. Not in that much of a hurry to see 'what's what' then.

Before going back into the cottage, Emma looked towards the church. Peaceful. No one in sight.

It wasn't really cold. Just scarf weather. Was she up to exploring, maybe find the waving stranger for herself? Why the hell not? Time she got a grip.

So, cloaking herself in the cheap jacket she'd bought yesterday, and a thicker skin, Emma left too.

Back in the kitchen, the forgotten bunch of flowers remained on the draining board, waiting for a vase. From the tightly configured petals of one of the blooms, crawled a single black earwig.

In the living room, the dull black eye of the webcam on Emma's 'safe' laptop stared at the empty sofa. It gave a single red blink when the front door banged shut.

Another insect had entered the house.

## 5

# WILLIAM AND JUDE

Gazing back at the cottage from the other side of the green, Emma resolved to get some blinds. She hadn't realised the extent to which the 'clear view' worked both ways. This may be a sleepy village, but she couldn't afford to tempt providence. The last thing she wanted was exposure.

Once next to the church, Emma wondered about the louring, self-important impression it had given the day she arrived. For all its swagger, close-up, she thought it a gentle building.

Josiah, her father, had been very religious. She tried to be enthusiastic about his faith and had borne communion classes with the sort of grace only a bored ten-year-old could muster. Not knowing much about what it meant, she'd taken the first Eucharist and obediently accompanied her parents every Sunday until teenage life got in the way. She grimaced at the recollection of the arguments it caused, when her mum would intervene and tell Josiah to back off. 'Leave her to it, Joe. She'll get there eventually.'

Emma stood awhile, silently reminiscing. As far back as she could remember, she'd always been very taken with her father's name and never called him by anything else. She'd loved how it sounded so archaic—biblical—and it fitted in so well with his spirituality and love of parish life. She sighed. His heart may have been broken when her mum died, but his faith never wavered.

Now here she was, not two feet away from her very own parish church.

She reached out to the stone brickwork, flattening her palm against the wall, connecting with it. Peering upward, from this perspective she could see the curved arches of the unstained triptych window looming overhead, adding a kind of miniature grandeur. The ledges were too high to look inside. If she wanted to see any more, she'd have to go in.

She caught sight of a row of primitive stone carvings, embedded just below the roof-line, spaced every ten feet or so. Intrigued, Emma followed the wall around, seeing if the pattern of faces and creatures continued as she walked. She took in each one: a single bird in flight, a goblin with a giant erect cock, a green man, a huge-breasted mermaid, and more. They guided her way to a long and wide gravel drive which curved from the church entrance for about fifty yards to where it met the Blaxton Road. She crunched her way along it towards a large scaffolded red sign, the gold letters upon which read:

## THE PARISH CHURCH OF ST. JUDE, FLAMMARK, IN THE DIOCESE OF SANDMARSH.

### SUNDAY SERVICE: 9.30am
### EVENSONG THURSDAYS: 7.00pm

## ALL ENQUIRIES TO THE REV. WILLIAM TURNER, VICAR OF THIS PARISH.

St. Jude, the patron saint of lost causes and desperation. How appropriate.

Emma turned to view the picture-postcard church. From her new perspective she realised the chimney she'd seen from the cottage window was not that at all but a sturdy stone arch with an in-built open window housing a bell, its rope hanging down into the interior.

She loved the building: the quirkiness of its carvings, the buried entrance within the ornate stone porch, everything about it. Even the cemetery. Looping around the back of the church, its mostly ancient gravestones were planted hugger-mugger in the midst of overlong grass, guarding the way to a large, imposing red-brick house. The vicarage, she supposed.

Emma felt even more connected to the church now she knew its name. Imbued with a growing sense of belonging, she completed her journey to the entrance feeling much less like an interloper. Josiah would certainly have loved it.

She stood before a large, arched oak door, stained and grooved with age and framed within elaborately carved stonework. She twisted the iron ring-handle to give a testing push. Surprisingly, it opened and

*... she felt a surge of wonder and warmth and comfort and welcome and belonging and she didn't want to leave and everything will be all right and she didn't need to worry any more and she will be safe here and will be protected so she ...*

A loud bang interrupted her reverie, and Emma shook her head and frowned, strangely disorientated. She discovered herself to be at the end of the church aisle, facing a statue. The patron saint, no doubt. Feeling a bit dizzy, a condition not helped by a strong and pervading scent of incense, she took some deep breaths. St. Jude's smelt Catholic. She hadn't learned much from her C of E communion classes, but she knew a denominational boundary when she crashed into one. Maybe she couldn't belong here after all.

Rubbish. She didn't need anyone's permission to visit an open church, Catholic or otherwise. She'd got this far; the Lord wouldn't strike her down because she wanted a quick butcher's around a choir stall.

Except the church had no choir stalls. Instead, neat rows of linked wooden chairs, twelve at a time, lay either side of her. Perched on the seats were colourful, tapestried kneeling cushions, an arty contrast to the plainness of the white-washed walls. Above her she could see a broad archway spanning the entire width of the nave, directing her focus through —what was it called … the chancel?—then through to the apse wherein lay an old carved table, clothed with a pristine white cotton runner, a plain wooden cross in the centre. The altar.

Moving a few steps back, now able to take in the church's three-stage composition from the inside, Emma did not get a sense of separate parts, just a gradual narrowing of the focus towards the altar. She understood the architecture now; how each section related to each other. Impressive.

Her eye was drawn to the triptych window which looked even more over-sized from the inside. Peering through its thick, ancient glass, she saw with some discomfort, how it back-dropped the interior of the nave with a view of her very own cottage. And its blindless windows. She really did have to do something about that!

She jumped at the sound of another loud bang. Then another. Unable to quite work out where they came from, Emma tilted her head, echo-locating. The noises were hardly conducive to prayerful meditation—not that she'd gone there for that purpose, though, if tortured, she might have said it'd crossed her mind. She jumped at a metallic clatter and her fingers moved to the comfort of her pendant, pulling it out from beneath her scarf. Building work, perhaps? Unlikely. It seemed to come from under the church.

Emma took it as a sign. To leave. She headed back towards the oak door. The shelves of hymnals and prayer books puzzled her, having not noticed them on the way in. Come to think of it, she couldn't remember entering the church in the first place. What the hell was wrong with her?

"Bloody thing..."

The sound of shuffling feet prefaced the appearance of a man in grubby blue overalls gradually emerging from a hole in the floor next to a staircase, far too busy swearing to notice he'd got company.

"Damned Bishop..." On finally seeing Emma, he stopped dead and grinned, shamefaced. The dog collar beneath the overalls gave away his identity. This could only be William Turner, her landlord, and priest of this parish.

"Oh, sorry! Pardon my French and the verbal abuse of a much-venerated fellow Christian. Welcome to St. Jude's! I'm afraid repairs are underway so we're a bit at sixes and sevens. Not strictly open for visitors."

"I'm sorry," Emma replied. "I've come over from the cottage—your cottage, I believe. I had the urge to explore."

"You're my new tenant? Emma, is it?"

The smile that grew on her face in response to this easy familiarity, suddenly froze, and instead of responding like any normal person, tears welled in her eyes. Her guard had been up for so long, she'd forgotten how to act naturally. Especially with a man.

Much too long after his question, she managed to reply, "Yes ... Emma."

He looked away; a possible acknowledgement that he'd picked up her agitation. Then he turned very kind brown eyes back to her and said, "Nice to meet you Emma, and welcome to Flammark. We hope you'll stay with us for a long time." He rubbed an oily mark on his forehead with even oilier fingers, making it a lot worse. He stared at his palms ruefully. "I'd shake your hand but—"

Emma's smile darted back for an instant. Nervously pushing her wiry hair behind her ears, she said, "It's very nice to meet you." Then, tongue-tied, blurted, "… but I have to go."

"No, wait, hang on." With the air of a man trying to find the right words he said, "I've an apology to make. I'm sorry. I should have come over to say hello and give you a proper welcome. I know Gabby visited, though, so I haven't felt too guilty. I hope you're settling in okay?"

"Erm … yes. Yes, I am. The cottage is nice. I like your church too."

"Thank you. Unfortunately, the church doesn't like me very much at the moment. The damned heating's broken down. Wouldn't you know, just as the weather's getting colder!"

"Gabby did mention it." Relaxing a little, she continued, "She also said your congregation had come down with something too. Sounds like bad luck."

"Bad luck, my are. Sorry, language again. I've been banging on to HQ in Sandmarsh for ages. Well, the bloomin' Bish'll have to shell out for a new boiler now, that's for sure. I've been having a go at it myself actually, but it's beyond me."

He moved towards the door, and asked nonchalantly, "Fancy a coffee?"

Surprised by the sudden invitation, Emma's instinct was to refuse. But despite herself, she liked him—liked a priest who could swear. He'd be safe enough, being a vicar and all that. And let's face it, she could do with some practice at being normal. "Thanks. I do actually. What do I call you? Vicar? Father?"

"Good God, no." He smiled. "I'm sorry, I should have introduced myself properly. My friends call me Will—except Gabby for some unknown reason. She always uses the full moniker."

Will locked the heavy door behind him and they left the church.

Emma asked, " What's with the gargoyles?"

Will looked bemused, then his face cleared as he saw her pointing at the carvings below the roofline. "Ah, you mean the corbels. They're not gargoyles. They're part of the structure that supports the roof. No one really knows exactly how they came about—not even the experts that occasionally descend upon us. All they can attest to is their pagan origins."

"I think they're interesting."

"Yeah. Churches like ours are uncommon and attract quite a lot of tourists. Some of the corbels are self-explanatory, like the green man, but others are just plain mystifying. God knows what a booby mermaid represented."

He turned to face the studded oak door. "And these are even ruder." He pointed to the embellished stone at the entrance, to what at first sight seemed to be an intricate web of roots and branches carved around the entire edge of the door frame. About two feet wide all round, the stone undulated and wove itself into mesmerising shapes. Looking more carefully, Emma could make out a tapestry of fauns and antlers and human faces, some with their tongues hanging out. Bare-breasted women, trapped within roots, were leered at by goblins with penises huge and erect.

She took a sudden step back.

"Shocked?" said the priest. "A lot of people are, you know."

"No … not really. I'm not prudish or anything like that." But Emma *was* shocked. She couldn't help but take the carvings personally, stunned for a moment by the notion she was just part of a long, long timeline of abuse and subjugation, and it made her feel … insignificant.

"They call it Romanesque. The carvings and corbels, et cetera. St. Judes was built in the 11th century by the Normans but there's evidence of even earlier worship here. Flammark and Sandmarsh are full of pagan burial sites, for example. All this," he waved his hands generally around the edges of the door, "was a way of exploiting the more … earthy traditions of our pre-christian ancestors."

"You mean they were lured in," said Emma

Will grinned. "Exactly."

He led her away and continued his tourist-guide chatter. It took Emma's mind off her reaction to the carvings and allowed her to take stock of her companion. A few inches taller, Will was wiry—athletic, even—with good, dark hair and very strong features. Maybe older than herself by a few years, so, mid-thirties? He walked with his head bowed slightly to reduce the height between them. It felt comfortable, diminishing her earlier awkwardness.

As they neared the vicarage, Emma remembered what Gabby had to say about it. A big affair, she'd suggested. Used for training purposes. But the scale of the enterprise surprised her. Though only two storeys high, it had the proportions of a small country manor, with no less than three chimneys and a series of mullioned windows around which huge swathes of ivy had been neatly cut. A gravel drive replaced what once must have been a huge garden, now reduced to two flower beds, either side of the porch. Full of dahlias.

"Wow," said Emma as they stepped on the path leading to the door. "This is some place!"

"It certainly is," Will grinned, sheepishly. "So big, in fact, the army commandeered it as a cottage hospital during both wars. The diocese once thought about letting it go, but we hold training sessions here and often use it as a retreat. It keeps me busy."

"I'm impressed, considering the church is ..." Emma became stuck for words. She didn't want to cause offence.

"Comparatively small." Will helped her out. "It's to do with the family that used to own the village. They wanted something substantial for their younger male offspring—the ones that wouldn't inherit. Church life provided a useful option, but they lived too well for it ever to be a humble endeavour. Size mattered." He chuckled. "Fortuitous for us, as it turned out. Churches like St. Judes are fast becoming historical treasures—I've already mentioned tourists—and the Bish likes it when we get conference bookings for historians and such like. We're quite the thing nowadays. I've even been on the telly!"

He let them into to a large glass porch, its windowsills covered with leggy geraniums and perspex racks of visitor guides, then unlocked a wide, red-painted front door. "Here we are, then," Will said. He pointed to a large old carver chair in the hall. "You can pop your things on there. They'll be safe enough, we've no bookings at the moment."

"Nice place," said Emma, looking around the panelled hallway.

"Yeah, it is. I've been here for about ten years now, but you know, to be honest, I prefer the old place—your cottage. Sometimes I wish..." he trailed off as he led her into a large kitchen and gestured for her to sit at its table.

"You wish...?"

"Oh, nothing. Ignore me. I'm a bit fed up, what with the heating going wrong, and—"

"The bug?"

"Bug?"

"The mystery illness affecting your congregation!"

"Ah yes, that. Gabby must have told you." He fell silent.

Less tense, and able for once to think about someone other than herself, Emma picked up on his preoccupation. Although cheerful enough, and performing his current pastoral duty admirably, under the surface there seemed a bleakness about Will, an elsewhereness.

Perhaps sensing her scrutiny, he said, "God, I'm not exactly being great company, am I?" He let out a sigh then gave a little shrug before changing the subject. "Tell me, how do you like Flammark?"

He was very easy to talk to. Emma actually chatted! She told him how much she liked the village and the cottage, about her job-hunting and meeting Gabby. But she made no mention of the waving woman, due in part to her neighbour's odd reaction. She didn't want to risk souring the mood.

Will made good coffee, and they had a second cup. After a moment's thought and completely out of the blue he said, "Robbie Mason needs a receptionist."

"Who?"

"Robbie Mason, our doctor. He's had a few temps, but none of them appear to be good enough." Adopting a deep timbre to his voice Will enunciated, "'Flibbertigibbets.'" He laughed. "That's what Robbie calls 'em. It seems they're all too young or too inexperienced or—well actually, let's leave it at too young. No empathy, apparently, especially with older patients." He paused then hastily added, "Not that you're old or anything—"

Emma, happy to pull him out of the hole he'd started to dig, said, "That sounds perfect. Except - I'm not exactly sure how long I'll be here. Definitely for the next six months. I ... I've a lot that needs to be ... sorted out."

He didn't pry. "I'll talk to Robbie and let you know, shall I?"

The phone rang. It struck Emma how long it had been since she'd heard the sound of an old telephone. She mentioned it when he returned.

"Sometimes we lose signal. No real reason as the mobile network's strong in these parts. I know it's down if the land-line rings."

"Is everything okay? You look worried."

"It was Connie Chater—she's been coming to St. Judes long before I started here. Her husband Sam's come down with the dreaded lurgy. She thinks he picked something up at the church last Sunday, probably because the heating's down."

The phone rang again. As Will stepped into the hall to take it, Emma rummaged in her bag to check the signal on her new pay-as-you-go phone. She didn't remember seeing a landline at the cottage and couldn't afford to be without the means to call for help.

Five bars, full signal. Strange.

Will returned in some agitation. "That's another gone."

"Do you know what's making them sick?"

"Well, that's the thing. There're at least ten people I know of who've been afflicted. No temperature or fever, just a kind of creeping fatigue. Like a sleeping sickness. It's keeping them inside. Robbie's stumped." As if in sympathy, Will scratched the back of his head, the faraway look back. Then, as if he'd made up his mind about something, he said. "I'm worried about you now, Emma. The last thing I want is for you to come down with it too. After all, you've only just arrived. We can't have you being ill."

She was just about to tell him about the signal on her mobile, when the phone rang again.

"Sorry, Emma, that might be another one."

"Don't worry about me, you answer it." She could see little point in lingering just to tell him her phone worked! "I'll see myself out. Thanks for the coffee."

She went with him to the hall and gathered her things before letting herself out. He gave her a smile and a parting wave before exclaiming down the mouthpiece he held, "Oh, I'm so sorry to hear that. I hope she gets better soon."

## ❧ 6 ❧
### WATCHING

The computer alerts him.

He sloughs off his clothes and sits naked in front of the laptop, rapt in what's on the screen, basking in his cleverness.

*There she is.*

*Thought you'd escaped? That I wouldn't find you ... that I couldn't spike your laptop? Silly girl. You took me to your office once, remember?*

*Tch, tch, tch. How many times have I told you to tape over the camera lens? You never know who might be watching.*

*How long should I wait before coming to get you? How long to weigh the pleasure of watching you, against the desire to catch you, hold you ...*

*... in the flesh.*

His hand moves to his cock while he watches her look down then back at him, down and back, as she hunts and pecks at the keyboard and reviews her work on the screen.

*Hunt, peck, review.*

*Hunt, peck.*

*Hunt ...*

*Getting into rhythm, he licks his lips; imagines her smell, her taste.*

*What he is going to do to her.*

*Something has caught her eye. She disappears from view. He hears nothing, then the microphone picks up a thudding noise. Someone at the door? Yes. Then talking.*

*Unable to listen and wank at the same time, he rests his hand and concentrates. Strains to hear.*

*Nothing.*

*The conversation fades; moves somewhere else.*

*He waits. And waits. He is a very patient man.*

*The talking gets louder, then there's a thud. The door again. More silence.*

*Gone.*

*But he is not disappointed. Or angry. He has compensation.*

*He closes the camera down, replaces his view of the back of a shitty sofa with a new file.*

*Her slideshow. His secret pictures of her sleeping, dressing.*

*That night, over the bed.*

*He sits back, spreads out his legs, and puts his hand to work again.*

## ❧ 7 ❧

## TROUBLE

**A**fter lunch a few days later, Will arrived at Emma's door, carrying more dahlias and looking terrible. His eyes were darker, sunken even, as if he hadn't slept, and a knot played in his forehead, a frown he couldn't lift.

Abject in apology, stumbling over his words, he said, "I am so s-sorry about the other day, not being ... being able to finish our conversation. The phone ... it barely stopped after you left."

Emma invited him in, shushing and muttering about it not being a big deal. They went through into the kitchen and she fussed a thank-you over the flowers, putting water in the sink for them. Later, when he'd left, they would go in the bin. She'd spotted the foul earwigs in the first bunch Gabby had picked—obviously from the flower beds in front of the vicarage—and didn't want any more visitations. She made coffee, found biscuits and sat with him at the table.

"You know," Will said, looking around wistfully, "I'd forgotten how peaceful this place is. It'll always be home for me. I really miss it."

"Yes, it's very quiet. I've taken quite a while to get used to the silence, but I think it's growing on me."

"You haven't lived in the countryside before." More of an observation than a question from Will as sipped his drink.

"No, not really. I'm a city girl."

"Why the change, then?"

"Oh, no reason. Well, yes there is a reason but—"

"It's okay, Emma," Will smiled. "I think I've picked up that there's something in your past, but it's your business. I'm here if you ever want to talk about it."

"I'll bear that in mind. Maybe one day I'll take you up on the offer." She smiled back, enjoying the easy relaxation she felt when talking to this man.

"I've come to let you know that Robbie Mason's up for it, if you are. You know, the receptionist job? He'll be available after surgery finishes this afternoon, around four-ish? I'm pretty sure it's yours if you want it. You look ... old and capable enough."

Emma smirked at the tease, remembering their conversation in the church. Will fell quiet, looking preoccupied again. Something else bothered him. Maybe there was another reason behind his visit. He seemed in the mood to talk—sometimes strangers had that effect—but he wasn't there yet.

"What's wrong, Will?"

No answer.

She resorted to teasing him back. "Not managed to fix the boiler?"

He gave a snort, then blurted, "It isn't just the boiler. Things have been going wrong for months."

"Things?"

"It doesn't matter, really. I only came over to apologise and let you know about the job. You've probably got enough problems without dealing with mine."

Emma didn't believe him for one minute. They both knew he had nothing to apologise for. He'd come over for another reason. Whatever was on his mind needed to come out.

She repeated, "Don't be silly. Tell me."

"I've been going over it all, and I can't help but think that everything started when young Abigail Chater disappeared."

"Abigail Chater? Wait, is she related to—" Emma tried to remember the conversation in the vicarage, "Connie?"

"Yeah. Connie is Abby's grandmother."

"And she disappeared? Did she run away?"

"We don't know. She was—is—a troubled girl. It's what the village called her—Trouble. Abigail's mother, Josie, hasn't had an easy time of it since her husband, Jim, died. That was about two years ago now. Not only did she have to cope with losing him she had to raise a difficult teenager. Without her father around, well, Abby went off the rails. She disappeared on her eighteenth birthday."

"What did the police say?"

"That's the problem." Will's frown deepened. "Having turned eighteen, she'd become an adult. They said to leave it a few days to see if she'd turn up. She didn't, but the police still dragged their feet. After some half-hearted enquiries, they decided there weren't enough resources to take the case further. Said there'd been no suspicious circumstances and she was old enough to make up her own mind about whether she wanted to stay or leave. To be honest, I think her reputation went before her—there'd been a few cautions. Petty pilfering, that sort of thing. Bottom line? They didn't want to know."

"But you don't think she went of her own accord?"

"No, I do not. I get that she was a problem - but less so in recent months. Abigail thought the world of Josie and Connie and I'm positive she wouldn't want them to worry about her.

Besides, she'd just got a place on a hairdressing course, and the salon in Flammark said they'd take her on as a junior. We all thought she'd got herself sorted."

"So," Emma said, refilling their cups, "what's this got to do with the church?"

Will let out a huge sigh. "I don't know. Nothing seems to have gone right since."

"Specifically?"

He fell silent again. Emma could wait.

"A few weeks after she disappeared, the Chaters started to get anonymous letters, really nasty stuff about Abby and her dad. They suggested that ... that all wasn't as it should have been between them."

Emma felt her chest tighten. She pushed her hair back and quietly cleared her throat, trying to ignore the thrumming in her ears. As usual in times of stress, her hand moved to the necklace Josiah had given her and an image of him floated into her mind, seeing her through the conversation, allowing her to throw some encouraging nods towards Will. His reply had hit too close to home for her to manage much more. There seemed to be no respite from the appetites of men. Even here.

"The notes stopped after a while. The police were interested at first, asked a few half-hearted questions, but couldn't find any real evidence that linked them to the disappearance. They put it down to native spite and that was that."

Emma swallowed, fixed her face in a way she hoped looked supportive.

"I spoke to the inspector in charge but talk about bloody useless! He just said they were making the usual enquiries, and they would let us know of any developments."

"And did they?"

"No. Josie tried to make some headway but was easily

fobbed off. That damned inspector—Holbrooke, I think he was called—intimidated the hell out of her. I went to the station with her a few times but got no joy either."

"Well, it doesn't sound right to me," Emma eventually managed, the noise in her ears easing. "Even adult disappearances merit some sort of investigation."

Will nodded his agreement, but she sensed more was to come.

"Then?"

He shook his head, his reluctance to continue, palpable.

"Go on, Will."

Like an expulsion, it came out. "Then the altar was desecrated."

"Desecrated?"

"Don't get me wrong, not like in the movies. Nothing ... Dennis Wheatley. No blood sacrifices or goat skulls or upside-down crosses—no chickens. Someone just came in and pissed over the altar cloth. But the stink really got to me. Knew what it was as soon as I entered the church. Utterly, utterly gross. Antithetical." He wrinkled his nose and shivered. "Though it happened nearly two months ago, the stench went bone deep. I'm sure it's gone, but it's stuck in my head and the reek's there every time I enter the church."

Emma thought back to her visit to St. Jude's. "I noticed the incense the other day. I just assumed that's how Catholics like their churches to smell."

"Good God, Emma! St. Jude's isn't Catholic!" The extremity of his indignation seemed to amuse him, and he laughed despite himself. "No, we occasionally use incense but not loads. It's the best mask against that smell I could think of, and seems appropriate. I expected some of the congregation to complain but I've had nothing so far."

He continued his story. "Thing is, he—definitely a bloke,

the mechanics of doing it, and all that—left another note, just like with the Chaters, same handwriting."

Fumbling in his jacket pocket, Will took out a crumpled, yellow-stained scrap of paper, placed in a small plastic wallet not much larger. He put it on the table with a flattening motion, allowing three words to emerge through its grubby transparency.

## I AM COME

Emma puzzled at it. "What does *that* mean?"

"God knows. I let Connie see it—didn't like bothering Josie—and she said it looked exactly like the others, same scratchy handwriting, as if it had been done with a quill and ink. I showed it to the police, but could I get them to display one iota of interest? Could I buggery! Weren't interested in forensics or anything like that. It was like they had a script: Abigail had left of her own accord and the notes weren't connected to her disappearance. The culprit had simply moved on to the church and would probably lose interest, like he'd done with the Chaters."

Will let out another exasperated sigh, as he stared down at the note. "It's turned into a damned obsession. Carry this blasted thing with me everywhere."

After a while Emma said, "And then this ... sleeping sickness began?"

"I'm not sure exactly when that started, but Robbie says some patients have been off work for months with it. It's definitely escalating. Only about twenty managed to get to church yesterday. This is a God-fearing village, Emma. The church is usually full."

"But *you* can't sleep, can you?"

Will threw her an amused look. "Does is show that badly?" Then his expression changed, became more quizzical.

"But ... funny you should say that. You're right. I'm lucky if I get a few hours kip. I'm absolutely exhausted." He breathed out yet another sigh. "But, you know, coming here to my old home, and talking to you, has been just the thing. I feel so much better." This rang true. Will's eyes had definitely lost some of their haunted look, and his knotty frown had eased.

They struck a companionable silence. How disparate their situations were! Her visit to St. Jude's had imbued her with a sense of safety and comfort; a feeling that forward movement might be possible. The weekend had been restful, in stark contrast to her first days at the cottage. On the other hand, inexplicable and awful events seemed to be plaguing Will. She'd only met him twice, but enough to sense his vulnerability. The burning question: could she afford the energy to get involved?

Life couldn't be put on hold forever. Hadn't this been what she'd hoped for? Something that would move her on, offer connection and relationship? It hadn't been a full week since she'd arrived, yet already she'd stopped listening for footsteps on the path and scanning the landscape every time she opened her door. Maybe she could afford to engage with Will's problems. Then Emma realized why. She could help because she wasn't the locus of the issues he faced, therefore —and it pained her to think it—she wasn't the victim.

Father William Turner was a troubled soul, and although Emma didn't know him that well his air of quiet desperation felt all too familiar. And it was liberating to feel of some use.

She knew exactly what to say next.

"I'm going to see Dr. Mason and have a chat about this job. Why don't you go into the second sitting room? I'm turning it into a study. Have a nap on the Chesterfield? There are a few throws on it and you can always put the gas fire on. If you're still asleep when I get back, I won't be able to disturb you when I come in. You can stay for tea if you like. I may be living here for now, but this is your home, after all. You obviously really need the rest."

Will stared at her, open-mouthed. Before giving him any chance to refuse she stepped into the living room, hastily gathered her things and left him to it.

## ❧ 8 ❧

## MASON

Driving away from Clearview, Emma mulled over Will's story. The last few weeks had obviously taken their toll on the priest. Why had the police been so complacent? The link between the note left on the altar and those sent to Josie Chater seemed crystal bloody clear to her, why not to them? The plod had got it wrong.

And what about this ... sleeping sickness? Strange. She was about to be interviewed by Flammark's own doctor, Robbie Mason. Perhaps she'd be able to find out more, assuming she got the job.

With time on her hands Emma drove the scenic route to the village centre, up to the Flammark Road, circling back towards Seely Tor, the large craggy hill which overlooked everything. It had a small carpark adjacent to an obvious viewing point. Leaving the jeep, she zipped her jacket against a sudden blast of cold, before strolling about the plateau. At its centre rested a huge Celtic cross. Signs of old offerings drew her in: straw crosses and dollies, long dead posies tied with string. She lingered there awhile before stepping onto the flat expanse of stone—granite probably—which acted as a huge viewing promontory. Stony outcrops grew out from the sides, smoothed over the centuries by the bottoms of countless individuals who, like her had been drawn to sit and ponder the view.

A breeze added to the chill, but Emma welcomed its freshness after being cooped up all weekend. She found a sheltered spot on which to perch, hoping the rural perspective would add meaning to her own.

Flammark was certainly a looker: a chocolate-box village right out of a fairy tale. Skirted by woods, at its apex stood St. Jude's from where the high street meandered down, on its way spurring random avenues of cottages and romantic terraces.

Absent-mindedly playing with her pendant, running her fingers around its gold setting, Emma gazed down at the places she'd yet to visit: a tiny park where dots of children now played on doll-sized swings and roundabouts; a village hall next to a school; and The Flammark Arms, once a coach house according to her internet research, now pink-washed and pretty for the tourist trade. People—maybe greeting, gossiping and going about their business—moved as pinpoints under the red and gold poplars that punctuated the square and surrounding shops. Having taken her fill, Emma raised her head and looked further, beyond Flammark to the Downs and, in the very far distance, the faint spire of Sandmarsh Cathedral, threading upwards through the faraway autumn mist, a needle in the clouds.

Breathing in the beauty and letting the vista fill and sustain her, Emma rested; moved her view inwards. Slowly, she visualized the locked box which lurked in the deepest recess of her mind: always there, never forgotten. Not to be opened under any circumstances, it contained the very worst memories of the past year, recollections to be locked away forever. Only with its help could she acknowledge what happened and maybe some day accept her past. So long as they were locked away, this single act of mindfulness meant she didn't need to relive the details as she had before the box was conceived. Day after day.

Refusing to think his name lest the casket be breached and its horrific contents come gorging out, Emma bowed her head, contemplating the single word that epitomised the deepest wound of all. Victim. Above everything he'd put her through, the rules, the mercurial moods and petty revenges —even that terrible, terrible week that she'd buried in the box's deepest corner—all were nothing compared to being this. Victimhood defines, and no matter how much she wanted to refuse its label, she would never be able to deny the emotional scars he left her with. Only manage them. Joining in the echoes of the many women who came before her and of those yet to come, Emma invoked the terrible clichéd lament: how could she possibly have let it all happen?

She may be safe, for now, but the bastard had still won; had stolen her home, her friends one by one, her job and the life she loved. She'd been the one to run away, who'd had to sacrifice everything to be free of him.

She sat a while, the box, tight-closed and darkly nested in the depths of her primitive brain, and allowed her thoughts to stray in tune with the sights and sounds of the autumnal landscape, resting a short while, in the cradle of normality.

After leaving Seely Tor, Emma took afternoon tea at *Food for Thought*, after which she revisited the scene of her earlier debacle—the loo—to freshen up ready for her interview. An elderly couple at the next table had saved her seat and as she returned to it, her heart sank a little as she saw Gabby, near the entrance, thick as thieves with the waitress. She didn't want to turn up late to the surgery.

"Yoo-hoo!" Gabby called, making a beeline for her table, giving Emma no time to use the cloak of invisibility afforded by her old mate, the laminated menu. "Oh, you're not leaving, are you? I've just finished work and popped in for a bite. We could have had a chin-wag."

"There'll be another time, Gabby. I didn't know you worked in Flammark."

"I'm at the community centre. We've got a lot going on. It's a library, advice centre, information point, everything. The council nearly closed us down to save money. Volunteers have to run it now." She paused for breath and sat down. "Just three days a week but it keeps me out of trouble. If you're interested, I could put a word in."

"Actually, I'm on my way to Dr. Mason's. He needs a receptionist. Will arranged an interview."

Gabby grew quiet and her face took on that serious look she had at the end of their conversation in the cottage. Like she had two personalities: one extrovert and chatty—a typical gossip—the other, somehow more centred. Astute. "Has he now?" she nodded, sagely. "Well good for him—and good for you."

Then, ebullience restored, Gabby said, "I think you and Robbie'll get on like a house on fire. He's a bit of a gruff-bucket but his heart's in the right place." Gabby looked round and leaned in conspiratorially. "You know, his wife died about two years ago and he's been in a bit of a mess ever since." Tapping her index finger on her temple, she continued, "Nearly had a breakdown. If it hadn't been for William he'd have gone under for sure." Gabby flared her nostrils as she inhaled and nodded knowingly at the weight of the information she'd just imparted.

Though the inside-info on the doctor might come in

useful, receiving it made Emma feel a bit awkward. Though not yet in his employ, it felt … unprofessional. "Gabby, honestly, I'd love to carry on chatting, but I really do have to go." Glancing at the clock above the counter, she continued, "I don't want to be late. The surgery's on the Flammark Road isn't it?"

"Yes, turn right out of the village. He's in a big Victorian villa on the left. Car park's in front, you can't miss it, it's the only house of its kind around here. I've told him, Robbie, it's far too big and ugly. Tried to get him to move somewhere smaller and away from all the memories but will he have it? No, he won't."

Emma gave a token smile and nodded as she moved with deliberate strides towards the till.  After paying, she turned to wave goodbye and genuinely grinned as she saw Gabby sitting down now deep in conversation with someone else, a full cake-stand already in front of her.

It was barely more than half-past three, but the evening had already begun to gather in. The square's mock-Victorian street lighting, more for charm than illumination, couldn't mitigate the gloom. The clock-tower loomed eerily upward, its face already lit, but no kids congregated beneath it now. The temperature had plummeted.

Emma easily found the surgery. As the jeep neared, she recognised the old house from Gabby's description, and turned in. Its austere proportions dominated the scene as she parked the car, an ugly profile standing out against the darkening sky. The only clue to its purpose, a brass plate, had been carefully inset onto the wall, swathes of thick ivy cut away from it. The surgery opening hours had been stamped into it with such permanence they looked as if they hadn't changed in years.

Checking her watch, Emma walked beneath the leaded glass lantern hanging within a large stone portico. She admired the wide, red-painted door and ran her fingers over its stained-glass insets, a poignant reminder of the fanlights above the windows in her old living room. She twisted the round brass handle and the door opened to reveal a beautiful, chequered tiled floor. The reception area must once have been a large hallway. Today, chairs were placed around two of the walls and a huge battered oak coffee table took centre stage, strewn untidily with sundry magazines and papers. One rug-lined corner contained a set of shelves on which children's books and toys jumbled together. A wide, roped-off staircase stood to the right. No doubt leading to the doctor's living quarters.

She took in the reception desk which was really nothing more than a large oak-panelled counter—pretty much everything seemed oversized here—behind which lay a computer, various notepads and an empty chair. She smiled to herself; the latest 'flibbertigibbet' must have gone home. Her voice, gently echoing, called, "Hello? Anyone here? Dr. Mason?"

No answer.

Two doors lay to her left. One, fully open, clearly led to a clinical area. Light and bright, fluorescent strips still on, it housed a large weighing scale, blood-pressure machine and the usual health warnings about smoking, alcohol and how to notice a stroke when you see one. She heard stirrings behind the second door labelled 'Dr. Robert Mason' upon which she duly knocked.

She hadn't known what to expect, but it certainly wasn't the cross, bear-like man who opened the door. "The surgery is closed, madam. I can't see anyone now, so I'd be grateful if you could make an appointment ..." he looked over Emma's shoulder and to the empty reception desk. Tutting and shaking his head, he sighed loudly and continued, "...tomorrow."

Will told her the doctor had a short fuse, but she didn't

think she'd be on its receiving end so soon. Large, red-bearded, with horn-rimmed, round spectacles, Mason looked stressed and tether-ended. But for all his gruffness she sensed a kind man within—no danger here—so managing a smile she said, "Dr. Mason, very pleased to meet you. My name is Emma Blake, William Turner said tha—"

The scowl on his face softened, "Ah, you're the lass renting Willy's cottage! Come in, come in! I was expecting you but completely forgot. I'm too buried in all this damnable paperwork."

Emma was still at 'Willy'. She was going to enjoy his Scottish lilt and the verbal eccentricities—to her ear—that went with it.

He let the door hang open so she could follow him into his office. Where she beheld utter chaos. A large bookshelf lined the wall behind his desk, groaning with the weight of piles and piles of precariously balanced, vertically stacked books, their spines leaning this way and that. An old open laptop, grinding and overdriving itself to death, sat on a desk covered in files and prescription pads and various pens. Apart from three empty chairs, the only other clear surface was a beautiful, leather-covered, pitch-pine examination table.

The doctor watched the horrified look on her face as she surveyed the room, whilst motioning her to sit on one of the chairs.

"I know, I know. But I'd forgotten you were coming, and it isn't usually like this." Then he sighed again. "Actually, that's a barefaced lie. Left to my own devices, it's only slightly better than this. Apparently, I am a piler, not a filer and I've obviously been expecting more than my recent receptionists can manage in a day's work. My wi… someone else used to organise everything—but that's a different story."

He paused and slumped down in his chair. "I'm in a mess, Miss Blake. No two ways about it. I can't get the help, and things have got worse over the last few months. I'm an irritable old bastard and this place doesn't suit any of the children the agency seems impelled to send me. I'm getting desperate!"

"So I see." Emma replied, looking around again. "I'm up for the challenge, if you'll have me!"

Mason tried, but obviously failed to hide a smile. He rummaged around in a fruitless search for a blank piece of paper. "Well we ought to go through some semblance of an interview, don't you think?" He gave up looking and sat back, all pretence of being prepared, gone.

"Is it all right if I call you Emma?"

She nodded.

"Okay. What brings you to Flammark then ... Emma?"

She kept it as vague as possible. "I used to work in HR for a big firm up north. Times being hard, they had to let me go. I needed a change, to ... cut some ties." She tried to hold his gaze but failed. Words were defeating her.

As if she'd taken some sort of truth serum she continued, "I really liked the look of Flammark. If I'm honest, though, it was just a pin in a map. I wish I could tell you more but ... can't." What was she saying!? Not only had she managed to reveal more than she wanted to, she was coming over as an irresponsible nitwit. Pathetic. Stupid, stupid, stupid!

The doctor studied her, his perceptive blue eyes seeming to see right through her. Apparently unfazed by her awkward silence, he asked, "Are you used to office work?"

Emma decided not to elucidate on her previous role, since it would over-qualify her for the current position. Instead she talked in general terms about organising abilities, her understanding of what reception duties entailed and of being a 'people-person'. Not a word of a lie, any of it. "I have my CV here, if you'd like to see it?"

Mason leant over the desk to take it. He gave it a cursory glance and said, "Excellent. Can you start right away?"

"Is that it? I mean—is that all? I'm happy to wait while you follow up on references."

"Ach, I know a worker when I see one, Emma, and you've come recommended by Willy. I'll have to make formal enquiries for the record, of course, but for now, that's more than enough for me. And to be honest, I wasn't joking when I said I was a desperate man. Let's see how we go, eh? Barring reports of any criminal tendencies, the job is here for as long as you need it—" He paused before continuing, "—or until whatever problem you're running away from goes away."

Really? Had she been that transparent?

"My current receptionist— and I use that word in the loosest possible sense—is on a rolling contract which, as I have told her more times than I can remember, may be cancelled at any time of my choosing. I am minded to choose now. Right now." He glanced at the huge grandfather clock in the corner of the room. "The agency doesn't close until five-thirty so your first task will be to ring them before you leave. Let them know their services are no longer required and from immediate effect." He wrote the number down on a scrap of paper. Emma noted with some amusement that he knew it by heart.

As she stepped back into the reception area to use the phone behind the counter, she grinned at hearing a gruff voice call from his office. "And I'll see you at eight-thirty sharp tomorrow morning. Sharp mind!"

## ❊ 9 ❊

## COMING, READY OR NOT

S omething.
    *A silent signal.*
    *Eyelids flick open.*

*Naked amidst a pile of her torn clothes and underwear, he remembers the excitement of destruction. How he exulted in it. How he would tear her to bits too.*

*Changing focus, he looks at the clock ticking away the seconds.*

*5am.*

*He feels a pull to stay, but it's a trivial urge and easily overcome. His wait is over, her time is up. He needs to pack and go.*

*He'll find a hole to hide in.*

*Far enough away from her to escape discovery, but close enough to watch her.*

*Whenever he chose.*

## ❧ 10 ❧

## COLD

The weather had turned. At eight o'clock that morning, the ice, ingrained into the very seams of the car, left Emma no choice but to use warm water to infiltrate the locks.

Why the hell didn't she buy de-icer when she had the chance? She couldn't afford to be late; she'd only had the job a few days. Damn, it would be ten minutes before she could safely set off and in this weather the roads would be hellish.

Once the jeep started she left the engine to do its thing and ran back into the house. She gathered up her shoulder bag and wound a thick scarf around her neck. Thank God for employment. It'd allowed her to use her depleted savings to beef up her wardrobe ready for winter. She really was coming out of herself. The parka she'd bought was a bright cherry red and it clashed beautifully with her hair.

After taking one final check round, she rushed out of the door and banged it shut. The mortice lock was sluggish. It took an age to turn the key.

Job done, she turned to make for the car. Instead she stood stock still on the doorstep.

The waving figure was back.

Taking shallow breaths, ears thrumming, Emma stared at it. This time the woman no longer stood in front of the church but *in the middle of the green*. Closer, her agitated waving seemed more urgent than ever and even more obviously aimed at Emma.

No way could this be an optical illusion, but, weirdly, despite the increased proximity, the woman's features remained as indistinct as ever. A black coat over a long skirt was still the only firm impression Emma managed to glean from the blurry visitation.

Torn between leaving and confronting the figure, Emma slid over the icy ground to pull open the defrosted passenger door. She threw in her handbag, slammed the door shut and whirled around, ready to run towards the desperate woman.

But no one was there.

Only the blank normality of St. Jude's faced her, silhouetted in the brightening morning, the frantic figure replaced by the dissipating fog of the car's exhaust.

Astonished, panting—peering—Emma stood stock still. But with the clock ticking, and with a new job to get to, she had little choice but to tear away her gaze and climb into the idling car.

How she made it to work on time turned out to be another mystery. The doctor had already unlocked the front door, so Emma hurried straight in, arriving as the grandfather clock in his office chimed the half hour. By the time he descended the stairs a few seconds later, she'd shrugged her coat to the floor and was giving a passable impression of being long settled behind the large counter.

"Good morning, Emma," said Mason. "Inauspicious weather. Are you ready for action?"

Trying to conceal much needed deep breaths, she replied, "Yep, as always, doctor."

"Right, lass. I think we know each other well enough for you to start calling me Robbie. You'd be one of the privileged few, mind."

Gabby had been right. Emma and the doctor—Robbie— were getting along very well. She liked him a lot. His outward severity and rough manner didn't put her off in the slightest. On the contrary, he made her feel safe, in the same way Josiah had.

The morning offered little challenge. No sickly hordes beat their way to her desk and, shoving the earlier exasperating events to the back of her mind, she fell into an easy rhythm, organising her workspace and putting files in order. Though the surgery had been quiet during her first days on the job, she'd busked her way through well enough, using gaps in patient arrivals to familiarise herself with the doctor's routines.

"It still hasn't picked up," Emma remarked. "Are there other doctors in Flammark?"

"Not in the village," he replied, "and I've asked around elsewhere. My colleagues are all busy as usual. It does surprise me. It's usually pretty manic at this time of the year, what with flu jabs and so on. The first cold snap brings people out in force. There has been something going around, so maybe my patients all still in bed." Though he made light of the situation, Emma could sense his words had a serious edge.

"The dreaded sleeping sickness?"

Robbie raised questioning eyebrows at her.

"Will told me about it. A few people have been missing services."

"Ach, well, I wouldn't call it a sleeping sickness. It's obviously an infection, but I'm unwilling to prescribe antibiotics till I know what we're up against. I've sent blood samples away for tests."

Blood samples? Sounded serious, and she'd be on hand to find out what was causing it all. No point in pushing it further, she said, "If it's still quiet this afternoon, I'll finish tidying up your office, if you like?"

As if all his Christmases had come at once, Robbie beamed. "With the greatest of pleasure."

Emma worked late. Driving home, she recalled that, being a Thursday, there'd be an Evensong at St. Jude's. Did she feel up to going?

She hadn't forgotten the deep sense of comfort she felt on first setting foot inside. Maybe she *would* like to attend a service. Perhaps the time had come to pick up from where she'd left off, when teenage angst and rebellion had made going to church an inconceivably uncool thing to do.

She hadn't seen Will since he'd visited her at the cottage. There'd been no sign of him on her return from the interview, though his grateful thankyou note told her he had taken up the offer of the Chesterfield. She wanted to know if it—she—had made a difference, and whether the rest had made him feel better.

All things considered she might as well dip a toe in holy waters again. Josiah would certainly approve. She liked it that thinking about St. Jude's strengthened her connection with her father—and her mum. Yes. She would definitely go.

Flickering strands of light danced before her as Emma entered the church. At the far end, in the apse, two candelabra had joined the wooden cross on the white altar cloth. More candles, in motley shapes and sizes, were arranged on the windowsills in the nave. Shadows on the whitewashed walls, played and danced to the chilly draughts left unmitigated by the broken boiler Will had been unable to fix.

Only five other hardy souls had braved the cold and were blanketed in the same sort of heavy clothing she herself wore —though definitely not as bright. They sat on the front-row chairs which had been unlinked and arranged into an informal semi-circle. On one of them sat Gabby, huddled in her mac, and next to her, the serious-faced estate agent, Michael Parker. Will, of course, and, surprisingly, Robbie. Gabby had told her Will had helped the doctor through the loss of his wife. He must have kept the faith.

The only person she didn't recognise was a dark-haired woman, possibly in her mid-forties, but maybe younger. The moving grimace she wore sent worry lines back and forth across her face. She turned away as Emma drew near.

Will did look a lot brighter. Coming forward to greet her, he took her hand in both of his and quietly mouthed, "Thank you ..." making it plain that he had stayed at the cottage to take up her offer of a nap. She smiled in response and with a vague gesture to the redundant light fixture above, mouthed back, "Why so dark?"

"Wiring," he whispered, with a roll of his eyes. Smiling, he led her to the small ensemble.

He broke the silence with a quiet introduction. "Emma. You are most welcome. I know you've met Michael and Gabby, and Robbie, of course. Let me introduce you to Mrs Chater—Josie."

This had to be the mother of the missing teenager, Abigail. Josie's pain was an extra presence all on its own. Emma couldn't imagine being in her shoes. The not-knowing.

Nodding Emma towards a spare chair near Josie, Will took his seat at the edge of the informal gathering. Part of it yet, somehow, apart from it. Tentatively, she also sat. Having never been to an Evensong before, taking her cue from the others, Emma guessed the right thing to do next was simply close her eyes.

She embraced the quiet. Breathed slowly. Exhaled the day's activity, one fret at a time. In its place, she inhaled the after-scent of incense, which grounded herself in the moment. In. Out. Allowed the deeply chilled, shadowy atmosphere to wrap tendrils of comfort around her.

She listened to Will's quiet words.

"We come together tonight in the peace of the Lord while we take this quiet moment to reflect upon the day, our tasks within it, and the people we have met."

She thought about Gabby. The intelligent look behind the gossipy exterior. *As if she were two different people.*

Then Robbie Mason, the stern Scot, the heartbroken man.

"We ask that we remember to bring your love into all our hearts, that we may offer comfort to others and, in our turn, be comforted ourselves..."

And she thought of the beckoning woman.

"A reading from Second Corinthians, Chapter One ..."

Who could she be? What did she want?

"*...And our hope for you is firm, because we know that just as you share in our sufferings, so also you share in our comfort...*"

The candlelight continued its dance on the walls, as if in response to the words of the priest, throwing ever taller shadows. Wilder they grew as freezing draughts increased in tandem with the bite of the strengthening wind outside. Will's words faded out as Emma watched the flickering candlelight, mesmerized by the shadows they spawned, black offspring of the tiny flames. They danced as they climbed, creeping ever upwards, looming above the tiny congregation.

Transfixed at the shadow-show, her stomach lurched as she watched the dark configurations morph into two discernible shapes. A narrow man and the shorter, curvier figure of a woman, both lewdly swaying, separating and joining, again and again. The scene towered above them, larger than life, perceptible as sin. The shadow man in aroused nakedness undulated behind the female shade, its arms dancing, arcing, drawing her into him. Or he into her.

Emma's bile rose and a scream pierced their prayers. Will stopped, mid-sentence. Then came another shriek, and another, echoing and bouncing off the walls, sounds so tortured they could hardly be borne.

Will sprang up and ran towards Emma. The shapes were still at it, why wouldn't they stop? On and on they danced, paralysing her, freezing her to the spot. There could be no doubt about the identity of the shadow man and his consort. The awful parody of a now unlocked memory would burn in her forever.

Blind panic transfixed her. Suffocating in the horror of what she saw, Emma turned to Will. He'd make them go away, wouldn't he?

But the priest had not gone to her, because to her utter, utter amazement, she had not made the noise.

The screams had come from Josie Chater.

## ❦ II ❧

## THE CHATERS

Will knelt before Josie, who, still screaming, stared fixedly at the walls—though as far as Emma could make out, the weaving shadows had retreated to their usual harmless flicker. He wore a stricken look as he tried to find the matter of it and help. Emma, momentarily incapable of rational thought, had barely enough wherewithal to make way for the doctor.

It took several minutes before Robbie could calm Josie's hysteria. Loud sobs racked her shaking body, as she gulped and choked in the freezing air. She called out her vanished daughter's name, over and over again. "Abby! Abby ..." Adding to the aftermath of Emma's own traumatic vision, the sounds of Josie's scalding grief made her skin crawl.

She looked on in stunned silence, unconsciously digging out her pendant from beneath her scarf, gripping and tugging at it for comfort. She knew what the shadows meant to her, but what horror had exposed itself to Josie?

Emma glanced at Gabby and Michael. Their expressions were unfathomable. Neither had moved from their seats as they watched the strange tableau: doctor, priest and sobbing woman.

"Emma. Emma!" Robbie shouted. "Lend us a hand, will you? I need to get Josie home and put to bed. Can you come with us?"

"Of ... of course," she replied. Pulling herself together, she leapt to Josie's side and gently held her arm, joining Robbie's efforts to get her to stand.

"Are *you* alright?" He said over Josie's head, his voice laced with concern.

"Yes, yes, fine," she lied. "Just a bit shocked."

"Aye. Isn't everyone! Well, we'd best be gone quickly. Out of the cold."

Slowly, they led Josie out of the church. Just before they got to the door, Gabby stole up to Emma from behind and grabbed her free arm, whispered in her ear. "This is more than just hysteria. We know you saw something too. We need to talk." What the hell? Emma stared blankly at her as they left the church, but she had no time to linger, only to get Josie into Robbie's car.

Soon they were off, his patient quiet now, staring ahead. Emma used the silence to try and process what happened. Because she didn't have a clue where to start. The shadows had performed a dumbshow of an event buried deep inside the lockbox in her mind. Having escaped, it would only torment her again if she couldn't put it back. But what—how —could this have happened? Her febrile imagination at work; activated by the stress of the past few weeks? But she'd been feeling better. And *Josie* had seen something too. This was a whole new ballpark of madness. On top of everything that haunted her, the last thing she expected was to be treated to some kind of ... what? Dual manifestation?

More questions assailed her as she remembered Gabby's words. *We know you saw something too. We need to talk.* What the hell was she on about? Was she and Michael connected in some weird way? And what could they possibly want to talk about?

Josie cut through her thoughts. "She's dead, in't she?"

Emma turned to her, asked gently, "Abigail?"

"Yeah," Josie whispered, "My Abby. I don't know how he did it. But he did it, alright. My Jim. I've seen it now. It was my Jim who killed her."

"Josie, what do you mean? What did you see?"

"I saw him with his hands around her neck. That's why she's gone. He's killed her."

Her eyes welled up again and she began to keen. Emma could do little more than take Josie's hand and squeeze it. No point in asking any more questions, her distress was too awful.

Soon Robbie turned off the main road. From what little could be made out in the dim yellow light of the streetlamps, rows of tightly packed, identically constructed dwellings suggested they were in a council estate. A few moments later they'd drawn up outside a small, semi-detached house.

"Best if I drop her off with her mother," said Robbie. "She's in no condition to go home."

They managed to get Josie out of the car and half-carried her to the door, pausing only to allow the doctor to get his bag from the boot. Vaguely, Emma supposed he must always have it with him. Connie answered after a few poundings from Robbie and looked frightened to death when she saw the state of her daughter.

"Goodness. Goodness me. Whatever's to do? What's happened, Josie?"

"She'll be all right, Connie," said Robbie, his voice clear and reassuring. "She's got a bit overwrought in the church. What with Jim's death and now Abby's disappearance, it's all been too much for her. She needs to get to bed. Will you lead on?"

"Of course!" Connie fussed ahead and left them to find their own way in. Shutting the door behind her, Emma let the stuffy warmth of the house envelop her as the others made their way up the narrow staircase.

She couldn't stop shivering. Beyond cold, Emma knew the shock of the shadow-show had set in, and though holding on to the puny hall radiator, she craved the comfort of a proper fire, which she could see burning, luring her in through the open door to the living room. Not thinking Connie would mind, she went in and slumped in the chair in front of the gas heater. Finding a modicum of calm, she listened to the muffled but diminishing cries upstairs, and breathed.

Ten minutes later Connie joined her. "Dr. Mason's given her an injection and she's starting to drop off. He said we could all do with a nice cuppa."

She bustled into the kitchen, and Emma, restored a little, followed. Connie continued, "I think he wants to keep me busy. Poor Josie, what do you think happened? Erm ... sorry, I don't know your name, dear—"

"Emma. My name's Emma. I've taken Clearview Cottage. The one over from the church?"

Connie nodded her recognition as she busied herself with a teapot and a tray of cups and saucers. Emma did her best to tell Josie's mother what happened but couldn't say much without sounding out of her mind.

"This is all because Abby went," said Connie after Emma had finished. "Josie had just got over Jim, and then Abigail left without a trace. No note, nothing." Connie's eyes welled, the tea she poured spilling into a saucer.

Emma took over. "Let's take these into the other room, shall we?" She picked up the tray and followed Connie who, herself now distraught, tearfully wrung her hands all the way back to the living room.

"This is Abby." Connie had picked up one of several framed photographs on the sideboard and was holding it for Emma.

Finding a surface on which to land the tray, she took the photograph. And gasped. "Connie, she's beautiful." No word of a lie. For some reason, she'd expected to see a selfie-obsessed teenager pursing her lips, duck-fashion, at the camera. Not in this instance. Emma could hardly tear her eyes away from the image before her.

Abigail Chater was an unusually beautiful young woman. She wore a wicked expression, eyes dancing with mischief and rebellion despite the static nature of the picture. Her heart-shaped face, delicate and lovely, was framed by blue-black hair, clipped up in an array of plaits and slides, with beaded braids reaching to and beyond her bosom. Adorning her neck were myriad chains and charms all seeming to glint in the glass of the frame, animating the photo. Emma admired her style. It reminded her of own half-hearted tendencies at that age. Goth-chic, they used to call it.

"Her hair is beautifully done," said Emma, so taken with the image she almost forgot that Abby may no longer be alive.

"Yes. She loved doing it. Wanted to be a hairdresser you know."

Connie took back the frame and placed it lovingly with the others. "She was the apple of her dad's eye." Connie nodded towards another picture, a large mountain of a man. Rough-hewn but handsome, with Josie buried within the arm he'd placed around her shoulder, he possessed the same heart-shaped face; not quite as pronounced, maybe, but the resemblance was striking.

The sound of Robbie's footsteps coming down the stairs broke the atmosphere. Emma offered him some tea.

"Josie's asleep now," he said, taking the proffered cup. "I've given her enough to sedate an elephant so she shouldn't wake up until the morning. But..." he gave them both a rueful look, "... it seems she wants to go to the police tomorrow. She has it in her head that Jim isn't dead."

The two women looked horrified. Connie sat down and patted at her throat. "Oh, I don't know about that. I don't like talking to the police. They never listened to us the first time, so I can't see how they'll listen now."

"She may think better of it when she wakes up in the morning, but I doubt it. She's set on it." Robbie took the tea in gulps. "I think she'll need someone to go with her. It won't serve anyone's interests for her to get hysterical again. To be honest, I don't think I'll be much use. I don't know what she's babbling on about. Jim's gone, I'm afraid, and that's that. Connie, will you go with her?"

Looking anywhere but at the doctor, Connie's reply bordered on the desperate. "And see that Inspector again? Ooh, I'm not sure that I can. He was bad enough the first time. I'll go but—"

"I'll do it," said Emma. "I'll make sure the police listen to whatever Josie has got to say. It's the least they can do. Will told me about the unacceptable way they behaved last time."

"You sure?" asked Robbie. "It's a bit above and beyond."

"I'm sure," said Emma.

Anything to shine a light on those terrible shadows.

## 12

### WESTEN

"What the fuck is this?"

Detective Inspector Jamie Westen strode into the squad room in Sandmarsh's Serious Crime Division. He followed the expletive by launching a thin file at his new team, its meagre contents spilling everywhere.

He stood before them, fulminating, ready to pile even more invective on the first person stupid enough to risk their career by answering him.

Pete Burrows, his sergeant, motioned someone to effect a retrieval mission. Twisting his head to take a quick look at a stray photograph, he ventured, "It's a misper file, sir."

"I know it's a fucking misper file. I'm also sufficiently in possession of my faculties to work out who the missing person is. What I don't know, is why it's still open and why it's so fucking thin!"

No answer.

"Right," Westen huffed. "Sergeant, enlighten us."

Burrows stood up. "The missing person is Abigail Chater,

Guv. She disappeared from Flammark Village—" he looked towards Westen, "That's ten miles out from—"

"I know where it fucking is. I might only have been here two days, but I can read a map. Get on with it."

"She disappeared six months ago, on her eighteenth birthday. We made the usual enquiries—"

"Usual?"

"Interviewed the family and what few friends she had. Father died two years earlier. Apart from the suddenness of the disappearance we found no other suspicious circumstances. She got herself into a bit of trouble here and there and most of the villagers we talked to didn't like her much, but apart from that, nothing out of the ordinary. She was of age, sir, so low priority."

Donna Stirling, one of the DCs in the team, having completed a search and rescue mission, handed the restored file to her sergeant. Burrows stopped improvising and opened it. "There were a few cautions for verbal abuse, some petty pilfering here and there, but nothing serious."

"Who put it on hold? Holly?"

"Yes sir." Burrows nodded in agreement. "Inspector Holbrooke, about two weeks before he retired."

"And there's been no action on it since?"

"The family received some anonymous letters, sir," Donna interjected, "but there were only a couple and they stopped soon enough."

"Oh. Did they? And did we also think it worth our while to—remind me what we do again—investigate?"

Burrows said, "Yes sir, but as you know, writers of anonymous letters are difficult to find at the best of times and—"

Weston cut him off, the palm of his hand up like a stiff flag. Nothing so far had been said that he didn't already know, but he wanted to put his new team through their paces.

Holbrooke's backsliding annoyed him. He needed to be sure they hadn't been infected with his incompetence. Wanted also to know if they needed a kick up their collective arse.

Facts sufficiently aired, Westen dialed down his temper, but not by much. "We need to put this fucking awful house in order. My second day and I've already set aside three—repeat, three—cases for review. What sort of piss-poor show are we running here, for Christ's sake? Have we checked farther afield, hit the databases? Checked for new developments?

He worked the uncomfortable silence. "The case is no longer shelved. We're reinvestigating. From scratch. Donna, get a board started, conference room in thirty."

The five-person team muttered as they turned back to their desks. Westen signalled Burrows to follow him to his office.

"Okay, Pete," he said, throwing himself down on the red studded-leather office chair left by his predecessor. He'd also been responsible for the stunningly kitsch matching desk, complete with blotter and an all-in-one inkstand and digital calendar. Westen hadn't found the time to get rid. "Tell me what I don't know."

Sitting in front of his new DI, Burrows reviewed the facts. "Connie Chater, the grandmother, started the ball rolling by making a call to report Abigail's disappearance the day after she'd gone missing. Her mother—that's Josie Chater, Guv—thought Abigail had stayed over at her best friend's house, as she often did. When she didn't come home, they—that's Josie and Connie—began to panic. It was me on the first visit, Guv. Took Donna as female support. They live out on Flammark's council estate. The grandmother was just about holding it together. The mother, not so much. In bits, actually. Both couldn't think why Abigail would leave home. To be honest, Guv, looked like a pretty routine runaway."

Westen didn't look convinced.

"We did a surface search of her bedroom. Bit of a goth-den. Black and purple affair. Her shoulder bag had gone. Oh, and a hair dryer too. Never without it, apparently. I remember the grandmother saying if she wasn't doing her own hair, it was someone else's. She was all set to start work in the village salon as a junior."

"Follow up?"

"The usual. Timings, last-seens, what she was wearing, et cetera. We interviewed a few friends—there weren't many. Bit of a loner, and I have to say, bit of a stunner too." Burrows, consulting the file, lingered a moment over the photograph they'd duplicated. "Her best mate, a Marsha Stubbs, didn't know anything about a stay-over, nor had Abigail confided any plans to go somewhere else. The Stubbs girl didn't seem that bothered, Guv. 'Doing her usual,' I think she put it."

"Holly?"

"We reported everything back. Holly himself had been a bit poorly. Nervous exhaustion, apparently. Had to spend a lot of time in bed. Later on, it got so bad he put his retirement forward by a couple of months. He lives in Flammark and knew the girl. Called her a waste of space and to do the basics and move on."

Westen shook his head. What had Holbrooke been thinking? "So, what about the letters?"

"They're the only odd thing about it all, Guv. They were pretty nasty," he took them out of the file to remind himself. "But, again, Holly thought nothing of them. Said Flammark, like any small village, had its fair share of gossip and spite. Abigail was trouble and everyone knew it. He thought they were just a way of letting off steam. Then all went quiet until the vicar rang, and we had to go out to the church."

"Come again?"

"Flammark Church, Guv, St. Jude's. Someone had left

another note and peed on the altar. 'orrible smell, apparently, or so Holly said."

"Holly? Holbrooke went there himself?"

"Yes, Guv. His report must be here somewhere." Burrows started to check through the slim folder.

"No, it isn't." said Westen. "There's nothing there about Detective Inspector Holbrooke going to question any vicar. Go on, see for yourself."

"Turner, Guv. The Reverend William Turner." Burrows was shaking his head as he shuffled the papers in the file, looking for the report. He gave it up, stumped.

Western grimaced. "I suppose it's a good job we're revisiting the case, then."

Donna tapped on the door, put her head round it.

"Guv. Sorry to interrupt, but there're two walk-ins downstairs. You got time to see them before we start? Think you might want to."

"Who are they, Donna?" Westen looked impatiently at his watch. His conversation with Burrows had genuinely infuriated him. He didn't want to start making enquiries that would call into question the behaviour of one of their own, retired or not. Especially as he'd just started at Sandmarsh. And he could do without needless fucking interruptions.

"Erm, it's Josie Chater, Abigail's mother. She's here with a friend. An Emma Blake."

The two senior detectives looked askance at each other."Perfect," said Westen. "Fucking perfect."

Westen told Donna to postpone the case meeting for an hour while he and Burrows headed for the downstairs interview room where the two women waited. He'd no idea what coincidence had brought Mrs. Chater and friend to his door, but given the negligence he'd so far uncovered, the least he could do was see what they had to say.

Polar opposites. The first, a sensitive type—wiry red hair, eye-wateringly bright red coat over skinny jeans—had an arm around the other. Quite clear which of the two was Josie. She sat slumped, leaning towards the red-head, worry lines etching her face, her chin tremulous. Westen felt a pang of compassion for her. Her daughter been missing for six months and his lot had come up with nothing. Worse still, not only was the file missing a report about the church shenanigans, it contained no record of any follow-up conversations or feedback to the family. Knowing Holbrooke's reputation, he'd bet the farm his predecessor had intimidated the hell out of this woman, rather than have her ask awkward questions.

So, with moral support at her side, was this interview some sort of recrimination at the lack of action? A dressing down? Perhaps not. Though clearly distressed, he sensed determination. Josie held eye contact with him. Something was definitely in the offing.

"Good morning, Mrs. Chater, and—"

"My name is Emma Blake. Josie invited me to come with her. We want to discuss Abigail's disappearance."

"I'm Detective Inspector Westen. This is my sergeant, DS Burrows. DI Holbrooke retired a few months back. I'm now in charge of the investigation. Have you any new information for us?"

Josie got straight into it. "I want to know where we are with our Abigail ... where you're up to with things. It's been ages since she went missing and we've heard nothing from you lot for months."

Westen cleared his throat as a throb of irritation began to form at his temple. Recrimination it was, then. "Perfectly understandable, Mrs. Chater, no problem at all. I've only been here a few days but have already begun to make—"

"Excuses, Inspector?"

Not such a sensitive soul then, our Miss Blake. Willing to take some flack, he offered a conciliatory smile. "Not at all. If I might continue? I have already identified Abigail's case as needing review. It has been six months since she disappeared, so—"

"—so you're inclined to close the case," Emma interrupted. "It won't wash, Inspector. Josie has been fobbed off for far too long and should at least have been given updates. It seems to her there's been no semblance of an investigation."

Tapping the file in front of him, trying to ignore the Blake woman's jibe, Westen kept his annoyance under control and continued from where he'd left off. "Although it is six months since she disappeared, we are looking to see how we can move the things on. I can assure you, Abby's case is still very much active, even if it has been—"

"Forgotten?" Emma interrupted.

Christ.

"Absolutely not. In fact, I have scheduled a conference about Abigail's disappearance this very morning."

"Good for you. There've been developments, then?"

"Not as such. But cases like this benefit from fresh eyes and—"

Josie intervened. "She's dead."

Quiet filled the room. Burrows sat up in his chair and began scribbling on a piece of scrap paper in the file. Westen made no move. Said nothing. Waited for Josie to talk.

She said, "I can't tell you why I know she's dead. I just know. She's dead and he killed her."

"Sorry, Mrs. Chater—may I call you Josie?" She gave a

little nod and Westen continued, "Josie, who is 'he'? Who do you think killed your daughter?"

"Jim."

"Jim?" Westen glanced at where Burrows' finger had planted itself on the shared file. "Your husband?"

"That's right. I don't know how. He's supposed to have been gone these two years. Car accident. But he did it, all right."

Loosening his tie slightly, Westen sat back. What a fucking waste of his time. Abigail Chater's disappearance solved by blinding new insight that her fucking dead father did it. Brilliant.

"Inspector," said Emma, "Josie received some—"

"Anonymous letters, I know," Westen snapped. He sat forward and whipped the notes out of the file, slapping them on the table.

## SINS OF THE FATHERS VISITED
## UPON YOUR GENERATION

And

## YOU SHOULD HAVE TOLD HER FATHER TO KEEP
## HIS FINGERS TO HIMSELF

Westen let their presence be felt. Josie, no stranger to the notes, shrank back when she saw them and started to cry. Emma tried to stem the flow with a steadying hand to her arm.

She asked, "Can I pick them up?"

"Of course," he shrugged. "All the forensics have been done."

While she read the notes Westen watched her, gauging her reaction at seeing them for the first time. She did nothing

to modulate the derision in her voice when she said, "Will—
that's our vicar— told me what the last Inspector said about
these notes. This was no prank. It feels there's more behind
them than spite. To me, it looks like the writer knew
something."

Westen couldn't agree with her more, but no way would
he admit it. This was fast becoming a clusterfuck of a day.

"All I can say, Miss Blake, is the case is being reviewed.
Every aspect will be looked at again." Then, turning away
from her, and tapping one of the notes Emma had put back
on the table, he said to Josie, "I assume D. I. Holbrooke ques-
tioned you about this six months ago, but I have to ask again.
Did you have any reason to believe Jim had ..."

"Been interfering with her?" Josie's sobs could no longer
be repressed. "No. I had no idea. I didn't believe it and I
wouldn't have had it. Not under my roof."

"*Didn't* believe it?" asked Emma, gently.

Josie looked at her, eyes full of tears. "The notes were
right, weren't they? I know that now, after ... after ... "

"Go on," Westen said, against his better judgement. What
fantasy would she come up with next?

"After last night, at the church, I don't know what to
think."

"The *church*? What happened at the church?"

He heard Emma take a deep, hesitant breath. As if
choosing her words very carefully, she said, "We attended an
Evensong service, Inspector. At St. Jude's."

Uh-oh. Here it comes ...

"Josie experienced a—sudden realisation. You may want
to call it an epiphany, or—a vision, but whatever the case, we
thought it best to ask if you could look again into the death
of Josie's husband. If she's right, it obviously means Jim
might not have died in a car accident and is very much alive."

"And this is your educated opinion, is it?"

The Blake woman glared back at him. He sensed something in the look. Not anger exactly, which is what he expected—intended even. No, it was more in the way of defiance, as if he was threatening her in some way.

"No, Inspector," she replied, "just a simple request. We would like you to re-investigate the car crash. After all, it's the very least you can do, isn't it? After all these months of doing nothing?"

Blasted woman needed to keep her nose out. For some reason, Westen desperately wanted to argue with her, to have a real ding-dong. But he had to face facts, she'd only spoken in the spirit of his own words he'd addressed the team with, earlier on.

He put a hand through his hair and made a deep inhalation. "Pete, get the file from the archive. Won't do any harm to take a look. But—" he said, turning to the two women, "No promises. I don't usually investigate on the basis of a vision, or a whim, or ... whatever ... but we will give it another look."

Josie and Emma turned to each other, relieved. Interview over, the policemen got up as the two women rose to leave.

"Thanks." said Josie. The other one managed a curt nod in his direction as Burrows saw them out.

Westen sat down again, deep in thought. On his sergeant's return, he blew out his cheeks."Well, Pete, what the fuck was that?"

## ⚜ 13 ⚜

## DEBRIEF

T he next evening, Emma became a reluctant visitor to the vicarage. Will had asked her over to get her take on what happened during Evensong so he wouldn't put his foot in it when he visited Josie. He had no idea the service had completely unnerved her too, almost shattering her fragile confidence. God knows where she got the strength from to confront that snarky inspector!

No way would she be able to reveal why the service had so terrified her. To do so would mean admitting she saw something too, and that would entail revealing her past. No way could she let that happen, not even to Will. But she had no excuse to offer for staying away, so here she was, in the vicarage library.

"What a collection!"

Emma, eyes everywhere, drank in the bookish atmosphere. The room seemed to go on forever, armchairs dotted here and there, each with its own side-table and lamp. Josiah would have loved it. "Is it usual for vicarages to have libraries?"

"No," Will laughed. "I should think they're very rare, but

I did explain that the house doubled as diocesan training centre. We keep the resources here and it's a great place for tutoring and personal study. Trainees come here all the time, sometimes just to get away."

Emma walked to one set of shelves and ran her hand over its leather-bound volumes.

Will moved to stand next to her. "They're mostly ecclesiastical in nature but my predecessor shared my passion for history, so I've been able to add to his collection." Then he pointed to a great oak desk under one of the library's two windows, a filing cabinet next to it. "I do all my work in here. I just love the atmosphere and the smell of the books. It's the only room in the house I really like."

A series of bound volumes with gold lettering caught her eye.

"Parish magazines," Will said. "St. Jude's has a long and well-documented history. Look at this." He drew her attention to a massive cabinet which took up most of one wall. Several drawers comprised its lower section, above which rested a series of glass-fronted cupboards, their shelves occupied by hundreds of rolled documents.

"Wow, that's massive! Pity the poor blokes who had to carry that in."

He laughed. "Yeah, well, it comes in sections, but you're right, it certainly is a solid piece of furniture."

Emma stepped over to it to take a closer look.

Will joined her. "Some of our oldest parish records."

"Shouldn't they be archived somewhere?"

"They came from the chancery at Sandmarsh Cathedral. There'd been a fire. Most of the records were saved but they didn't restore it as a diocesan office so some were returned to their original churches. There isn't much of value here, but it is nice to have them."

"Won't they deteriorate?"

"No more than they might have done in the chancery. They weren't exactly hermetically sealed, and there's not a lot of light in here, and having so many books tends to soak up the humidity. The cabinet keeps them dry enough. I'll show you some later, if you like."

"What's that?" asked Emma, pointing to a small black casket in the centre of the cabinet.

"Ah, yes, an interesting relic from the Blaxton fire."

"Another fire?"

"Yeah. The Blaxtons owned most of Flammark at one time. Their family seat, Blaxton Hall, burned down just before the Second World War started. Some were killed in action during the Great War, then more in the flu epidemic that followed. The family had no time to properly recover before the fire finished off the line once and for all." He took on a deeply sonorous tone of mock seriousness as he pointed at the box. "This was prised from the burnt, blackened and very dead hand of the last patriarch, George."

"Will, that's horrendous!"

He shrugged. "I should have more respect, I suppose, but I don't. They were a terrible family and the village is better off without them. I know it's a horrible thing to say but it's what I feel. It's interesting that nothing survived the fire except for this. No one had any idea why George had clung on to it, there must surely have been more valuable things to save. The parish didn't know what to do with it, so it was brought here. It's been on display ever since."

Emma shuddered and crossed her arms, rubbing them.

Will must have noticed because he said, "Sorry. Didn't mean to weird you out. Come to think about it, it *is* a bit chilly in here. Let's sit down."

They moved towards two deep leather armchairs resting either side of an open fire, promising comfort, tempting disclosure. But despite the lovely room, and pleasant company, Emma would not be falling for their charms this night. Not after the shadow show.

Will had already brought in a rather posh trolley, bedecked with a very ornate teapot, two cheery china cups on matching saucers, milk, sugar and chocolate biscuits. After they sat he began pouring.

"Come on then, Emma, spill the beans. I haven't seen poor Josie since Evensong, and I don't want to say the wrong thing."

She accepted the cup he offered and began.

"As you know, Robbie asked me to go with him to take Josie home." She pushed her hair back behind her ears, stalling for time, wondering how to play it. She decided no harm would come by telling him about her conversation with Josie. "She said she knew Abigail was dead and that Jim had killed her."

"Bloody hell. What made her say that?"

Not yet knowing how to frame an answer, Emma let his question hang. "We took her straight to Connie's."

Will nodded. "Good call on Robbie's part. She's not coping, which is hardly surprising. Husband gone, daughter missing. I can't begin to imagine."

Taking a sip from her cup, Emma said, "She was in a terrible state. All the way to bed she kept wailing, about Abigail and Jim."

Emma filled him in with the details, about what Josie thought she saw, the conclusions she'd come to about her husband and how they'd both gone to the police the next morning to get them to look again at Jim's accident.

"It is physically impossible for Jim to have killed Abigail. I officiated at his funeral! That was what..? Two years ago!"

"I know, Robbie told me."

"God alive." Will interweaved his fingers and rested his chin on them, elbows on his armchair. "What I can't get my head around, is what triggered it all? What happened in the church to make Josie scream like that?"

Emma stuck to the facts. "She saw something in the shadows the candles had thrown onto the walls."

There, she'd said it!

To avoid incriminating herself in the lunacy, she pressed on. "Josie said … said they revealed Jim and Abigail. Together. And that her father had his hands around Abby's neck."

Eyes wide, Will hung on every word. *"That's* what made her want to go back to the police?"

Emma nodded. "Robbie didn't think it a good idea for her to go on her own. He couldn't get his head around what she'd said and didn't feel he'd be much use to her. Connie looked scared to death, so I volunteered to go with her."

Finally, he said, "She saw this in the shadows, you say?"

"Yes."

Elbows on his armchair, Will steepled his hands and stared into the fire, his gaze lost in the flames as they licked round the coals.

"Robbie ranted about it as he drove me home. Called them hallucinations and doubted the police would give her the time of day."

"Typical Robbie," Will tutted. "Well, I don't know what went down between you all at the station but their new inspector—Westfield is it?—paid me a visit this morning."

Thankful for the change in subject, Emma said, "Westen?"

"That's it, Westen. He told me they were reviewing the case and asked about the desecration and the note. He was really cross I still had it. All but accused me of withholding important information, for goodness sake! The man whipped out an evidence bag and took the note away. I'm glad really. It'd been burning a hole in my pocket for much too long. He mentioned he was going to visit the site of Jim's crash, but he didn't tell me why."

Will poured another two cups.

"He asked after you, actually."

"Me! Why?"

"Just wanted to know how long you've been in the village, and what connection you had with the Chaters. What did you make of him?"

"Hmm. I'm glad he took us seriously enough to open the case, but I didn't take to him. Too up himself. I suppose arrogance is inbred in that sort. I have to admit, though, he handled Josie very well."

The two of them grew silent, mulling things over.

"May I ask you something, Emma? About that night?"

Forgetting to sip, she took in too much of her drink and tried not to pull a face as she held the hot tea in her mouth, swallowing it in bits so as not to make an embarrassing gulp. Aiming for nonchalance, she said, "Go ahead."

"Do *you* believe she saw something? In the shadows?"

Should she tell him? Risk it now and the thread would be loose, maybe he'd pull and pull on it until …

Without making eye-contact, she replied, "Yes. Yes, I do."

Her breath quickened in the silence that followed, waiting for the inevitable questions. But, to her relief, Will sighed and changed the subject completely, as if sensing her discomfort. Changing the mood altogether, he leant forward and said with a wink, "Would you like to have a rummage inside my cabinet?"

Emma chuckled at the innuendo, relieved she'd dodged the bullet of disclosure. "How can I refuse?"

They spent a companionable hour looking through some of the library documents, at the end of which, though not particularly late, Emma began stifling yawns.

"Tired?" asked Will.

"I didn't think I was, but … yes. It's time to go. I should have an early night." The stress of the past few days had definitely caught up with her. "I don't suppose you'd see me over the green, would you? I came the long way round, following the road and under the streetlights. I don't feel up to the return journey and I haven't got a torch."

"Of course not! Happy to. I've plenty of spares too, for the visitors, you know. You can keep one, if you like."

The frost had barely let up since Evensong. The wiring still hadn't been fixed and the absence of exterior lighting made everywhere pitch black. At the edge of the green he said, "Here, take my arm. The ground can be very uneven."

As they picked their way along by torchlight, Will said, "Sunday tomorrow, Emma. Will I be seeing you in church?"

She sighed. It would be a while until she'd feel able to set foot in there again. The last service had afforded more than enough excitement for one week.

"Actually, Will, I think Jude will have to give me a miss. I'm going to have a lie-in."

She snuggled further into her parka as they crossed more of the exposed space towards the cottage. An icy blast suddenly assailed her and for no reason, the hairs on the back of her neck rose and her temples throbbed with sudden tension. Sensing movement, she spun round, listened.

Nothing ... something.

"What's up?" said Will.

She peered into the dark. "I'm sure I heard something. Listen!" They shone their torches behind them, but the short-range beams were useless. She definitely sensed something.

Cold and unnerved, Emma grasped Will's arm even tighter as they hastened towards the cottage. When they reached the step, she unlocked the door and quickly flipped the light switch next to it.

"Night, Em, sleep well. Thanks for coming over tonight."

"Goodnight, Will. Thanks for walking me."

She waved him on his way, standing on the threshold, illuminated from behind by the living room light. Holding her breath, she listened intently, as she watched the priest disappear into the night.

Nothing.

Blasted by another wave of cold, Emma shivered as she made her way inside.

## ❧ 14 ❧

## RAGE
### A FUCKING PRIEST!

He gazes in the mirror of the squalid bathroom, breathing up a storm. Every moment he thinks about what he saw last night, fuels his temper.

The two of them, arm in arm.

Hand in glove.

So besotted with each other, his presence behind a gravestone had gone totally unnoticed. He could have reached out. Touched her. But they were oblivious. Too busy rubbing up to each other.

She'd told the priest all about him, hadn't she? Confessed her soul to him. And we know who she'll have blamed.

Well, wrong, wrong again.

Bitch.

Everything is down to her. Shallow, ungrateful; like all women, unable to do what she's told.

A fucking priest, for Christ's sake!

He doesn't bother fighting the flames of incandescent anger that burn him. He fans them, embraces them, welcomes their hot touch.

She needs a lesson. So does the priest.

Grievance etches the face that stares back at him, his mind's eye *seeing them together; naked, entwined—against him. His nostrils flare as he inhales his fury; eyes engorged, blackened with rage.*

*It is exhilarating.*

*Before his frenzy can peak, an unfamiliar impulse takes him.*

*He reaches for his razor, slides out its blade.*

*Some internal resistance makes his hand shake. But he swats it away. It is nothing.*

*The first cut along the flesh of his stomach isn't deep. It doesn't have to be.*

*Hurts.*

*Wave after wave of satiating pain sweeps over him.*

*Why has he never done this before?*

*Moments later, the climax over, he takes a step backwards and cocks his head, the better to admire his handiwork. Tch. So much blood! It obstructs the clarity of the strokes he has made.*

*He picks up a towel to stem the flow but the human in him takes over.*

*And he falls to the floor in a faint.*

## ACCIDENT INVESTIGATION

Westen delayed their visit to Jim Chater's accident scene until after morning briefing so they could park at the roadside without causing a jam.

"So, Guv, I think it was ..." Burrows, against the biting wind, gripping a hand-drawn map from the Chater file, stamped out five large paces and announced, "... here."

He landed almost exactly in front of a "Welcome to Sandmarsh" sign. Only a straggly patch of verge where the grass hadn't recovered properly showed there'd been an accident there.

"Okay," said Westen. 'Talk me through it."

There were aspects of the Chater case that really bugged him. His conversation with William Turner confirmed his worst fears. Evidence had been ignored. Why the hell did Holly allow the anonymous note to stay in Turner's possession? Thank Christ the priest had foresight enough to bag the thing. It left reasonable hope that forensics would turn something up.

The accident report annoyed him too. He hadn't set much

store by what Josie Chater had to say—fucking epiphanies—but he felt he owed her a look, since she'd all but been ignored by his predecessor. After giving it the once-over, like everything else in this case, he found the report had big gaps. These, more than the desire to soothe the grief of a deranged widow, provided the prime motivation for visiting the scene. He needed to see it for himself.

He watched his sergeant turn the map this way and that, getting the proper orientation. "The van, a blue Ford Transit, fishtailed off the road here, sir, just before the sign. SOCOs reckon it must have been going a fair whack. Their analysis of the skid-marks, density and so on, had the speed at about eighty or ninety."

"Ninety miles an hour," Westen ruminated. "It's a wonder the van could take it. Remind me, what time was this?"

"No cameras on this stretch sir, and no witnesses. The flames caught the attention of the farmer," Burrows nodded vaguely over the fence. "Thought vandals were on his land, so he came out to check and found the burning vehicle. Called it in at ..." he looked in the file. "12.30 am."

Westen nodded. He knew all the details, of course, but things had a way of looking different in situ. He was having to shout now against loud gusts of wind, so strong they whipped at his overcoat. "Hell of a speed."

"Yes, sir. In a hurry, for sure."

"And he was coming from..?"

"Flammark, sir. Chater was the village locksmith. His wife said he came back from his last call at about seven pm."

"Anything significant to the case about the callout?"

Burrows pressed his lips and shook his head. "Not in itself, Guv. Young couple got him out. They'd been away for the day and on arrival home, couldn't find their keys."

"What about later? What time did he leave home, again?"

"That's the thing, sir. Mrs. Chater didn't know he'd gone

out. The family were in bed by eleven and Chater must have slipped out later. It was only when Family Liaison knocked on their door first thing, did they notice he'd gone. Wife and daughter were in a bad way when we spoke to them later. Abigail could hardly speak."

"So, two years ago, she'd be, what, sixteen?"

Burrows nodded. "To the day."

The loud ringtone of Burrows' phone pierced the noisy wind. "'Hang on, Guv." He took it out and turned, allowing his back to take the full force of the buffeting, a hand at his other ear to mitigate the noise. Westen saw his sergeant's head jerk upright. "All right, thanks. I'll tell him."

"What's up, Pete?"

"Morgue, Guv. Pathologist on the case was Savage. He heads up the department now. Bit ...eccentric ... but knows his stuff. He's free in about an hour."

"Right. Let's get out of this bloody wind."

In the relative calm of the car's interior, Westen took the file from Burrows and opened it, gazed out at the crash site then down again, frowning. "What do you think happened here, Pete?"

"Well, Chater was going hell for leather. And with no street lighting, anything could have caused it. An animal on the road, maybe, another car ..."

"State of the road?"

"Good. It'd been resurfaced six months prior to the accident, and it was a dry night."

Westen said, "File says tox screens were useless. Couldn't establish alcohol levels."

"Yep. Body too far gone. The heat was so intense, parts of it had vaporised. But both Mrs. Chaters said he was tee-total, and he'd certainly not been drinking at home earlier. Something in Jim's family way back, apparently, put him off. Wouldn't touch a drop."

"Then it's probably safe to assume he wasn't pissed." Westen sat awhile, thinking. Suddenly he burst out, "Fucking zebras!"

Burrows threw a double-take. "Come again, sir?"

"If he'd been bladdered, then it's a simple assumption that he'd put his foot down, and for whatever reason, lost control. Straightforward. Makes the case a horse. If, on the other hand, he was stone cold sober, then we're looking for a more exotic explanation. It's a zebra."

Warming to his theme, Westen continued, "If Chater hadn't been pissed, it's a different matter altogether. What happened that caused him to be travelling at that speed in the first place? What else then took place that caused him to swerve onto the verge?" He consulted the file again. "Ground visibility was good. Was he on high beam?"

"Yes, sir. That was established that when they rescued the vehicle. Headlight switch full on."

"Therefore, if he'd seen an animal or some such—even an oncoming car—there's a likelihood he'd have been able to veer round it."

"Yes, sir, though the speed he was doing would have cut his response time. He'd only have a split second."

And that's when Westen gave voice to the problem that had bugged him all along. "True, but consider this, if he was travelling at that speed—drunk or not—would he have the strength to pull this ninety?" He jabbed his thumb at a photo of the wreckage. "Look at it. One minute he's on the road, the next he's right-angles to it. It's far too acute. Whatever might have been in his way, avoiding it at that speed would have landed him at least fifty yards further on and certainly at much less of an angle. Maybe even overturned. It's clear enough from the pictures, but it's only when you see the actual crash site do you fully realise the extremity of that turn. It's impossible."

Westen took out the copies of the flash photography taken on the night of the crash. "See for yourself. The skid marks start here, when he hit the brakes." He pointed to the heavy black lines on the photo. "Then they turn inwards, what, only five meters before he crashed at the sign? I'll say it again, at that speed it's a fucking impossible turn. And this file, look at it! A handful of photographs and the flimsiest accident report I've ever seen. Why was nothing queried or flagged up at the time?"

Burrows pursed his lips and shrugged. "I wasn't on that night, Guv, but I've a mate in Accident Investigation. I'll see what I can dig up if you like?"

"Why don't you do just that. It beats working by psychical fucking forces."

Burrows fell quiet. No doubt to defend the honour of his old boss he said, "It had been one of those weeks, Guv. We'd been working with the Drug Squad on—"

Weston cut him off. "I don't care if the whole fucking cast of Breaking Bad descended on us, if there's an accident you fucking investigate it. Properly. Thoroughly. And you do the paperwork."

Except for the sound of the odd gust of wind and whoosh from a passing vehicle, silence filled the car. Lost for words, the familiar angry throb returned to Westen's temple. He hated incompetence.

But he couldn't do much about that now. He needed to get on. "Remember what the Chater woman said at the station? 'She's dead and he killed her?'"

"Guv?"

"If her husband was responsible for the girl's disappearance and possible death, *a whole two years later*, then it couldn't have been him in the van. He would have had to fake his death. But this is Flammark for Christ's Sake, not fucking Chicago."

He looked back at the file and slapped his hand down on it, frustrated that its contents weren't speaking to him. "We've established the body was part-vaporised. We are certain it was Jim Chater's, aren't we? I mean, these dental records are accurate?"

"We have to assume so, Guv, if they're in the file. It'd take an inferno to destroy teeth."

"Well, I'm not assuming anything. The first thing you do when you get back to the station is check everything again."

"Will do, Guv. There's also his wedding ring, don't forget. They found it on the floor next to the body. Badly charred, but it seemed to escape the worst effect of the fire. We could still make out some of the inscription on the back." He reached over and picked out its photograph from the open file on Westen's lap. "Mrs. Chater made a positive identification at the time. Told us he couldn't get it off and it was starting to bite into his finger. Apparently, he intended to go to the jewellers and get it removed and extended."

Weston internalised a shudder. Terrible way to go. Then this talk about the ring brought back to him the words of the second anonymous letter.

*You should have told her father to keep his fingers to himself.*

Was all this about incest?

Chater might well have harboured inappropriate thoughts towards his daughter. Christ, for all Westen knew, he might have acted upon them. But nothing he'd seen so far went even near to suggest he'd escaped the crash, holed up somewhere, then, a whole two years later, abducted and killed his daughter. That was a zebra too far. No, Josie Chater had got it plain wrong. If her husband's dental records matched the body then the remains were, categorically, his. No doubt about it. No way could he have been involved either in Abby's disappearance or possible death.

So much for bloody female intuition.

Nevertheless, there were aspects of this case which were too suspicious to ignore. Westen couldn't shelve it yet, and certainly not until he'd got to the bottom of Holbrooke's incompetence.

Westen said, "Right, I've had enough. Let's talk to Savage —hell of a name for a pathologist, by the way. See if he can tell us anything else. Get him to confirm those dental records again."

He cleared up the file and kept it on his knee as Burrows drove them away. He mulled over what got them out here in the first place: the interview with Josie Chater and the redhead. Turner told him Emma Blake had just settled into these parts. A newcomer. Bit of a firecracker too.

Well, he'd have to disappoint the two women. Pending Burrows' review and confirmation from Savage, it was clear Jim Chater had suffered a horrible and unquestionable death. But the crash site raised more questions. As the car made its way to the morgue, Westen let out an exasperated sigh.

Fucking zebras.

## ❧ 16 ❧

## SIGHTING

Emma stood side-by-side with the doctor as they sorted through the last of his overcrowded filing cabinets. Their hard work had paid off and his office had been transformed.

"I hear you've been out with Josie Chater. It'll do her the world of good," said Robbie.

"I hope so," Emma replied. "I've taken her into the village a few times for a bit of window shopping and a bite to eat. Nothing too strenuous. Connie's very protective of her, isn't she?"

"Terrified she'll have a breakdown, no doubt. She seemed definitely on the verge of one at the church."

That had been over two weeks ago. Not a word had crossed their lips about that episode until now.

"Did she ever tell you about—" he let the words hang, unable to give them proper completion.

"Her 'hallucinations'?"

"Aye. What else could they have been, Emma?"

"You're a man of science, Robbie. I'm not going to share something you might find ridiculous."

"Then there was all that nonsense about her husband. The man's been dead these two years."

"See?"

He held her gaze for a few moments before looking down. "I don't like what's happening here, Emma. Not one bit. It's as if the village is going into some kind of self-imposed lockdown. Stasis. The sickness has started to escalate, and people aren't getting better. I can't find out what it is."

"The tests?"

"Negative for flu, gastroenteritis, measles and any other malaise-inducing viruses in the known universe. It's beyond me, Emma. Look around. Empty. Whenever have you known a doctor's surgery to have no patients?"

"Never," she admitted.

"It bothers me. It bothers me greatly, because I don't understand it." A frown played on Robbie's brow. "What use is a doctor if he can't give a diagnosis at a time like this?" He shook his head. "At least we've had no new cases today, and you and I are okay. Maybe we've dodged a bullet."

"Let's hope so."

They looked up at the sound of the front door opening followed by footsteps on the tiles. Emma was about to leave Robbie's office to greet the visitor when she saw Gabby had already made it to the surgery door.

"Hello, you two," she said. "Gosh, it's really, really dead in here isn't it?"

"I should hope not, Gabby," said Robby. "Last time I checked, we two were very much alive."

Gabby put her tongue out at him. The grin which emerged from his plentiful red beard surprised Emma. It never dawned on her they may be friends.

"I'm at a loose end," said Gabby. "It's nearly lunchtime and I wondered if Emma fancied a coffee?"

Emma looked at her watch, about to demur, but before

she could say anything Robbie pre-empted her. "It's all right. You go and have a chinwag with the Gab, here."

"You sure? It's a bit early."

"So long as you're back for afternoon surgery, I think I can cope."

Emma, happy to take the break, collected her things. Once outside she teased, "The Gab? As in 'gift of'?"

Gabby giggled. "Robbie's a love. He really went through the mill when his wife died. I didn't like to see him dwell on things, rattling around in that big old house, so I did my best to coax him out of it. We used to go on lots of bus trips, train journeys, that sort of thing. Any excuse to take his mind off what happened. Poured his heart out, he did, poor dear."

The bustle of market day had returned to the square, as shoppers, unaffected by the sickness, went about their business, even though the temperature had barely risen above freezing.

They browsed for half an hour or so. What a difference a few weeks could make! The last time Emma braved the market, she'd nearly turned tail and driven back home. Gabby had played her part in stopping her. If she hadn't been in the café at just the right time, hadn't rescued her with tissues and tea, things might have turned out tragically different. Emma felt her confidence increasing, the compulsion to keep looking over her shoulder had all but disappeared.

A pretty, cherry-red tote-bag caught her eye and she haggled for it while Gabby headed for the sweet stall. Then, rather than sit in for lunch, they decided to buy take-away from the usual assemblage of catering vans. Despite the cold, Emma felt in a salad mood, Gabby plumped for a pasty and both treated themselves to a cake. They popped their purchases into Emma's new bag as they turned away to decide where to eat.

"You seem to be very fond of this colour," teased Gabby,

as she looked at Emma's parka. "Haven't you had enough of red?"

Emma laughed. "I know! I have absolutely no idea where that came from. I can't seem to get enough of the colour. I always used to go for greens and purples. You know, because —" she pointed to her hair, currently burnishing in the late autumn sun.

"Well, it does clash a bit," chuckled Gabby. "But why not? You certainly couldn't be missed in a crowd!"

They stood awhile, trying to decide where to eat. "I know where we can go," said Gabby. "Follow—"

Before she could finish, Emma stopped dead and grabbed her friend's arm.

A horribly familiar figure was watching them from the other side of the square.

Her mouth dried up.

She peered back, not really sure. Then suddenly, he darted off towards the car park.

It was him.

"Are you alright, dearie?" Gabby asked, with obvious concern. "You've gone white as a sheet."

Without replying, Emma let go of Gabby's arm. She sprinted towards where she'd last seen the man, wanting absolute confirmation. She had to know. Had to.

Having reached the car park, she stopped, chest heaving for breath, neck craning. She saw something ... then nothing. Just a few vehicles making for the exit, none of which she recognised.

Panting still, more with fright than exertion, Emma dropped her bag, their take-away lunch spilling all over the cobbles. Hands on her knees she bent over, trying to catch her breath, knowing she'd been right, praying she'd been wrong.

When was she going to be free of this shit?

"Are you going to tell me about it?" Gabby, suddenly next to her, put an arm over her shoulders holding her friend, right there, on the edge of the car park, for as long as it took. When Emma started to unfold herself upright Gabby let go, but Emma reached for her hand, hoping to borrow its strength.

"Are you going to tell me, Emma?"

Something about her tone pulled her back from the brink. Gabby had been like this before. One minute all freckles and smiles and gossip; the next, profoundly serious, the entire timbre of her voice changed. Like in the kitchen when she told her about the waving woman, then again, in the church with Josie.

*We know you saw something too. We need to talk.*

"It's all right. I've got you," Gabby said, still in her 'other' voice. "Come on. I know where we can go."

Emma, eyes everywhere—looking over her shoulder—started to move. They came to a building just off the square. On the frontage, huge red letters on a white sign proclaimed it to be: COMMUNITY CENTRE. The place where Gabby worked. Fumbling around in the capacious pocket of her mac, she fished out a large bunch of keys and offered one up to the thick, glass entrance door.

"You've had a nasty shock. It's very quiet in here and you can get your bearings back. Everyone's sick. I've been working on my own for nearly a week, so we won't be interrupted."

Despite her preoccupations, Emma still couldn't get over the sustained change in Gabby's tone. She brooked no argument either and Emma felt compelled to follow her in.

She was in too much of a state to take in many details about the place. She sensed rather than saw the books, carousels and computers that populated the colourful space. Most importantly, it was warm and quiet and—

"Where's the loo. I'm going to throw up."

She bolted to where Gabby pointed and heaved herself through the door. But her retching-in-the-loo habit was doomed to failure this time, as with no warning at all, the world went black.

～

"Thank goodness, I thought you were a gonner for a moment."

Emma came round to the sensation of having her hand patted. She moved her other hand and fingered the grain of what felt like plastic carpet then lifted her head to find her feet sitting in the lap of a purple monkey.

"W-what..?"

"Take your time. You had a funny turn in the loo. We brought you into the children's library, away from the windows, for privacy."

Extricating her hand from Gabby's, she put it on the floor and pushed herself to a seated position, releasing her feet from what she now saw had not been a weird hallucination but a child's chair. She gratefully took swigs from a bottle of water her friend handed to her.

"Can we sit somewhere else? That monkey's freaking me out."

"Of course," Gabby laughed. "Let's go through to where the adults play."

Clutching the water bottle, with Gabby's help, Emma slowly clambered up. She followed Gabby past a huge see-through bookshelf that acted as a room divider between what was obviously a children's play area, and the main library.

Gabby walked to a partitioned-off kitchen area. "I'll make us some tea, won't be long. Sit on one of the sofas, Emma, and get your bearings. You remember Michael, don't you? I called him to help me with you when you fainted."

Still dazed and disoriented, Emma stared at the estate agent, the last person in the world she expected to have to thank for picking her up from a toilet floor. Embarrassed, she slumped down on the sofa opposite to where he sat, perched on an uncomfortable-looking red plastic chair. She threw him a polite smile but didn't have a clue what to say to him, so she swigged more water and waited for Gabby, and, hopefully, some illumination as to how she'd got there.

She didn't need her. As she drank, the light began to dawn all by itself.

The look on her face must have given her away. Michael called out, "She's remembered!" Gabby came in straight away and sat next to Emma. Jerking her head in the direction of the kitchen, she said to Michael, "Give us a minute."

She picked up Emma's hand and started patting it again. "There, there, dear. You've had a nasty shock. Breathe. Try to relax. Do you feel up to talking about it?"

Emma raised utterly distraught eyes to her friend. She clung onto her pendant so hard its edges dug into her palms. Shaking her head slowly, out came, "I … can't. I just … can't."

Perhaps to divert her, Gabby said, "That's such a lovely pendant. May I see it? Can you take it off?"

Confused, but for some reason unable to resist the request, Emma passed Gabby the water bottle and unclasped the necklace.

Michael came out of the kitchen, carrying a tray.

"Look at this, Michael. Emma's pendant. Isn't it beautiful?" Turning back to her friend she asked, "Where did you get it?"

Emma's brain felt disconnected and fuzzy. "Josiah … that

is, my father gave it to me after my first Communion. I always wear it."

"Do you? So lovely. Where did he get it from? Did he buy it specially?"

"No. It's a family heirloom."

"I see."

Gabby held the pendant up to the light and Emma watched as the gold setting glinted and twisted and fascinated. She forgot to be distressed in the overwhelming effort it took to keep her eyes open. All she could hear was the sound of her friend's voice.

"Such a lovely necklace, Emma. So much history it could tell us. Can you tell us your history, Emma. Can you tell us what brought you here?"

Sleepily, Emma replied, "I can't. It's in my box."

"Which box, Emma? Tell us."

"The one in my head," she murmured. "Where I lock away the bad."

"Good. Very good. You're doing very well."

Gabby continued to swing the pendant and Emma's eyes closed.

"Now, Emma, listen very carefully. The box. The box in your head. I want you to open it for us."

## 🌿 17 🌿

## REVELATIONS

Emma woke the next day with buzzing in her ears. Her mobile. Half asleep, she frantically patted the top of her bedside table, chasing it across the surface to get the damned thing to stop. To speed things along, she opened her eyes only to clamp them shut again. For some unfathomable reason, she hadn't closed her curtains before going to bed and though the sun was low and weak, its rays still stung.

The call was from Robbie.

"Emma! I'm just ringing to see if you're okay! Gabby told me what happened."

"Did she?" Emma replied, twisting away from the window as she sat up. She rubbed her eyes and yawned. A faint recollection that something important happened to her yesterday hovered at the edge of her brain, but she couldn't quite grasp it. Hoping for clarification, she said, "What did Gabby say?"

"That you took a funny turn in the market and you needed to go home and lie down."

"Shit, Robbie," Emma said, flinging the covers off. Finding herself fully dressed, she exclaimed, "What the—"

"Emma? Are you sure you're okay?"

"Yes, yes I'm fine," she lied, trying to manage the conversation in tandem with working out what the hell had happened. "I've overslept, that's all. Don't worry, I'm on my way!"

"No! Emma, no. Gabby was quite clear you needed to rest. All's well here." He paused, sounding a little awkward. "I just hope you haven't caught the sickness. I've added you to my rounds this afternoon, then we can decide if you're well enough to work tomorrow. If not, I'll ring the agency. Listen to me now. I insist."

"Well, okay, I won't come in. But I don't need you to visit. Honestly, I'm feeling fine … and very embarrassed." She could have added mystified to the list.

"Well, lass, so long as you're sure." His pause felt doubtful. "I … I'll see you tomorrow, then."

"Yes. And Robbie—thanks for ringing."

"No problem at all. You take care now."

After ending the call, Emma sat on the edge of her bed and closed her eyes, hoping some quiet concentration would retrieve her memory.

If she'd had what Gabby called 'a funny turn' why did she feel so refreshed, like she'd taken a load off? She'd slept great —best night in months. But it seemed to have come at a cost. Apart from work in the morning and buying lunch with Gabby, the rest of the day was a complete blank.

Still no clearer, and with her mouth parched, craving coffee, she clambered off the bed. Yawning again, she made her way downstairs to the kitchen. A note rested on the table.

.  .  .

*Dear Emma,*

*I hope you're feeling a bit better. You were so tired when we got home, all you wanted to do was sleep. I hope you didn't mind me putting you to bed and leaving you to it.*

*I've let Robbie know you took a bit poorly, and he's fine with you having the day off.*

*I'm not going to be at home for the rest of the week, but if you need anything, give me a ring. I've left my mobile number on the Clearview sheet.*

*Love, Gabby.*

The sound of her friend's voice in her mind as Emma read the words of the note, hit the recall button. She clutched the back of a kitchen chair, fighting a sudden onset of nausea.

She'd seen him. He was here. In Flammark.

No wonder she'd had a 'funny turn.' Had she fainted, then? Emma rushed into the front room and peered through the window. The jeep rested in its usual place. Gabby must have driven them back.

Emma needed to think; needed to get her head straight. After all these weeks, gaining confidence and valuable perspective, it was as if he'd snapped his fingers at her fragile equilibrium and blown it all away.

Her mouth even drier now, Emma returned to the kitchen and fumbled at the switches on the coffee maker. She reached for a mug, but it dropped from her hands, shattering on the kitchen floor. The crack of the impact whipped through the air. A pause—a hiatus—then the tears came. She kneeled, racked with anguished sobs, trying to pick up the scattered shards as waves and waves of memory and recognition flooded in. The figure in the square had been only too familiar. There was no room for doubt. He'd found her and she couldn't stay.

She had no idea how long she stayed on her knees but the cold floor made them ache and she came to herself. On automatic, she got out the dustpan and started brushing up the mess. The simple action calmed her. Afterwards, Emma sat at the table and, chin in hand, found herself listening to the homely chugging of the coffee machine. Taking in the aroma and, absent-mindedly dragging her pendant back and forth on its chain, she stared through the kitchen window at the landscape beyond, realising with a profound sense of belonging just how much she loved it here.

Realistically, what were her options? It took months of planning to escape from him the first time, not to mention all her savings. And where would she go? This had been an all-or-nothing move and so far, it had worked. Flammark made her feel better. Emma didn't want to leave and why should she? He'd forced her out of one home, hell would freeze over before she'd let him do it again.

A faint smile surprised her. Clearview really did live up to its name.

All very well talking the talk, though. She'd need support and lots of it. Her friends may have wondered about her past —what had brought her here—but they knew nothing. Getting help meant opening up to someone, and no way was she going to do that.

The phone rang again. Will this time. "Hi Emma, you all right?"

"You've been talking to Gabby, haven't you?"

"Yes. How did you know? She said you were okay but that you had a bit of a turn and needed to sleep it off and that you'd probably appreciate a call."

"Someone needs to tell that woman about boundaries."

He laughed. "I know. She's a force of nature, but she does see things others don't. I like to think of it as a gift. For example, she said that after you wake up you may find your-self at a bit of a loose end."

"Well, though I need to talk to Gabby about minding her

own bloody business, I can't deny she's right. I have the whole day ahead of me and not much to do with it."

"Okay," said Will. "That being the case—and you've not to worry—I've had a break-in at the vicarage. Strangely enough, they've taken an interest in those parish records in the library cabinet. There's glass everywhere. The documents have been pulled out and thrown around."

"As if you haven't enough on your plate. Have any of them been taken?"

"I called the police and Westen sent his sergeant over. It surprised me, actually. You hear tell of the police not being that bothered about burglaries and I thought they'd just give me a crime number. But it seems they're keeping an eye on us, what with the Chater case being reopened. Anyway, he came with a fingerprint technician and took a statement. They want me to go through everything and give them a list of what's missing. I wasn't up for doing it last night and just wondered..?"

"Say no more, Will. Love to. Give me an hour."

Emma took her time walking over the green. She didn't feel she could go two steps without scanning the landscape and looking over her shoulder. But rather than panic and wanting to flee, she remembered her resolve and thought instead about future possibilities, and how she might go about getting help. It might have to come to police involvement—they might not take her seriously. Then there'd be statements, and restraining orders, all of which had been terrifying prospects before. She felt stronger now, though, fortified by the presence of good friends. Will, Gabby—even Robbie. They gave her the energy to fight.

She would consider going to the police. But maybe not quite yet.

By the time she knocked on the vicarage door she'd persuaded herself that, as a first step, she might—just might —be prepared to have a conversation with Will. Get it all out of her system, get some external perspective. He was a vicar, after all. He'd no doubt have come across stories like her's before.

Will opened the door at her knock, and they went straight through to the library. "God, what a mess!" Emma exclaimed.

"I know," said Will. "It isn't a good look, is it?"

They viewed the carnage. As he'd said, the locus of the break-in centred around the huge cabinet. It was still standing—it would have taken a Herculean effort to pull it over—but its doors had been yanked open with such force, the glass had exploded into thousands of fragments which now glinted on the jumbled mass of documents which scattered the floor. The small black casket rested on its side amongst them.

"Have you any idea who might have done it?" asked Emma, shaking her head in disgust. "Or why?"

"Haven't a clue. Whoever it was confined their activities to this room. Everywhere else has been left alone. They were definitely after something in that cabinet."

"The police have given the go ahead to clear it up?"

"Yeah, no problem. They took a few fingerprints— including mine for elimination—but they weren't hopeful."

They got right down to her second clear-up of the day. Will provided cushions to kneel on while they picked up the larger pieces of glass first. It took them half the morning before they'd cleared enough away to start rescuing the documents. After carefully blowing and dusting down each page Emma handed them over, one by one. Will, having freed up all the space on his huge desk, gently placed them on it, dusting them a second time, ordering and nesting them like a game of patience.

They broke for lunch but didn't linger over it. Afterwards, with more picking and brushing and a thorough vacuum, they were finally able to stand freely on the carpet and survey the neat array of documents on the desk together with a set of shelves he'd pressed into service as overspill.

"You know, I've had them all these years, and have some idea of what they contain, but I never found the time to really scrutinize them."

"Some of them do look really old."

"Flammark's part of an ancient estate."

"So I understand. I read about the ruins on the council website before I came and presumed they belonged to the landowners."

"Yeah. Blaxton Hall used to be the largest country house in the South of England," Will said. "Blaxton money and influence have been here for centuries but, as I think I've said before, not in a good way."

"You mentioned there'd been a fire?"

"A conflagration, by all accounts. George Blaxton and his daughter, Sophie, were killed together with the last of their sons, Edwin. It could have been a lot worse. Another son, Edmund, and his wife and child—can't remember their names—had left to find pastures new only a few months before. Must have been terrible. It left the hall irretrievably damaged and unsafe, so they had to demolish. All that's left are a few foundation stones and the standing remains of the family chapel—what we hereabouts just call the Ruins."

He started to rifle through the papers, still mindful of any missed crumb or shard of glass.

"I didn't realise there were so many," said Emma.

"There's a couple of hundred here, some merely fragments. A drop in the ocean. As I told you before, everything of any real value has been archived."

"The Blaxton family name comes up an awful lot, doesn't it?"

"That's hardly surprising. You have to remember that church livings were once at the behest of the landowners, and their fates intertwined. Remember, when you first saw the size of the vicarage? I said then that several lesser members of the Blaxton family took up the parish living, at one time or another."

"Common practice, I believe," Emma said. "Weren't they used by the aristocracy to occupy their feckless dimwits?" She chuckled. "Present company excepted, of course."

"Of course!" Will acknowledged, giving a mock bow. "And you'd be right. Church livings in those days didn't have to take much effort. The lazy ones could get away with organising a service every week—a major festival, or two—and whipping up a sermon. That, together with saying the odd prayer occasionally, job done."

"Tch."

"Take this chap, for example."

Emma looked at the document, a yellowed piece of unlined paper printed with the name and coat of arms of Sandmarsh Cathedral under which were the words:

*The Investiture of the Reverend Ronald Markham as vicar and priest of St. Jude's Church, Flammark. July 1806.'*

"Was he related to the Blaxton family?"

"No. He was given the living by old Thomas Blaxton, who owed thousands in gambling debts to the Earl of Tewkesbury.

They were written off on condition the living was given over to his youngest. Nasty piece of work, by all accounts."

"Who, Ronald?"

"Yeah. Rumours about his marriage. Don't know much more about it, except she died. Horse-riding accident apparently, or so it appeared on the death certificate. She's buried in the churchyard next to her husband." He nodded in the direction of the library window.

"My God. What happened to him?"

"He didn't outlive her for long. I have the parish accounts for that period." Going to one of the bookcases, he took out a thick leather-bound volume. He carefully opened it up and gently turned the pages until he found what he was looking for and stood next to her with it.

"See here?"

"Yes. *'Twenty bottles of brandy at three shillings and sixpence each.'* Wow, that sounds a lot for then. What's that in today's money?"

"Oh, a good hundred and fifty quid. I'd say cause of death was either bankruptcy, a sclerotic liver or both."

Emma chuckled at the gallows humour. Then they both jumped. The little casket which Will had placed on the windowsill while they cleared up, had dropped onto the desk.

"That's weird," said Will.

Emma stepped over to retrieve it. Touching it felt like electricity had tingled her fingertip and she drew her hand quickly back in surprise. She couldn't account for the sensation. The box could hardly have got hot since it had been sitting on a drafty window ledge. She was about to examine it more closely when something on a fragment of script seemed to catch the light. It shimmered, somehow, and drew her attention away from the casket. But she didn't put it down, preferring to hold it in one hand whilst she picked up the small piece of paper in the other.

Written upon it was a series of notes, with the title: *Prayers of Intercession. 10th October, 1697*

"Goodness, this must be one of the oldest documents you've got!"

Will put the account book back and came to look over her shoulder at what she'd found. "Ah yes. It will be. 1697 marked the incumbency of the first vicar of Flammark. He had a rather grand name: Sebastian Gerard. Funny, I thought all the valuable fragments had been archived. I must set this aside."

"I hadn't realised dates were written as they are today."

"Absolutely. They're a vital part of evolved civilisations. Formats don't change much over time. They carry too much legal weight." He returned to the shelves.

"I've got a tiny piece about Gerard here." He pulled out a book entitled, *'The Ecclesiastical History of Southern England'* and after consulting the index came upon a chronological list of incumbents of St. Judes's. He read out:

"*Sebastian Gerard, first vicar of Flammarque, had a short incumbency. Installed in the April of 1697, he died only nine months later under very suspicious circumstances, being at continual loggerheads with the estate's owner, Henry Blackstone.*'"

"Blackstone!" Emma exclaimed. "Is that the origin—"

"—of the Blaxton family? Yes. The Blackstone history lives up to its name. Generations of male children—very few daughters—produced what people today would call a culture of toxic masculinity. In those days they'd simply be called blackguards."

"Well they were patriarchal times, weren't they? Women have always been … used and abused." She sighed. It had all been going so well.

"Oh, I agree, though have to say the Blackstones were an exceptionally brutal lot. At the risk of repeating myself too much, Flammark is well rid of them."

Emma looked down at the intercession again. "These look like the actual notes Gerard took with him as he led the prayers that day."

"Yes," Will agreed, "they probably are."

Squinting at a line in the text, trying to decipher the handwriting, Emma said, "Will … does this say what I think it does?"

He followed her finger, and read aloud from Gerard's archaic secretary script:

"'*We pray for the whole of the parish of Flammarque, that we be released from the lassitude that hath afflicted us.*'"

"Lassitude," said Emma, frowning a little. She made a little laugh. "Maybe they had a dose of the sleeping sickness too!"

Will looked at her askance and scoffed, "Don't be daft."

"I'm not! What's lassitude if it isn't some kind of sleeping sickness? One that's come over an entire community—the '*Parish of Flammarque*' no less?"

She was reading on now. "And look at this!"

Slowly, getting the hang of the handwriting, with Will's help she read out the words of the second intercession:

"'*Hear … our prayer as we think of our patron … Henry Blackstone and his wife, Mary, that their daughter, Margaret, missing these last weeks, will be returned to us unharmed.*'"

"Gosh, that is a coincidence," said Will. "They had a missing girl too!"

Emma felt a catch in the back of her throat, a rising stress. Her brain told her there was nothing to see here, just a silly confluence of events. But instinct told her otherwise, in fact, the steady pressure she felt increased so much she could feel each thump of her heart.

A sudden thought occurred to her. She said, "Will, why do you think someone broke in?"

"What do you mean?"

"The cabinet is the only thing they've touched. What's been stolen from it?"

"I can't be sure until I check all this," he said, pointing to the desk. "I have a record of its contents somewhere, but on the face of it, I have to admit the collection does seem to be intact."

Emma stood locked in thought, her brain on overdrive. "What if the intention wasn't to steal anything? Instead, what if someone wanted to draw your attention to the documents? You've got to admit, the intercessions are one hell of a find."

"But who would do that? Over the years, I've rarely opened the cabinet, so hardly anyone knows what's in here. And why couldn't whoever it was simply tell us about it, instead of faking a burglary?"

"I have absolutely no idea. It's completely bonkers. But so is the sickness that Robbie can't diagnose, and the blind eye the police took over Abby. So is Josie's certainty that Jim killed her."

Not to mention the waving figure, the shadows in the church. Losing her memory.

Emma put the intercession down. She suddenly remembered the casket she still held and looked at it again. It felt a heft beyond its size, made of some kind of stone. Was there something inside? She tried to open it but could see no mechanism with which to do so. She shook it, turned it upside down and searched for hidden catches. Nothing.

Will watched her, a look of amusement all over his face. "You won't be able to open it."

"Have you got the key?"

"There's no keyhole. As far as I know, the box has always remained locked. It's one of my parlour tricks. I think every trainee and curate that's stayed here has had a go."

"So, nobody knows if there's anything inside?"

"Nope. Though if there was, we'd hear it rattling or moving about, wouldn't we?"

"The carving's so intricate. I can't quite make it out, is this a ... bird?"

"It is. The box is so old the edges have worn a bit. The image also appears on the family coat-of-arms. It's a blackbird."

Emma felt the blood drain from her face. She saw it now —how could she have missed it? The etched surface suddenly made complete and familiar sense. Swaying slightly, as if it were a hot coal she dropped the casket; looked for a chair or something to hang on to, as her hand flew to her throat to worry at her pendant.

"Are you okay?" said Will, coming over. Gently, he caught her arm and led her to one of the armchairs by the fire. "You've gone drip white. Shall I ring Robbie?"

She shook her head. "No. Nope, I'll be alright. Just a sudden headache. Robbie will only fuss."

"Do you want me to walk you back to the cottage?"

"No, I'll be fine. I think I need some fresh air. Sorry. Could I ... could I possibly ask you to you get my coat?"

"Of course! Hang on, won't be sec." And with that he hurried out of the room.

In the few moments it took him to return with Emma's parka, she'd got up, whisked the little black casket off the rug and slipped it into her bag.

## ❧ 18 ❧

## DAWNING

*L*ook *at this Michael, isn't it beautiful … beautiful … an
heirloom. Take it off … take it off … take it off …*
　　Gabby's face filled her entire vision and Emma's
breaths came quick and hot, as she struggled to escape her
friend's gaze. But her leaden limbs wouldn't move. Suddenly
the visage morphed into Michael's and he stared at Emma, a
penetrating glare that thrust itself deep, then deeper still,
into her consciousness. She tried to cry out but the black
wing of a bird covered her mouth, its feathers choking her,
stopping her from screaming. She flung her head one way,
then the other, squirming beneath the piercing gaze of
Michael's stony eyes. Then the face changed again, and her ex
was there, with his pretty-boy looks and twisted smile,
weighing her down, suffocating … sucking the life out of her
…

Dragging herself out of sleep, drenched in sweat, her forehead deep into a pillow, Emma hauled herself up at the
sound of her alarm. She panted with exhaustion her head
filled with a thick soup of memories she thought she'd locked
away. Desolate she sat, in the dark of the morning, surveying

the sea of bedclothes she'd tangled with, sick with the knowledge that, somehow, all her memories had escaped.

She opened the curtains. Bleak. Grey. Cold.

Like an automaton, she went to the bathroom, showered then dressed. Trying not to think, she partitioned the nightmare and made her bed, ignoring the trouble she was in for as long as she possibly could.

A few hours later, work proved a different kind of bad dream. Closing down her mind meant closing herself off to Robbie and despite all his irritating efforts to cheer her up, she'd only been able to raise wan smiles and charity laughs. Eventually he said, "Are you sure you're all right, lass? If you need a few more days off, that's perfectly acceptable."

"Yes. No. Really, I'm okay. I … I've had some bad news, that's all. This is the best place for me, Robbie. I need to keep busy."

To stop the doctor from fussing, she allowed him to take her temperature, but didn't want to open her mouth to let him press her tongue and check her throat. It would feel like one more violation and she didn't want to think of Robbie's actions in that way. So he had to make do with brewing her some coffee, telling her not to, "… budge from the desk until lunch time."

He needn't have worried. The phone hardly stopped ringing with patients either cancelling appointments or asking for the doctor to phone or visit. On the one hand Emma was glad of the occupation, but the obvious escalation in the sickness—or should she call it lassitude?—worried her and added to the thickening dread which had begun as soon as she recognised the carvings on the small black casket she'd stolen from the vicarage. It had not left her bag since.

The phones died down after about eleven o'clock. Robbie decided to abandon afternoon surgery in favour of making direct rounds. Since people clearly didn't want to expose themselves to possible contagion and come to him, he must go to them. Emma baulked at the decision. What the hell was she going to do with herself for the rest of the afternoon? Go mad?

An hour later they locked the door for the rest of the day. They devised new opening hours and Emma organised a sign displaying the changes. She pinned a copy to the door before going back to her desk, sure she could find a bit of filing to do.

"How about I make you some lunch, Emma?" Robbie stood at the foot of the stairs concern written all over his face. "You're worrying me. Let me feed you."

Why not? It would at least take her mind off herself for a while.

Emma picked up her bag and followed him upstairs—she hadn't been in his private domain before. The oak panels in reception continued upwards before giving way to a wide landing. Two doors were open on her right. As she passed, she glimpsed a huge, comfortable living room, with a single leather chair next to a large, ornately tiled fireplace. Over it, a beautiful, gold-framed, foxed mirror hung over the mantlepiece.

Next door, her passing curiosity revealed Robbie's study, looking not dissimilar to the state of his surgery office when she first arrived. She managed a half-smile to herself. She could see herself sorting that out for him too.

Before walking through into the kitchen, another set of stairs appeared, obviously leading to the bedrooms. Echoing Gabby, she remarked, "This is an enormous place for you to rattle about on your own in, Robbie. Ever thought of downsizing?"

"Never. The best memories of my life are in this house." Emma noticed his clipped Scottish undertones were coming through more strongly now. "I cannot conceive of ever leaving. Now, do you like soup? I always have a pot on the go for my lunch and I can make it stretch."

"Soup would be fine, Robbie, thanks."

She gazed around as she sat at a pine table, her interest piqued. "Such a massive kitchen! I've never seen one this size on an upper floor before."

"The house originally had six bedrooms, four on this floor and two upstairs. We knocked through two of them to make this so we could convert the whole of the ground floor as a surgery. What do you think?"

"It's ... amazing."

"Also one of the reasons I don't want to give the place up. I've a large workshop in the back garden and am a fairly decent carpenter. I made all the pine units here myself." He surveyed his handiwork like a proud father. "We hunted down as many period pieces as we could—went all over the country—"

He stopped for a moment, swallowed hard before continuing. "See the Aga? It's one of the originals from the thirties. Cost a bloody fortune and Joanie—my wife—spent weeks restoring it before we had it converted to gas and installed."

Emma nodded. She could only wonder at the kind of relationship that could make a man still mourn so deeply for his wife, two years after she'd passed away.

"Now, Emma, food." He took off the lid of an over-sized enamel bread bin and cut chunks off what looked like a homemade loaf. "I have some chocolate cake left over. We can have that later."

Finally, he had succeeded in putting a genuine smile on her face. "Did you make the cake as well as the soup and bread?" Emma asked.

"Aye. I did.

They fell into a friendly silence as they ate. This had been a good idea. The food revived her and the pall that hung over her felt less heavy. Without really thinking, Emma said, "Robbie, how long have you known Gabby?"

His ginger beard made way for a smile. "That woman is a law unto herself. I met her when we first came to Flammark twenty-five years ago and as far as I know, she's not had a moment's illness in her life. She never once stepped into the surgery, until the day after my wife died."

He paused to tear off a piece of bread. "I'm not a … demonstrative man, Emma. Not very sociable. But Gabby has this ability to make you feel very comfortable in her presence. She saw me through. Simple as that. I'm glad she's attached herself to you. If ever you were in trouble, she'd be the one to go to."

Gabby. Seemingly all-knowing, a finger in every pie. She'd been the very first person Emma had met in Flammark, rescuing her in the café with tissues and tea, and knocking—thumping—at her door after the appearance of the waving woman. There too during the shadow show, and, of course, the day before yesterday, holding her in the car park after she'd seen *him*. She remembered going with her to the community centre.

Without warning Gabby's face loomed up in her mind's eye; a terrible, unwanted echo of the morning's terrible dream. In a blinding moment she knew. Knew how her memories had escaped; remembered that, somehow, Gabby had got inside her head.

"—Emma, Emma?" Robbie's voice faded in. "I'm getting really worried now, lass. You left us for a minute!"

She shook her head slightly, returning to the now. Stone cold anger replaced her former numbness. How dare she? How fucking *dare* she?! But Emma held her outrage at bay for Robbie's sake. If nothing else the realisation had at least got her brain working again. As she busied herself eating a slice of his chocolate cake, she felt it processing away, filling in the gaps. Though she could not recall the detailed content of her 'conversation' with Gabby and Michael, she was definitely getting the edited highlights.

Eventually, up to speed and wrapping her fury in a kind of weird calm, she got through the cake and pushed away the plate. "Robbie, that was fantastic. I'm stuffed."

"I'm glad to hear it. I'm also pleased to see some colour in those cheeks of yours. You look positively flushed. I was going to suggest you go home and take a nap."

Despite herself, she had to admit the meal had been very good and she was struck yet again at what an amazing husband he must have made. Lucky Joanie.

The food had not just filled her stomach, it had revitalised her. She'd deal with Gabby later. But no way was she going to nap—she'd had more than enough bloody sleep. Besides, Robbie might be able to shed some light on the Blackstone family and help her to process what she'd learned at the vicarage.

"Robbie," Emma asked. "Would you ever diagnose the sleeping sickness as ... lassitude?"

"What a strange question! An interesting one, though. It did use to be a stated medical condition back in the day. The term comes from the Latin, *lassitudo*, meaning weary, and was commonly used before medicine became a developed science."

Good old Robbie, ever the textbook.

"But we're not talking about mere tiredness here. Medically, fatigue relates to muscle weakness. Muscle tissue often presents with nothing wrong when tested. That's why our 'sleeping sickness' as you put it, is such a sod to pin down—if it isn't a virus."

"Can these things lie dormant, say over a century or more, and then become active again?"

Robbie shook his head and laughed. "Tch, lass, whatever's

put that into your head? Nonsense. The only thing that allows a pathogen to do that is if it emerged after being frozen. Ice-age or laboratory frozen. I don't think either applies to Flammark. No, this is a existing bug to be sure, but one we'll find. We must rest our hopes on science."

Emma nodded as if she agreed with him, but she wasn't going to disclose her true reasons for asking. He'd think there really was something wrong with her.

Robbie rose from the table and began gathering the dishes. "I'll be off soon to make my rounds. Since we're closed all afternoon, you'll have more time off to recuperate from, what did the Gab say? Your 'funny turn.' What're you going to do with it?"

"I've a bit of filing to do, and I'll have to stay to book appointments."

"Ach, leave that. Use call forwarding and I'll pick them up. Take the afternoon off?"

"Another? Robbie, this last week I've been more out of the surgery than in it!"

"That's okay. We're in special circumstances. What about paying Sandmarsh a visit? I don't think you've been there yet. Get some fresh air, see the sights. It may be winter but there's lots to discover."

Not a bad idea. She could go to the cathedral library— Will had been effusive about it, though she doubted it would offer much in the way of fresh air.

"You know what, Robbie, I think I might."

## ❧ 19 ❧

## PATTERNS

Sandmarsh attracted thousands of tourists every year. Even in early winter it had a lot to offer. Besides visiting the cathedral, people could walk its famous ghost trails, gawp at ancient stones and burial sites and shop for dreamcatchers and incense in the Goth shops.

Such delights were not top priority for Emma that afternoon. Fuelling her new obsession with the Blackstone family prevailed instead. As she drew into the municipal car park opposite the cathedral, she suspected *he'd* got a room here—well, either here or Ledbridge—so she was especially on her guard. However, as she crossed the road to the cathedral approach, she saw nothing to raise her anxiety levels further than they were already. Paradoxically, part of her hoped he was watching her; wanted him to know she functioned without him and that seeing him hadn't made her hide away, shivering under a duvet. But it was a small part. A very small part.

Massive, compared to St. Jude's, the cathedral had all the signature features of a straightforward Norman foundation. There was nothing Romanesque about its hundreds of round-arched windows and flying buttresses. No gargoyles or weird corbels. There were three towers, one of which sported the tall spire she viewed that day, as she sat on Seely Tor. Not that she could see much of it from where she stood now.

Head up, her eyes everywhere, she strolled through the open, studded oak doors of the cathedral entrance and bought a guidebook at the tourist point. It told her the library was housed in the basement and described the location as unusual, since normally a higher percentage of a cathedral's footprint was given over to crypts rather than books. Something to do with Sandmarsh having for centuries been what the guide book stated as: a *prestigious centre of learning.*

Emma found it easily enough and stood at the top of a series of stone steps which marked the library's threshold. Despite being only on a single level, what it lacked in height it made up for in scale and appeared much larger than she'd envisaged. From her vantage point she saw the extent of its bookcases and display cabinets, some even lit to show off its most prized volumes. Brass lamps with green shades rested on ancient tables upon which priests and scholars had studied their faith for centuries. The room, enshrouded by church silence and musty incense, drew her in.

She took the broad steps and walked over to a wide, semi-circular oak desk. Emma assumed the tall man behind it was the librarian, but his dog collar and cassock left room for doubt, so tentatively she asked, "I'm interested in the history of the parish of Flammark. Will Turner is the priest there and—"

The young priest interrupted, "Oh yes, I know Will very well. He was my pastoral tutor. I'm Peter Martin. Do send him my best regards. The vicarage library is wonderful."

Grateful for the friendly tone of the conversation, Emma continued, "I'm particularly looking for any records you may have concerning the family who owned the parish living, the Blaxtons or Blackstones as they were originally known. I'm not sure when the name change happened."

Peter replied, "Yes, we do have some books that might be of interest. The Blackstone name changed at the turn of the nineteenth century, if I remember correctly. The family had a notorious reputation for violence and dissolution, so they tried for a reboot. Unsuccessfully, as it happened."

"I'm impressed you know so much about it!"

"I have one of those minds. It's why I'm of more use here than in a parish, or so my elders and betters tell me. I don't disagree."

As if to prove their point, he continued, "Did you know that Edward Blackstone owned one of the largest sugar plantations in the West Indies? All those slaves! That's where all the later wealth came from, of course. Before that, the Blackstones played a big part in the Civil War – taking the king's side, of course. Backed the wrong horse there!"

Emma laughed politely. "If you could show me where I might read more? The date 1697 is of particular interest. And I also want to see a genealogy. Will had one and I hoped you'd have something similar."

"1697. Let's see ..." Peter took her over to a remote set of shelves at the far side of the library and before long took down three large tomes of varying thickness. Emma couldn't imagine they'd be a popular read and she thought it to the cathedral's great credit that he didn't have to blow any dust off them.

"I'm afraid we don't allow photocopying of our antiquarian titles. They need careful handling. You'll have to take notes - or you can use your mobile to take pictures, of course."

"Don't worry, Peter. I've come prepared!"

He smiled and seeing she had no further need of his help,

floated in his cassock back to the main desk. She shrugged off her coat and sat on an ancient bench, took out the pad and pens she'd bought on her way in and, taking a deep breath, surveyed at the volumes in front of her.

They were all histories of the Blackstone family, though written in relatively modern times. The slimmest book, but still substantial, outlined the Blackstone genealogy going back as far as the 15th century. She could see for herself that many branches had died out, except, interestingly enough, for the one whose members remained closest to the family seat in Flammark.

Anxiously, she fumbled at the pages, wanting and yet not wanting to see what she had really come for. She followed her finger down all the branches until coming upon the descendants of George Blaxton, born 1885. He married Alexandre Collins in 1906 and had eight sons—only one daughter—the youngest of which was Edmund, born in 1913. Then suddenly, there it was, in black and white, the name she feared would be there.

Josiah Blaxton, born 1936.

Her knuckles turned white as she gripped her pen. How could this be possible? Opening her bag, she lifted out the black casket and placed it on the table. She took off her necklace and put that there too. Desolately, she stared from one to the other, at the identically wrought image on both artefacts. A blackbird.

Josiah never talked about his family. She racked her brains, drawing a blank on any reference or comment or link to his past. Only one recollection came to mind—she hadn't thought anything of it at the time. Her father had been offered the chance of promotion down South and refused to take it. She'd found her mother in floods of tears, not because he turned good money down, but because he wouldn't tell her why. It all made complete sense now.

According to Will, only three family members had been found in the aftermath of the fire at Blaxton Hall. George, his daughter Sophie, and other son Edwin. He'd said Josiah's father had left the family before their old home burnt down, having made off with his wife and child. Something must have put the fear of God into Edmund. Not only did he take his family away he'd gone to great pains to ensure Josiah, and *his* offspring—herself—didn't return either.

But her grandfather obviously hadn't been able to cut all ties. He'd retained one precious thing and passed it on to his son. She picked up the blackbird pendant. It proved beyond any shadow of a doubt that she was a Blackstone daughter.

Time ticked past as she stared at the book, then at the pendant, then the box and back, as she tried to make sense of the connection and its ramifications. One thing for sure, her arrival in Flammark had been no 'pin in the map' exercise. Any illusions she'd harboured about controlling her own fate were dead in the water.

Gabby's round, plump face came back to her, in the same way it had loomed in her dream. Control. What a bloody farce. Emma had no control - over anything. Even her mind seemed to be fair game for her so-called friend. And what was *she* up to?

What was she supposed to do now? Run away again? Her stomach lurched as the full extent of her situation dawned. That wasn't going to happen, though not because of any determination on her part. She had a terrible feeling that whatever brought her here was not going to let her leave.

Emma's hand moved to her neck. Unable to bear the absence of her pendant, she picked it up and fastened it back again. It had always helped her to think straight and now she needed its comfort and help more than ever. As soon as her fingers rubbed against its familiar edges, she felt calmer and realised the only thing that would give her some forward movement—a handle on the situation—was information. She needed answers, and for this purpose at least, she'd found the right place. All her instincts screamed that the sickness—the lassitude—was somehow significant, and that whatever was happening to Flammark now, and that included the disappearance of Abigail Chater, had happened before.

Emma came back to the books. One turned out to be the same ecclesiastical history that Will had read from, so she set that aside. The third volume was entitled: *"The Blackstone Family."* Tentatively fingering the embossed coat-of-arms beneath the title, Emma could both see and feel the image of the blackbird incorporated into its decorative flourishes. Tugging at her necklace with one hand, she used the other to turn the pages straight to the chapters which dealt with their activities in the 17th century.

Success. More details about Henry Blackstone and his parish priest:

*1697 proved a difficult year for both Flammark and the Black-stones as a confluence of events disturbed the peace of the parish. The inhabitants were struck down by an unknown dis-ease which curtailed all activity in the fields. Trading activities ceased for two whole months and many people, without the support of the tight-pursed lord of the manor, starved to death.*

*His family received comeuppance for its miserly ways when a major scandal rocked the county. Margaret, their only daughter, vanished on her sixteenth birthday, never to be found. Henry, whom some suspected to have had some involvement in her disappearance, in one of his rages, (see p. 220), later set upon his wife, Mary. Her dead body, much abused and with a cord and its marks around her neck, was discovered by the vicar of the parish, Father Sebastian Gerard. Witnesses (see {3} below) told of a terrible confrontation between the priest and Blackstone, culminating in a vicious attack from which injuries Gerard did not recover.*

*Henry killed himself before he could be brought to justice. Cf: p320*

As the note directed her, holding the pages carefully by their corners, she skipped forward, thinking she might find even more details of Henry's dastardly ways. Instead, the direction pertained to another generation of Blackstones, this time from 1810.

As with his forebear, Henry, Thomas Blackstone's marriage also ended in tragedy and with marked parallels. Of a similar disposition, rumour had it that he murdered Josephine, his only daughter, also sixteen, though no legal proceedings were ever set in motion against him. To add to the family's woes, his wife, Marianne, died the following day, though no record of the cause exists.

Emma's pulse raced as she read:

*Thomas Blackstone, known for his rages, railed against the church for not burying the bodies of his wife and daughter quickly enough. They were held in their coffins for several weeks before burial as no gravedigger or celebrants were available, having succumbed to a strange sickness which had cursed the village before. When the funeral did take place witnesses described the stench of decomposition as unbearable.*

This made it the second reference to a sickness, and this time as a repeating phenomenon. And it had been framed in the language of evil. Was the notion of a curse meant to be taken literally?

During the next hour or so, Emma's studies revealed further cycles of violence and abuse unleashed on her kind by generations of Blackstone misogyny. She wasn't naïve, knew the history of the world had been built on the violent suppression of the feminine, it was her own lived experience. But it was extreme within this family. It defined them.

And when it got bad, really bad, the village got sick. Going back and forth to the shelves and indexes, she unearthed no less than six examples, over a period of about three hundred years, where these circumstances exactly aligned. In every one of them except for Henry, the lord of the manor, his wife, and their daughter perished amidst a community so bed-ridden it couldn't raise a finger to help.

God knows what remained unrecorded, or how far back this went.

Eventually, Emma straightened up and put her palms against the crook of her back while she arched and stretched. In her bones she knew she was connected to the cycle, but couldn't fathom how. Had some unconscious feat of magical thinking brought her here? Something more sinister? If so, what? To what end? The Blackstones were no more. The fire had seen to that. Okay, she might be a long-lost daughter, but whatever weirdness had brought her to Flammark, there was no 'father' around to see her off. What was the point?

Emma's efforts to rationalise her fears didn't work. The village's current sickness gnawed at her. As did Abigail's disappearance and the questionable death of her father, Jim, though how that linked to the Blackstone family, God alone knew.

For no compelling reason, Emma opened the genealogy again and browsed the pages of dead family trees, loosely reflecting on the different branches of the Blackstone family spawned by all those angry sons, finally ended by conflagration. As she browsed, a delayed reaction to something she'd glimpsed jolted her. She turned the pages back and forth, trying to locate it.

Eventually she found it, her eyes resting upon a minor branch of the family dated somewhere towards the end of the eighteenth century. It contained the names of only three people.

They were Georgina Blackstone and John Chaytor.

And they'd had a son.

# FAMILY MATTERS

Wired yet shell-shocked, Emma left the cathedral. Taking deep breaths of fresh air, she perched on one of the street benches and fished out her mobile.

The phone rang only once before Gabby's scatty voice came down the line. "Emma! What a lovely surprise ... are you okay? Feeling better? You had a really, really, funny…"

"Cut the crap Gabby, I need to talk to *you*, not the person you've been pretending to be. When are you due back? On your note, you wrote you'd be away for a week."

Long pause. As if she her reply needed a lot of thought. "Actually, I decided to come back early. I'm in the village now. Do you want to come to the centre?"

"No! I never want to set foot in that place again. You did something to me, didn't you? I've been remembering things."

"Shall I come to the cottage? We can talk it all through there."

"That works. I'm in Sandmarsh at the moment—"

*"Sandmarsh?"*

"Yes, I've been doing some research and I—well, I think I

may be in trouble. Though it pains me to say it, I believe you may be able to help."

"I'll come over about seven. That should give you time to—"

"Seven it is."

Emma thrust the phone back in her bag as she made her way to the jeep. Talking to Gabby made her angry, and not just about what happened at the community centre. The woman had lied to her. She hadn't left the village; she'd been there all the bloody time!

Preoccupied by her discoveries, Emma forgot to worry about being watched. She received a grim reminder, when, by the lights in the car park she saw a note had been thrust behind one of the wipers of her jeep. In an all-too-familiar handwriting it simply said:

## I SEE YOU

Without thinking, she whirled around and screamed, *"Do you? DO YOU? WELL, SEE THIS, YOU BASTARD!"* She tore the note into tiny pieces and threw them in the air, oblivious to any surprised or disapproving glances her outburst might have attracted. She scrambled into the car, reversed out and screeched away.

Men. Fuck the lot of them.

By some miracle she made it home safely, rocking the little jeep as she slammed out of it. The front door of the cottage got the same treatment. Throwing her bag on the sofa, she ran upstairs, hoping a hot shower would get rid of the dirt that had been dished out by everything she'd read that afternoon.

When Gabby knocked on the door—dead on time—Emma opened it and let it hang before nodding her inside, unable to form enough words to greet her properly. Hair still damp, she went through into the kitchen, presuming Gabby would follow.

She thumped around the room, rattling the cupboard doors to within an inch of their lives. Gabby watched, a frown playing on her face. When the filter holder of the coffee machine finally defeated her, Gabby gently took Emma's arm, and led her to a seat at the kitchen table. "Slow and steady. Breathe. I'll make the coffee."

As Gabby took over, Emma spoke to her back. "You *did* do something to me in the Centre, didn't you?"

The back stiffened.

"It was to do with my pendant, wasn't it? You got me to give it to you. Did you—I can't believe I'm saying this— hypnotise me with it?"

"I'm sorry, Emma, I really am," said Gabby, turning round to face her, before leaning against the worktop. "We really didn't have any choice."

"We?"

"Don't you remember? Michael was there too."

"Was he?" She flushed as she remembered."What was he doing there?"

"We're—I suppose you'd call it co-workers. We've known for some time that Flammark is a special place. It succumbs to certain ... forces. People like us are stationed here to watch and, as far as we can, protect."

"What do you mean, 'people like us?'"

Gabby waited, letting Emma put it together. When the light-bulb moment finally came—especially on top of all the other revelations—it hit Emma like a blow. Their names! Gabby and Michael.

It started as a ripple, like an electrically charged shiver that worked its way upwards from her stomach, discharging through her mouth in a bark of bizarre laughter. Then another one—and another. Terrible, funny, ludicrous thoughts assailed her. None of them making any sense! The world as she knew it was collapsing around her, and she was falling with it. When uncontrollable sobs joined her howls, Gabby stepped in.

Emma heard the slap across her face before she felt it.

Afterwards, the angel plopped onto the chair next to her and held her hand, letting Emma cry it all out.

Then, as in that first time in the café, her friend rescued her with a tissue, this time torn from a kitchen roll. Emma eventually managed, "Jesus, Gabby."

"Well, let's not bring Him into this. And don't get ahead of yourself. We're only pale copies of the real thing. Flammark may be in deep trouble but not enough to warrant the attention of the heavy mob. We aren't without some influence, it's just very limited. By and large, it's usually the wisdom of humans that wins the day. Free will and all that."

Emma's sobs may have subsided, but her mind raced like hell, trying to weigh the unbelievable against the incredible. *In her kitchen, no less.*

"I can see you're feeling a bit calmer," the real Gabby said. Then, with a business-like exhalation, she continued, "On the phone you said something about being in trouble."

"Yes," replied Emma, mopping up and blowing her nose. "But before we get to that, tell me what really happened at the Centre; what you did and why. I need to be able to trust you—no matter who … what you are."

Gabby nodded in agreement. "Fair enough, I suppose."

She got up, poured two coffees and returned to the table with them.

"If you've been doing your research into Flammark, you'll know about the Blackstone Curse."

The Curse. They were going to do this, weren't they? They were actually going to talk about it as if it properly existed.

Emma went along with it. "I think 'know' is too strong a word. Yes, I have been reading up on the Blackstones. Every so often, some kind of … I'm not sure what to call it—a killing pattern? Anyway something takes hold of the village."

"That's right," said Gabby. "It's triggered by the confluence of an aggressive father, his wife and a comely daughter."

"Like with the Chater family?"

"Oh, well done. Yes, you have been doing your homework. It's a lesser line and has erupted mildly in the past. Josie wasn't involved but we definitely picked something up about Jim and Abigail. You may have seen a photograph of her. She is very comely indeed."

"Yes, I saw one when we took Josie back after that Evensong service a few weeks ago."

"Ah … and what a performance that was. Knocked you both for six, didn't it?"

Emma worried at her necklace as she nodded.

"The evil behind the curse was playing with you. No real harm done, the church is protected by centuries of prayer, but it wanted its presence felt; wanted to stir the pot. It also what confirmed to us that you were a person of interest."

"But we saw different things…"

"Yes, Emma. I know what you saw. You told us."

"So, at the Centre. You did hypnotise me."

"I did. We knew you were connected to the curse in some way, but we didn't know how. Michael's suspicions were aroused when you first contacted the agents about Clearview. You sounded so desperate he turned other enquiries about it away and waited for you to arrive. And I'm so sorry about what you've gone through. You must have suffered terribly."

Emma had nothing to say about this. She wanted to have a real go at Gabby and demand what gave her the right to do what she did: invading her mind and her privacy, opening her precious lockbox, allowing her memories to prey on her. But she had more pressing questions.

She took off her pendant and put it on the table. "This really interested you, didn't it? You even asked me about it when you came with those flowers that time."

She went into the living room and brought back her bag with the notes she'd taken in the cathedral library. She spread out the handwritten copy of the Blackstone/Blaxton family tree—she'd only gone back as far as the middle of the nineteenth century—and pointed to the name of one of the eight sons born to George Blaxton, Edmund, born in 1913. Then to the name of his wife and finally to Josiah.

Gabby picked up the paper and looked down at it as she spoke. Her face melted into a smile of fond recognition. "Ah yes. It seems that in Edmund, the Blaxtons spawned the only son ever to have a decent moral compass. He was a serious lad, devoted to his mother. The pendant was originally hers. She knew about the curse, all right, and no doubt told him all about it. Though in the throes of the illness that eventually killed her, she begged him to leave, and he did, never to return. Murial, his wife, was happy to go. Sir George had taken a fancy to her, you see, so they up and left and took baby Josiah with them."

Gabby took a sip of coffee, obviously mulling, remembering events no one of her apparent age should have been able to recollect.

"Edmund joined the army—which took him and his young family completely off our radar. Then came the fire. After the chaos of the war he must have got a new identity—an easy thing to do then, since he could have stolen the tags of any dead soldier and reported him missing in action. Even then he managed to take on a similar surname—Blake. Then he settled far away from the family seat."

"But he never forgot his roots, did he?" said Emma,

picking up the pendant. "Couldn't resist passing something from his past on to his son, and through him, to me."

She rummaged in her bag and held out the little black casket in her palm, as always slightly surprised at how heavy it was for its size. "I hope I'll be forgiven for stealing this from Will. I'll give it back."

She pointed out the carvings of a little bird on each of its sides. She lifted up her necklace and looked at it as it swung to and fro in the kitchen light.

"Josiah gave it to me on my first communion. I've always loved it. My bird pendant."

Gabby said nothing, just waited.

"I'm a Blackstone daughter, aren't I?"

"Yes, Emma," Gabby nodded. "I'm very much afraid you are."

"Flammark wasn't a pin in a map after all."

"No. It needed you back."

"But why? Is it to do with the Chaters? With Jim's accident?"

"Yes. It's where it all went wrong. Why you're here and why it's all my fault."

"*Your* fault?"

Gabby pressed her lips together and grimaced. "Our time in the village was nearly over. After the fire, we thought the curse had died with it, so we were on a watching brief, just to check. We were told to give it fifty years or so then we would be moved on. At first, we didn't see the cycle emerge in Jim because it didn't come with its precursor—the sickness. Probably something to do with the weaker family connection. And, as I just said, Josie was unaffected. But it soon became obvious that something was amiss, some echo of the curse at work. I watched the sudden surge of temper Jim struggled with, saw his desire for Abigail and his self-loathing at feeling it."

"You mean, Jim was going to—"

"Oh yes. Without a doubt. From the earliest times, they were possessed of a hatred for women so powerful it eventually became a force all of its own, separate and distinct, blighting the family and infecting the village whenever a rare daughter was born." She pushed her cup away and put her head in her hands. "I felt Abby's fear as Jim entered her bedroom on the night of his accident, and her despair as he made his intentions clear. She wasn't to know it, but he was at the mercy of a depraved force neither of them couldn't possibly understand."

"Did he—" Emma couldn't complete the sentence.

Gabby shook her head. "No. This is the problem. We ... interfered. I couldn't let it happen. We're supposed to contain, not meddle. But I'd become fond of Abby and, when I realized that Jim had lost control, we lifted the veil, just for a few minutes. Michael didn't want us to do it. He said we should let the cycle complete. Then the line would end and the curse with it."

Gabby wrung her hands. "People like us are supposed to be ... disinterested in our human companions. Properly *in* the world, but not *of* it. But I couldn't let any harm come to Abby. So, we cleared his mind and let him come to his senses for as long as we were able—as I've said, the Blackstone curse is very powerful. He realised what he was about to do to his precious, precious daughter, and tore himself away, left the house and drove from Flammark as fast as his van could take him."

"Then he crashed," said Emma. "I went with Josie to the police. She wanted them to investigate it. The shadows convinced her he was still alive."

"The shadows lied, another sadistic turn of the screw. No, Jim's very dead. The curse wouldn't let him leave the village; it needed him too much to let him go. He might have been part of a minor line, but he still had Blackstone blood in him. But it went too far, and we saw the accident yards from the parish boundary. The van had been going hell for leather then it suddenly twisted in its tracks and burst into flames. Bless the poor man, he must have fought that wheel for miles before he died. Heroic, really."

"So, it lost Jim and needs to have another go. To finish the cycle?"

"We think so. Something terrible is on its way, Emma. The sickness is strong and is closing the village down. This time it won't brook any interference or allow any means of escape."

Emma ran her tongue around her dry lips, foreboding building inside her. "What are we going to do?"

"Honestly? It's hard to say. With Jim gone, the evil behind the curse is desperate. It is literally at the end of the line. We think it somehow tethered itself to your partner and used him to get you here. We don't think it's finished with him by any means."

"Whoa. Hang on." Emma formed a white-knuckle fist and banged it on the table as it occurred to her what Gabby might actually be saying. "Are you suggesting—what? That everything I've gone through; the hell that's been my life this last year, wasn't because I'd chosen the wrong man?"

No, no, no, no, no. No way. No bloody way. This opened an entirely new can of worms. "You're telling me that's how this ... curse ... brought me here? That he was its ... instrument?"

"Your partner may have been as innocent as you are, or he may have had latent tendencies the curse could exploit. Personally, I think the latter is more likely, that way he wouldn't see what he did to you as being particularly out of character. Effective possession is a gradual process, Emma. If he'd been virtuous, he'd have noticed his behaviour change and been driven mad long before it completely took him over. But that's just an opinion. I might be wrong. It could be the curse needed a total innocent to attract you enough to let him court you, closing in on him only after he made you his partner. Either way, yes, you could say he was the instrument, willing or not."

Emma got up and paced the kitchen, processing, working up a storm. The scale of the manipulation almost took her breath away.

"What am I supposed to think about him now? Will I ever know whether he was innocent or not? Am I supposed to feel sorry for him; go back to him if—when—all this is over? Because I'll tell you now, that ain't gonna happen."

Then she rounded on Gabby. "And what bloody good are you lot? Jim's dead, Abby's gone, my life's been wrecked, together with every bloody Blackstone daughter there's ever been. What the fuck are you here for?"

Gabby remained implacable. "We do what we can to protect and contain the threat. Evil has a habit of spilling over and we were put here to watch and make sure it was contained only within the village." She bowed her head and said with some contrition, "Except, you're right. What good am I? I've undone centuries of work. Because I meddled with Jim and Abby, the curse was forced to look further afield and found you. Worse, it possessed someone with absolutely no connection to the Blackstone line. It will learn that if it can do this once, it can do it again and will be impossible to contain. Imagine this loose in the world! We've got to stop it. Got to."

"Well, if it needs three components, the man, the wife and the daughter, it's screwed anyway. There's only me and … him. No kids."

"It's cleverer than you think, and it's having to adapt. In a way you are a wife—a partner—to a Blackstone incarnate, a man possessed by its evil. You're a daughter too. Josiah's daughter, another Blackstone. Two for one. The cycle doesn't need anyone else."

Emma grew quiet as the enormity of the situation began to dawn. Then in a further wave of realisation she exclaimed, "Will! Will's involved too, isn't he?"

"I'm afraid so. Priests have always played their part in the pattern, but not always. Evil needs to deprave and destroy. It grows in the corrupted hearts of men; it must be ended by those that are righteous. Priests are classic targets and inevitably get caught in the crossfire. Michael and I dare not intervene again—you've only got to see what happened over Jim and Abby to see why, so yes, we think he will be involved in some way."

"So ... do we have a plan?"

"I can't lie to you, Emma. Not really. As I have said, we have useful but limited power. But we do have knowledge, centuries of knowledge about how this thing works. And we have a lot of faith. In you. You are the strongest daughter we have ever come across."

"Me, strong? You've got to be kidding me."

"Look how far you've come. Look at the courage it took to get here."

"Huh, frying pan and fire come to mind."

"That may be true, but we've seen how strong you really are. How confident, despite everything that's happened. And I think you've forgotten something. You have defeated it before."

"How so?"

"You locked him away, remember? A simple and symbolic act of mindfulness that helped you to function and move forward. A weaker soul could not have conceived doing that, let alone make it work."

Emma stared at the black casket, mulling over its odd synergy with the box she had in her head.

"Do not forget," said Gabby. "You made an important alliance with Will. You are fond of him, have strong bonds with him, though you've only known each other for a short while. These also will sustain you."

"I'm going to tell him, you know. All of it, including about you."

"I hope you do. I don't think it will surprise him much—we go back a long way, and he'll put things together. All of us need to be on our guard; be *ready*. The Blackstone curse has everyone in place now, and the sickness is deepening. It won't be long before it makes its move."

## ❧ 21 ❧

## SUNDAY

Emma just about managed to keep it all together until Sunday.

For her conversation with Will, she hoped to channel the comfort and strength she'd felt during her very first visit to St. Jude's. If she really had become embroiled in the eternal battle between good and evil, she may as well tool up by going to the Eucharist.

The wiring hadn't yet been fixed, so candles still pervaded the church. They were necessary. The black clouds which had kept her grim company on the way over had managed to suck out most of the light, offsetting the benefits afforded by the huge triptych window. Though she'd just about got over the traumatic events of her first Evensong, Emma's heart always quickened a little as she entered the church, as it did now, as she moved to the end of a row near the back.

Only three other people seemed to have dodged the sickness, none of whom she recognised. No sign of Gabby, Michael or Robbie. Good. She could concentrate on the service, use it to summon all her composure. Choosing the church as the place to tell Will everything had been a good call. What better place to drop a spiritual bombshell?

Despite the pathetic turnout, the service was beautiful. Will had an exceptional tenor voice; unaccompanied, since the seat in front of the small electronic organ stood empty. Emma recognised *In the Bleak Midwinter*—even joined in—and could hardly believe the title of one of the other carols. *Gabrielle's Message*. Perhaps, on some level, Gabby's true self had always been in his consciousness.

The Eucharist moved her. She held her blackbird pendant as she received the bread and wine from Will, using the sacrament to connect, not with her distant ancestors—evil abusers of women and priests—but with her father and grandfather, who'd done everything possible to protect their families from them.

She remained at her seat after the service had finished, waiting for Will to join her after the usual farewell chats outside. The strategically placed convector heaters did little to keep away the cold, and she curled her fists inside her mittens as she whiled away the time, watching her warm breath turn to mist in the almost-freezing air.

"You made it, then," said Will who'd come in without her noticing.

"Don't *do* that!" she exclaimed, as she turned to face him. "I hate it when people make me jump."

"Sorry about that. Did you enjoy the service?" He grinned as he tweaked the prayer mats and collected in the few service sheets the tiny congregation had used.

"I did. I'd forgotten we were getting so close to Christmas."

"I know! It's only three weeks away."

"Strange," Emma sighed. "On the one hand, it seems like I've only been here a few weeks and yet at the same time, ages ago since I first arrived."

"That's because you belong here."

"Belong?" The word hung in the air as she shifted back in her chair and surveyed the church. Despite everything, she did feel part of it. "Yes, I suppose I do." Then she shrugged and let out another long sigh. "Will, can we talk?"

Will raised a curious eyebrow and replied, "Sure. Shall we go back to the vicarage?"

"Erm … no. I'd rather do it here."

"This sounds serious." Will strode to the back of the church, closed the oak door and slid one of its heavy iron bolts. He grabbed a cardigan from behind the pulpit and brought the heater closer. Unhitching one of the seats, he turned it around and sat before her, placing his palms on each thigh.

"Tell me."

Out it came. No hesitation, no preamble. Emma just got on with it, describing her research at the Cathedral, and about being a Blackstone daughter. To his great credit, Will remained calm and expressionless throughout, giving Emma the confidence to let go and say what she needed to.

Until she told him about Gabby and Michael.

As she pressed on through her tale, the blood slowly began to drain away from Will's face. Clearly exercised by her words, not for one moment did he move or take his eyes off her. Years of confessionals in all their forms could not possibly have prepared him for this. His furrowed brow said it all, shifting between expressions of shock and incredulity, until, when she'd finished, his countenance eventually settled into a look of stunned acceptance.

After she'd fallen silent, he said, "Is that everything?"

"No, not quite everything." She remained composed and quiet, readying both of them for the next disclosure. "I know I've been the bearer of impossible news. Given the subject matter, I thought the church was the best place to break it to you, and to return this."

Guiltily, she reached into her bag and took out the little black box. "I'm so sorry. I don't really know what got into me. When I picked it up the other day, it didn't seem to want me to let it go." She took off her mitts as she prepared to handle the treasure for one last time, before noticing a trace of a twinkle in Will's eye.

"Aha! I thought you might have picked it up. Have to admit, I did scratch my head about it, but thought it might turn up again."

"I quite understand if you want to press charges!" she smiled, reluctantly holding out the little object.

"No. I'm only its guardian. It's a Blackstone box, so it really belongs … to you."

She traced the carvings with her cold fingers as she held it out to him. The stone seemed to warm to her touch. "It was the image of the bird that started everything."

"Which led me to tell you about the blackbird on the Blackstone coat-of-arms," said Will, "It's the same as on your pendant?"

She leant forward, holding her necklace out to him by its curlicued setting. The blackbird, cameoed against an even blacker setting, would have been invisible to a casual observer. Her secret icon.

"I've always loved it, but Josiah would never tell me anything about it other than his grandmother had given it to his father before he left to join the army."

Will observed the two items. The bird in the stone of the pendant and that in the embossed carving on the box, were unmistakably derived from the same imagination. "I've always known the Blackstones were evil. You can't be a priest in this place without understanding that. They may have died out …" Will bowed his head at Emma, "… well, so we thought, but the hurt lives on. I hear village-talk about them even now. How they afflicted their families back in the day. People were beaten and worked to death; land taken from them. You already know how I feel about them. I said it all the other day, after the break-in."

Will suddenly stopped speaking. He rolled his eyes and gasped. "I bet all that was Gabby's doing, you know. The 'burglary?' No such bloody thing. She just wanted to get our attention. Point us in the right direction."

"Aren't you ... amazed about Gabby?" Emma almost felt disappointed. After the initial shock had worn off, he barely seemed fazed.

"Yes," he said, quietly. "Of course, I am."

But Emma was not convinced, and she let him sit awhile to think about her question some more. He stared into the middle distance, still and expressionless, until a sublime grin spread across his face. "Of course I'm amazed, but that's become a meaningless, overused word' too much of a surface expression to properly describe how I feel."

"Which is?" Emma ventured.

"Truly? I feel comprehensively, profoundly ... blessed." Will fell still, his expression changing. Clearly more pennies from his past were dropping. Then he said, "I've known Gabby all my life and, well, knowing what she's like and how she operates, it's all very clear now. Let's face it, Em, what person in my position could feel anything *but* blessed? I'm a priest, for God's sake, and I have been visited upon!"

Emma could see a visible change in her friend, Will's face having lost the haunted look it had worn over the past few months. He appeared more grounded. Resolute. "I do have a question, though. If even the angels of heaven haven't been able to prevent the Blackstone curse from having its way, what's changed? How are we to make any difference?"

"Well," replied Emma, blowing out her cheeks. "It's the

last chance saloon. I seem to be the end of the Blackstone line proper, but as I'm female, it's had to deploy special measures to complete the cycle."

"You've got more to tell me, haven't you?"

"Yes," she nodded. Paused. She was not looking forward to the next bit. "Will, I'm not only a Blackstone daughter. I'm also a 'wife.'"

A frown returned to his forehead. "Sorry, I don't follow."

She explained how Gabby and Michael had thwarted the curse by saving Abigail from her father; how then it had been forced to look further afield for another host, after Jim was killed trying to make his escape from Flammark.

"It's why I'm here."

"Sorry, I know I'm being really dim, but I'm still not getting it."

"I think … I think it's time I told you everything. About what brought me here and … why. It won't make for easy listening—God, talking about it's going to be hard enough—but if I get it all out in the open, it will explain a lot and I'd feel …" she struggled to find the right word.

"Relieved?" Will said.

She paused for a moment, then looking into the middle distance, towards the altar, she said, "Cleansed. Cleansed is a much better word."

"Tell me."

I won't use his name. Won't ever use his name.

We met about eighteen months ago at a works party. Being in HR, knowing most of the people there, I was drawn to a face I didn't recognise. He came up to our table—there were a few of us, all mates—he'd such an easy manner, people just shoved up and made room for him. Next to me.

His eyes never left my face. He made me feel great, as if I was the only person in the room.

We drank a few drinks, hit the dance floor, then left early. I lived only a few miles away from the club and had taxied it, expecting to come back pissed. When he asked if he could walk me home, I said yes. Midnight, a beautiful starry sky, a light breeze blowing the cobwebs away—the perfect romantic dream.

As we walked, we held hands and talked. About everything and nothing. He seemed the most amusing, charming, fantastic man. He teased me when I complained my feet were killing me, and then laughed when I took my shoes off. I walked the last half-mile barefoot, with his arm around me.

We stood outside my house for ages, but he wouldn't come in, no doorstep kiss—nothing. What a man!

I looked him up at work. Turned out he'd never even been on the payroll. He'd gate-crashed the club. Stupid, I know, but I felt really flattered.

When I asked him about it, he said I'd worked 'my magic on him' the day he first saw me in a bookshop in town, during his lunchbreak. Apparently, I'd spoken to him about a magazine he'd been browsing. He said he knew I was a regular at the bookshop and had asked an assistant if he knew where I worked. From there he was able to track me down.

I know, I know! That should've got the alarm bells ringing. All that rubbish about the assistant—he must have followed me back to work. But it didn't. When you start to fall in love, your perceptions get very selective. Men like him know what they're doing. Flattery, inveigling. All grist to the mill.

He came around most nights; didn't much like me to go to his. I went once or twice, mind, but he knew I didn't really like it. He said he bought the flat from an old girlfriend, and that she hadn't looked after it properly. He'd done it up, decorated it top to bottom. I used to tease him about having OCD. Everywhere spotless, everything place-perfect. Sterile.

Even thinking about it makes me shudder. Lots of greys and neutrals. Total contrast to mine. I loved my house so much and made it warm, welcoming.

I inherited it from my parents. Mum died of a stroke about five years ago and Josiah—that's my father, I always called him that—just seemed to lose the will shortly after. Couldn't cope. He died of a broken heart.

Anyway, my so-called boyfriend began calling me a couple of times a day and came over most evenings. Before I knew it, he'd moved in. We still had fun, but we went out less and less until every night we'd just sit in. One of us would cook— well, to be honest, usually him. He told me I was no gourmet chef and, anyway, he knew more about cooking. Then we might watch a bit of telly before going to bed. Had sex—sort of. Looking back, I'm not sure I ever really turned him on. I fancied him no end at first and liked sex a lot, always have. And he excelled at it. But after a while, it just ... fizzled out.

Things grew into a sort of pattern. He didn't like me to interrupt it, wouldn't have my friends over—and I never saw any of his, ever. I thought he got on really well with mine, like at the works party, and at first, he did. They thought him a bit opinionated, but witty— charming. I didn't like the way he started to talk about them at home, though. Calling them losers, that sort of thing. I remember we had an argument about it one night. 'Aren't my friends good enough?'

No, they weren't. He told me not to encourage them by ringing them up or taking their calls. They were pathetic and I deserved better.

I know how all this sounds, by the way. Should have seen the signs, right? Let's face it, they were pretty classic and glaringly obvious to anyone with half a brain. But, when you're in love with ... no ... when you're in *thrall* to someone like him, there is no 'reason', there is no brain. It's all about how he makes you feel, about him and about yourself. Even after the sex stopped, he still somehow managed to make me feel comfortable, safe. You start to forget that you ever really coped without him. He tells you that he loves you, even though you have all these faults, and you start to realise, if he leaves, you'll be on your own forever.

The same didn't seem to apply to him, though. He had a life. I see that now. Started to see it then. I'm not saying there was anyone else. I'll give him his due, we were an exclusive couple. An *extremely* exclusive couple. No strangers allowed. But he had an important job and that involved a fair bit of travel.

He worked in research and development for a big engineering firm. Never told me exactly what he did. Too complicated for me to understand, apparently. He took me to a few professional gigs in the early days. He guest lectured at science and engineering conventions. I sat in on one once, and realised he'd been right. I managed the first fifteen minutes on fluorocarbons and polymers before giving up. Being a Humanities graduate, it was total Greek to me. The next couple of sessions he took me to, I dutifully toured the promotional stalls with him, but opted for reading in a café when he gave his lectures.

After a while, I cried off going altogether. I'd begun to enjoy the time away from him. Have to admit, the house had been getting me down—everywhere had become too bloody neat. So, with the place to myself, I'd pig out, get a takeaway, that sort of thing. You could call it a rebellion, I suppose.

But one weekend, he came home early before I had time to tidy up. The mess made him furious, incandescent. I told him it was my home, and I'd do what I bloody well liked in it.

Things went from bad to worse. He screamed at me, yelled so much the couple next door came round.

It escalated from there ... from the neighbours' visit. He let them in, all charm and smiles. But he switched those off as soon as he closed the door. He stormed upstairs and I followed him up an hour or so later. Fool that I was, I'd tidied everywhere up, apologised. My fault ... I shouldn't have made him so angry ... Then we had sex.

I'd never felt him so ...

He ...

... held me down and whispered foul things about how much I enjoyed having him ... inside me ...

... because whores like me always wanted it. Then ...

was he ...

... deep enough, was he big enough, was he messy enough for me? Should he have torn my clothes off and left them on the floor? Should he get the couple next door in to watch, so I can have more attention?

This isn't easy for me, Will, but it helps to know someone else understands what he's capable of.

From then on, he showed no semblance of the man I'd first met. The neighbour coming, and ... the rest of it ... triggered a new phase. He didn't like me to sleep with my back to him, so he'd wake me up, three, maybe four times a night, and make me turn round. I had no clue if he slept but I knew he watched. All the bloody time, watching me. He reduced his lecture tours to the bare minimum and always made it home before I got back from work. He even suggested I give it up altogether, since he earned enough for both of us.

He'd ring me three, sometimes four times a day, checking when I'd be home. Home. Hah. He'd throw a fit if he found anything out of place. And he'd started decorating the bedroom.

Grey.

An old friend rang me. She'd been recovering from cancer treatment and I hadn't seen her in ages. The chemo had finished, and did I fancy meeting up? I thought he was cooking dinner. Wrong. He came from nowhere and grabbed my phone, mid-conversation, started shouting down it to 'shut the fuck up and leave us alone.'

He ordered me in that shouting whisper of his, to go upstairs and wait for him. In shock at what he'd just said to my friend—my friend who was frightened she might be dying for God's sake—I just stood there. Then he pushed me towards the stairs, and, shaking—petrified—I did what he told me to. Rather that, than endure another of his rages.

I'm not going to tell you what happened next.

Then and throughout the rest of the week.

Just know it was so terrible and painful—I was in agony. Had to take time off work.

I thought about telling the police, but knew he'd only turn on the charm. Anyway, he'd shredded my confidence. Why would they believe me? There were injuries, for sure, but largely invisible and mostly mental and I'd spent so much time covering it all up I felt complicit somehow, like I only had myself to blame. I know they're set up for this sort of thing now, but it's a long, complicated and terrible road. There'd be restraining orders, he'd ignore them; then solicitors and courts and cross-examinations and ... where would I go? He sure as hell wouldn't leave. Who could I stay with? I have no relatives, no family. There'd only been Mum and Josiah. Sure, I once had friends, but I couldn't bear the idea of turning up on their doorstep and having to tell them—admit what had been happening.

The only way forward was to run away.

So, I saved—still had my own bank account, thank God—and waited, biding my time for an opportunity.

One work event he couldn't get out of entailed a trip to

Ireland every year to attend the firm's annual conference, months away: but it was my chance. Now I knew the score, I could keep my head down, hold things together. There'd been no more violence. He'd got what he wanted. Control and compliance. Sex was off the table, thank God. We'd got back into the old telly and bed routine.

I planned everything around the date, even packed a small bag that I hid in a box of my parents' things. When the time finally came, he was really apologetic at having to leave me. Asked if I'd be all right on my own, hoped I wouldn't get into any trouble. He'd leave on the Tuesday, stay over, then come back the next day on the earliest ferry he could.

I double-checked the conference details—that he'd given me the right date—just in case of a trap or a test. Not only did it exist, the firm's website had a picture of his butter-wouldn't-melt-in-the-mouth face, captioned with him as the bloody keynote speaker! I expected him home on the Wednesday night but left in the morning, in case he came back early.

And here I am.

So is he.

I saw him in Flammark the day before yesterday, when Gabby brought me home.

A pall of quiet grew inside the church once Emma had finished. She was done. Her cold hands still grasped the stone box as she sunk into the chair, waiting for whatever came next.

"I am so sorry, Em. I cannot begin to comprehend what he put you through."

She tried to look him in the face but failed. "Thank you. I

wasn't going to tell you—tell anyone, in fact. I didn't want to be ... judged."

"Judged! God alive, Em, how could anyone judge you? What happened was all on him. It took enormous courage to do what you did—"

"What, run away?"

"No. Take back control. Start a new life."

Emma rummaged in her coat pocket and took out a tissue. No tears came, but huge sighs took away her breath. She squeezed at the rag of paper, then squeezed it again as she coped with the emotional aftermath of her disclosure.

Hesitantly, not wanting to interrupt the catharsis, Will said, "So, Gabby—and you—think this man has been under the Blackstone influence all this time?"

"Yes," Emma nodded. "I've gone over and over it. He certainly could look like a man possessed." She gave a little ironic laugh, "You know, the person who first coined that cliché had no idea!" She played at the tissue, tearing it to bits. "I just can't bring myself to believe the Blackstone evil was in him from day one. When we first met, he was so ... perfect. But it wasn't real. Just a ruse to reel me in. God, Will, I thought coming here was my escape plan. But it was his, all along."

Will went quiet for a while before saying, "I can see how you might think that, Em, but there is another way of looking at it."

Emma cocked her head. "What do you mean?"

"Well, in a way, *when* it took him over is irrelevant. What we have to focus on, is that at one time, there was an innocent soul inside the man. Don't get me wrong, I'm not trying to excuse what he did—God, far from it—just that if he wasn't acting on his own volition, then maybe something of the man you loved is still there."

Emma fell silent. All the time she'd gone and over her

conversation with Gabby, this angle had not occurred to her. Then, out of nowhere, a sudden rage blindsided her.

Standing up, she shouted, "So, *he's* the victim now?"

Will looked up and held her gaze. "No, Em, what he did to you was vile and unconscionable. No question. I suppose what I'm really asking is, can we hold him wholly responsible?"

"Oh, this just gets better and better." Emma paced up the aisle. Fighting the impulse to scream, she faced the altar and said, "Do you think he knew what was happening to him? If so, I'd like to think he put up some kind of bloody fight."

"I honestly don't know. I'm no psychologist, and I'm fairly new to the concept of possession, but I suspect the curse would have chosen the line of least resistance; someone whose tendencies it recognised. You intimated he'd always been a control freak - with his OCD? His flat? If so, he might not have realised what was happening to him."

At this, Emma's eyes finally filled with tears. "I can't bear it. Can't afford to think about him. All these months I've programmed myself not to. I can't give headspace to consider how *he's* been affected by all this." Quiet, sobbing hiccups overtook her. "I'm terrified of him, Will. Terrified of what he —it—wants to do to me. I don't have the capacity to analyse or feel sorry for him."

Will, out of his seat, joined her at the altar. He put a gentle arm out. She leaned into it, happy to accept its friendly comfort.

"No one's saying you should," said Will. "It's something to bear in mind for the future, perhaps. Once this is all over. And until then, you have friends here that you can rely on to support you. You can defo count me in!"

Despite herself, this made her smile. After her crying subsided, she said, "Everything's been turned on its head. What's going to happen? What am I going to do?"

"Well, that part's easy," said Will. "I'll show you."

The priest unwound his arm and moved away to take two embroidered cushions off their seats. He returned to her side and put them next to each other on the floor.

Then they knelt together and prayed.

# MARKING TERRITORY

C learview Cottage.

Shit hole.

Master of her universe, he exposes his cock and lays face down on the sofa.

Imagines her beneath him.

He moves to an old rhythm, leaking but not wasting his essence, for this is not his purpose.

He sits on the armchair next to the glowing embers of the fading fire, wipes the tatty cushions with himself.

Transgression being thirsty work, he strolls to the kitchen. Enclosing as much of the tap in his mouth as he can, he drinks deeply, wetly spreading his saliva all over it. He opens every cupboard, touches every cup and licks every one of her pretty plates, before pressing his still exposed penis against the four sides of the kitchen table.

He follows her scent upstairs to the bedroom. Sniffs the air, breathes the familiar perfume.

Opens the wardrobe. Recognises nothing, handles everything. Shuts it again.

Opens her drawers, fingers her underwear.

As on the sofa, so with the bed. He thrusts almost to the point *beyond which he cannot contain himself, before stopping. For this is not his purpose.*

*He gets up. Smoothing away all surface traces of his presence, he leaves for the bathroom, where she always keeps the laundry bag.*

*Unwashed panties. He covers his face with a pair, inhales their musk. Beyond any control now, he holds his cock with them, masturbates with them and explodes into them, emitting strangled gasps of pleasure before wiping himself with the fluffy peach towel she'd hung neatly over the bath.*

*Spent, he places his hands on either side of the sink, and bows his head, gathering himself. He looks at the mirror, and at the red line above his right eyebrow. Leaning in, he examines it closely and curves his cracked lips upwards, wondering if he has time to cut another one to match.*

*But he hasn't. Her Evensong habit lasts half an hour at most. She may come back with the fucking priest she's fucking—or she may not. Just enough time to pen a little love letter.*

*He lets himself out and swaggers, his back to the broken door. Arms wide open, he stands to face the church, defying its candlelit windows, his dick exposed to the elements, bladder bursting.*

*Turning, he wraps something around the handle, then steps back. He pisses, arcing his stream on the painted, broken door, aiming for maximum coverage, ending with a steamy flourish on her doorstep.*

*For this had been his purpose.*

## ❦  23  ❦

## CALL OUT

I t was taking a hell of a long time to sort out Holly's naff paperwork. All things considered, Westen thought it a lucky break that, after all his earlier concerns, he'd come across only one really questionable case. The Chaters. He sat with the file in front of him, chin in hand under the light of his angle-poise, the main lights dimmed. He liked working late. It meant delaying his return to an empty flat.

His phone rang. A call from the desk sergeant.

"Sir, William Turner at St. Jude's in Flammark has just rung in. There's been another break-in, but this time at a cottage he's renting out. He wants someone over there straight away."

Westen looked up at the clock, surprised to find it nearly nine. No wonder he was fucking starving. "Can't uniform deal with it?"

"Doesn't sound that straightforward, sir. Nothing taken, but it could be a nasty one. Door broken in and urinated over. Turner's very agitated and the tenant's upset. Says the same thing happened at the church a few months ago, and you'd want to know about it. I could send someone from the night watch, if you like, if you want to get home?"

The altar desecration. Was he active again?

"No, Sarge, that's all right, I'll see to it. Text me the address. What's the name of the tenant?"

"It's an Emma Blake, sir."

The redhead.

"Sir, did you get that? Sir … ?"

"Yes, yes. On my way."

He arrived at Clearview half an hour later. He had thought about getting a petrol station sandwich on the way but decided against it—something about this case made him eager to get there. He'd been flooring it but eased up as he passed Jim Chater's crash site. No point in taking any chances.

Drawing up to the cottage, he saw the rigid outline of William Turner waiting for him at the end of the path.

"Thank you for coming so promptly, Inspector," the priest said.

Westen nodded and walked past him up the path. His nose wrinkled with disgust as Turner, following him, continued quietly, "Stinks, doesn't it?"

An understatement. The sulphrous ammonia fumes hit home, getting stronger as he neared the door. He side-stepped a pool of vomit just before the front step.

From behind, Turner was saying, "My fault, sorry. I know I've probably contaminated the scene and all that, but I couldn't help it. Brought back the …"

"… smell of the altar?"

"Yeah. We found the door hung open like this. The lock's broken and there's a problem with the hinges. We didn't go in and we haven't touched anything. I don't know if Emma noticed it before I got her away, but there's this too ..." He pointed out the lacy outline of some cloth wrapped around the door handle.

"You didn't do the stupid thing and go in?"

" Of course not. Emma was beside herself, so I took taken her back to the vicarage. Called you guys from there." A sudden look of horror flashed across his face. "Bloody hell, you don't think he could still be in there, do you?"

"No. We'll check, obviously, but he had plenty of time to leave, and this," he pointed to the handle, "looks like a departure note. You haven't touched it, or anything else for that matter, right?"

"Absolutely not."

"Okay, before we go any further, I need to make a call."

Western walked to the end of the path, took out his mobile and speed-dialled his sergeant's number. Out of earshot he said, "Pete, I got a call-out about an intruder down in Flammark. I'm on the scene. Nothing taken but looks like the phantom altar piddler's back. Get down here. We need to check the place is clear—and wake up forensics. I'm texting you the address."

Westen looked at Turner's drawn and worried face as he said to his phone, "... Yes, I know what fucking time it is and no, it can't wait till tomorrow. Just tell them to get their finger out ... yep, it is someone we know ... Emma Blake ... My thoughts exactly, it may well be connected to the Chater case."

Westen ended the conversation and turned to the priest. "The door was ajar, you say?"

"Yes."

"I won't go inside until my sergeant gets here. Did you say Miss Blake was at the vicarage?"

"Yes. Emma attended Evensong, then we went there for some coffee and a chat afterwards. It looks like ..."

"Looks like what, sir?"

"Nothing, Inspector. Just ... nothing."

As Turner ran his hand through his hair, Westen could see the pallor of shock on his face. And something else. Something the priest was keeping back.

"Do you, or Miss Blake, know who's responsible?"

"She's very upset. Actually, that doesn't go near to describing it."

"I'll ask you again, sir, if you don't mind. Do you, or Miss Blake, suspect who might have done this?"

"Possibly. She has—had—a partner. It seems he might have followed her here, to Flammark."

"Okay. And do we know the name of this ... partner and where he might be now? We're going to need a statement."

"I think she understands that, Inspector. Do you want Emma back here now? As I said, she's very upset and it's going to get very late ..."

"Under these circumstances, I don't think so. If this is connected to the desecration then it links to the Chater case, so we'll need to give the cottage a once-over and that will take time. Tomorrow morning will be soon enough." Westen peered more closely at the lacy door handle, compressed his lips and frowned. "But we shouldn't wait longer than that if instead we've got an active and obviously dangerous stalker situation. From the looks—and smell of it—there'll be plenty of DNA to harvest. We'll need fingerprints for elimination and she's going to have to tell us if anything's been taken. It'll be a while before the techies arrive. Is there somewhere safe she can stay? She shouldn't be on her own."

"I've plenty of spare rooms at the vicarage."

Westen eyed him for a moment, weighing him up. Were they an item? Bit dodgy having her stay with him, being a priest and all that, but, ultimately, none of his business. And what was he not telling him?

"I'll pick her up first thing," Westen said. Maybe she'd be more forthcoming. Priests were a tricky lot. Always thinking they had interests to protect, which meant having truths to hide. "Shall we say eight-thirty? You can come with her, if you like."

"Can't. I've a funeral in the next parish. I'll tell her the arrangements when I get back and let you know if there's a problem."

Turner started back across the green, leaving Westen alone with his thoughts. Although he suggested to Pete Burrows that this was connected to the incident at the church six months ago, he felt pretty sure the object wrapped around the handle of Emma's door made this incident more than just a repeat performance. Either the perpetrator was escalating, or they were looking at a different one.

He didn't have long to wait for his sergeant. Burrows arrived with two SOCOs, who immediately got to work on the front door. Westen sat in his sergeant's car and updated him.

When he finished, Burrows said, "While we've a minute, Guv ..."

"Go on."

"I made some enquiries with my mate in traffic. You know, about the Chater crash and why there wasn't much in the file."

"Okay ..."

"Well he—that's my mate—said Holly was in a hell of state that night. Didn't seem to know up from down. They thought the same as you, that the crash was well-nigh impossible and wanted to investigate it further. Seriously, Guv, he tore them a new one. Called my mate all the names under the sun and said that he would be reporting him first thing if

he didn't come up with a sensible report by the next day. So
…"

"So, he came up with a sensible report. A very thin, very scanty, but a very sensible report."

"Yes, Guv." Burrows admitted. "And there's something else."

"This is turning into one of those fucking nights. All right, what?"

"Holly was off sick for quite a while before he retired, but rumour has it that's not the only reason why he left early."

"Surprise me."

"Apparently, it was all about Mrs. Holbrooke. Mental issues." Burrows tapped his temple with his forefinger. "She'd made a few scenes in Flammark village, screaming her head off, apparently. Happened once too often. After a shop-keeper made a formal complaint, Holly sorted it on the QT. Then he got sick and the next thing, he'd left."

"Poor Holbrooke. I had no idea. How is she now?"

"Not good, Guv. Not good at all."

Westen let out a quiet whistle. "You never know what's going on in people's lives. It doesn't let him off bullying Traffic and back-pedalling on Abby Chater's disappearance, though. There's stuff going on here I can't pin down. Even the priest is hiding something. I can feel it. I told you this case was a zebra."

He didn't have time to drill down further. One of the techies was waving them in.

There didn't seem to be any sign of damage and the place looked undisturbed, but they were ushered into the kitchen straight away. A note rested on the pepper pot. It simply said:

*Thank you for having me. I'm so looking forward to returning the compliment.*

*You can do so much better than a priest. I promise. xxx*

Burrows bagged it, and together they followed the SOCO upstairs to Blake's bedroom. Using an ALS lamp, he showed them an array of tiny fluorescences on the duvet cover.

"Semen?" asked Westen. "There isn't much of it."

The SOCO said, "We'll have to test it for sure but looks that way to me. There are faint but similar stains all over the place: cushions downstairs, on the sofa. It's a DNA fest. Looks like chappie saved himself for the finale in her knickers. You'll have to check they're her's, of course, but we had a quick butcher's in the drawer here and found others that were the same sort."

"Fingerprints?"

"Multiple. So far, three or four different sets. Good chance of one set being identified as his if we can eliminate the homeowner."

"She's a tenant," said Burrows, "but the house will have been cleaned before it was let, so there's a reasonable chance of matching a set to the perp. Not to mention his very generous donation of DNA."

The SOCOs moved outside to finish their work under the area lighting units they set up. There wasn't much to report. They deprioritised the vomit on the Inspector's instructions and found no sign of any footprints. Soon they were on their way, leaving Westen and Burrows to themselves.

Having gone through the house one last time, the two ended up in the living room. "What do you think, Pete?"

"Not our church piddler, sir. Definitely something else going on."

"And?"

"The note. Different to the three we've already got. He knows her."

"Agreed. What else?"

"Either they had a sexual relationship, or he wants one. He smeared himself all over the show."

"Yep. Sick fuck. Turner told me his tenant might have a stalker. She knows who it is, all right."

Taking a last look round, he said, "I don't like this, Pete. He'll be back."

They moved towards the door, ready to leave. "Did the SOCOs fix up a temporary padlock?"

"Yeah, they weren't happy about it but I know they carry them just in case." He waved a small key in the air. They turned off the light and secured the door. Burrows produced a roll of blue and white tape and stapled it to the door as he unwound it.

Clearview cottage. Crime scene.

## ❧ 24 ❧

## OUT IN THE OPEN

The stench of urine permeated the air, as Emma walked up her garden path with the police. Since the ammonia had matured, it stank even worse than the previous evening.

Emma's mouth filled with saliva and she feared the coffee in her otherwise empty stomach would regurgitate and add yet another bodily discharge to the scene. She kept it down, hating every step she made, loathing that he had violated her home—*her*—yet again. Westen had brought a female DC with him, introduced to her as Donna Stirling. It was she who unlocked the padlock and entered first.

Lips curled in disgust, Emma hesitated and half-stumbled over the step, bothered about what she might tread in. Perhaps out of instinct, Westen touched her elbow. She flashed him an angry look and shrugged it away from him.

Silently, they moved through the cottage, taking stock. Nothing looked out of place and, as far as she could see, nothing taken. Apart from the front door, no damage either, thank God.

Familiar thrumming started in her ears. When Will had

returned to the vicarage last night, they'd resorted to the whisky bottle to calm both their nerves, knowing the break-in to be a significant escalation.

He had made a move.

The pressure at her temples added to her hangover and the nausea returned but she clung onto her composure for dear life. The last thing she wanted was to embarrass herself in front of Inspector Snark. She desperately wanted him and the policewoman he'd dragged along, to go, but they would have questions and she had already gone over everything with Will and why couldn't they just go, go and let her work things out by herself for once in her life?

"Care to tell us about him?" asked Westen.

"Him?" She almost laughed. What could she tell them? That she'd escaped from her ex and he'd followed her? Neither statement was necessarily true. She hadn't really escaped, and the creature that visited the cottage last night wasn't really him either!

Possibly.

"Miss Blake ... May I call you Emma?"

She gave him no answer.

"Emma, it's obvious to us you know the perpetrator. Turner told us you had a partner and that he may have followed you to Flammark. Is that correct?"

She paused before nodding.

Emma gave Westen a hostile stare. He was going to be no bloody use. Despite what all this looked like, there was so much more to it. More than he would ever be able to understand. But the look on his face told her he wasn't going to back off. Though he said no more, she knew his question was still in play.

"Yes," she sighed. "I left about three months ago. Our relationship ... broke down."

"Emma," Donna said gently, "Was he ever ... violent towards you?"

Tears welling in frustration and remembrance, Emma could only nod again.

Donna asked, "Did you file a complaint against him?"

Emma stayed quiet. Surely, they knew people in her situation didn't complain. Jesus, she couldn't conceive what he'd have done to her if she had. Still controlling the urge to disgorge the vicarage coffee, Emma also tried to swallow a growing fury.

"Miss Blake." Westen, clearly impatient, resorted back to formality. "Leaving home seemed a very ... drastic thing to do. Are you sure you're not here because someone else is? William Turner, perhaps?"

That was it. That was bloody it. Incandescent, she erupted. "W-What the fuck does that mean? What are you s-suggesting? That Will and I are having an affair? That this is j-just jealous payback? Christ almighty! And you people wonder why you can't get us to talk to you. In a minute, you're going to suggest it's all my fault, with your wheedlings and your insinuations. You make me sss-sick. Get out. Just ... get the fuck out."

Donna, frowning a little at her boss, took a step towards her, but Emma would have none of it.

Still seething, she held up both palms to the policewoman and took two steps back. "Get away from me. Leave. Will told me you'd done all your ... tests and things last night. You don't need to stay. I don't want you in my home."

Westen looked at his DC and offered what seemed a semi-apologetic shrug. He gave her the nod to carry on.

Donna said, "Emma."

She bristled. Turned her back on both of them. Refused to speak.

Trying to get through, Donna said, "Emma, I can see why

you're angry, but we don't think it's safe for you to be here on your own. There are some things you don't know that we have to tell you."

She gave them nothing.

"Emma," Westen said, talking to her back, an apology in his tone. "I realise I came over a bit harsh, but I've a job to do and I needed to get you to talk. We have to find this man, and quickly, because we know you have a problem on your hands. Come into the kitchen with us. We need to sit down."

She swung round and glared at him. "No."

Westen and Stirling exchanged looks and he indicated that his DC should continue regardless. She took out the evidence bag with the note inside and showed Emma. Half registering what it was, she slowly grasped it while still staring daggers at the inspector. She looked down at the bag and winced as she recognised the handwriting. Donna said, "Did he write this?"

Emma's eyes filled with tears again, but she shook them away, stubbornly trying to get back some control. She managed another nod.

Donna continued. "And there are … residues, Emma."

She almost laughed."Residues? What 'residues'?"

"There's not much of a way we can dress this one up, Emma." said Westen. "He left semen. There are traces of it everywhere. On the sofa, the chair, in the kitchen, and quite a lot of it on your bed, I'm afraid. Then there's this." He took out a second evidence bag.

Her hand flew to her pendant as she looked along a familiar line of lace, and Emma began to sway, despite herself, in Westen's direction. He caught her before her knees buckled completely, and half-carried her into the kitchen where she could sit down.

"Has he done anything on … this?" Emma said, looking down at the wooden chair he was aiming her at.

Westen, still with a steadying arm around her, shook his head, and said gently, "No. No traces on the chairs."

He let her sit, and Donna brought her a glass of water, fresh from the tap. Emma sipped, as she processed what Westen had told her. Now she knew why he'd brought female support with him.

"I'm sorry, Emma, but we do need to ask you a few more questions." Westen brought forward the evidence bags again.

Donna said, "We found this knotted around your door handle. It's full of ... ejaculate. It's a pretty extreme thing for him to do. We think he'll be back. We think you're in quite a lot of danger."

The appearance of the second evidence bag finally broke the dam and compromised all her efforts to contain herself. All very well, these esoteric conversations about abstract curses and evil ancestors but when it came down to it he'd been terrifying her for months, both mentally and physically. Her fear of him had such substance she could almost touch it.

And that's how she'd felt even before setting foot in Flammark. Now, his squalid essence, disgustingly encrusted in the folds of her knickers, had become exhibit A in a seedy plastic bag. Existential proof that the foe she faced today was of a completely different order of magnitude from the one she'd left behind. Utterly and inconceivably terrifying.

Her mind turned to Gabby's words. *"We think the curse has tethered itself to your partner—used him to get you here. We don't think it's finished with him."* So it had proved. The evil had taken root and was growing. Eventually it would overcome him completely. She doubted the curse could be lifted by a mere arrest, but they were all now locked into the Flammark cycle—police included. There was little choice but to follow its direction of travel. For now, at least.

To her relief, Westen, having exchanged meaningful

expressions with Donna, left the two women alone. With the inspector in the next room, Emma breathed easier. The policewoman offered her a small pack of tissues and eventually, face wet and snotty, she got up and washed herself at the sink, using more of Donna's tissues to dry herself. She didn't want to use the towel.

"Emma, we need you to come to the station and make a statement. Would that be okay?"

Standing in the kitchen, she looked out of her favourite window, as she had the other day after she caught sight of him in the village. She bowed to the inevitable.

"Yes."

RESPITE

They took her fingerprints, for elimination, and Emma made the dreaded statement. Though definitely an ordeal, the extent of the relief she felt after giving it surprised her. Even better, as she prepared to leave the police station, she found a text from Will, inviting her to take lunch with him at the Flammark Arms. Westen himself gave her a lift.

On the way, he said, "Thanks for coming in ... Emma. I read your statement. You've been through a lot. And you probably haven't told us the half of it."

She pressed her lips together and nodded grimly, but she had nothing more to say. "What happens next?"

"Once we find him, he'll be detained, interviewed, then put away until the magistrate's hearing. We're going for aggravated burglary, since the threat to your safety is high. We'll keep you updated."

Emma shuddered. She doubted he'd make it easy for the police to find him, but even if they did, she also wondered what difference capture would make. Surely, he—it— wouldn't be contained that easily?

"If the CPS agrees with the charge, we can remand him. Then he'll be off the streets. I don't know how long it'll be before we get him, though. Donna tells me you'll be staying at the vicarage?"

"Yes. As I told her, it's a training centre. It's set up for residential visitors."

"Well, be careful. Don't go out alone. I hope you won't have too long a wait. I can't see it'll take us long to pick him up."

Westen drove into the pub car park and idled the car. He turned to her, smiling. "Have a good lunch then go back with Turner. Try to not worry. We're on it."

Emma didn't go as far as to wave goodbye to Westen but stood and watched him go as he drove away. She certainly felt warmer towards him. Even without fully disclosing the darker aspects of the case, after the surprisingly sensitive treatment afforded her at the station, she could consider him —and Donna—as allies. Feeling more positive than she'd any right to be, she took her growling stomach into the pub.

The perfect place.

A traditional affair, the vast public bar of the Flammark Arms revealed a vista of spindle-legged tables and chairs, oak beams and wainscoting. She walked towards the well-stocked bar, the dappled rays of the wintry sun playing all over her as they beamed through the Georgian windows panes. A welcome oasis of calm.

Emma exchanged a few pleasantries with the barman, ordered a restorative gin and tonic, and turned to find a seat. Not a huge task, since the place contained only four other customers. On her way to a table, a group of framed photographs drew her eye, under a sign that read:

## PEOPLE AND PLACES OF OLD FLAMMARK

She peered at the black and white photographs. Some places were easily recognisable. The Arms itself, for one, had barely changed—though she doubted the current pink wash would be the colour of choice then.

There were images of St. Jude's, and several of the square. In the older photographs, there'd been a large village cross at the corner of Flammark and Blaxton Road. It looked very similar to the one on Seely Tor. Had it been relocated for some reason? It looked too old to be moved. Surely there'd be heritage objections?

Dominating the display hung an enormous, framed photograph. Depicting a huge, ugly mansion, it owned the landscape. Doric columns, portico and endless windows, emblematic of the conspicuous consumption of the Regency era, exuded ostentation. Yet it paraded no gentility, and would not have inspired, say, a Jane Austen novel. This was a masculine beast of a house, standing dark and proud above the other pictures. Interest piqued, Emma got on her toes to see the copperplate script below the image.

## BLAXTON HALL

"Brute of a place, isn't it?"

She whirled round. "Will! Stop making me jump like that!" She clutched at her chest as she turned back to the picture. "Yes. It's truly enormous. The carriage parked in front gives away its scale. It must have needed hundreds of servants to keep it going."

"The family were major players. Indomitable. They needed a house to match and more than just servants to keep it going. They must have had almost as many gardeners. Look at the size of the lawn! And you can just see to the side, the start of the greenhousing. They used to grow pineapples. One of the most labour-intensive fruits ever to darken our land. It makes me shudder. It really does, the level of exploitation it took to sustain these manors, their servants not much better off than the slave labour on their plantations."

"I talked about that with Peter." On seeing Will raise a questioning eyebrow, she said, "Peter Martin ... from the cathedral? He was the librarian. He asked me to remember him to you. Sorry, I completely forgot."

"Peter." Will smiled. "I'm glad you met him. Mind like a steel trap. Wasted on parish life." He paused. "I don't see him very often, now."

"So he said!"

Her heart thumped harder as she gazed at another photograph, this time a family portrait. She looked around surreptitiously and took it off the wall. "Can we sit down? I want to look at this more closely."

The actuality of holding her family was not lost on her, as she and Will gravitated toward a large open fire. They sat as near to it as comfort would allow. Will took a few gulps from his pint and stared at the flames, clearly giving Emma quiet space to drink in the details within the photograph. Her family. *Her family.* Nothing she'd heard about the Blackstones could possibly endear them to her. They were monstrous, evil people who had preyed on the village—and now beyond—for hundreds of years and yet ... and yet ... they were not to be denied. They were her family. She was one of them.

"When was this taken? There isn't a date underneath?"

No sooner had Will shrugged than she had taken another sly glance at the bar and flipped the frame over to get at the backing. Using her fingernail, she prised open the metal claws that held everything together. After it fell apart, she saw the frame was too small for the portrait. It had covered the printed date at the bottom. "The Blackstone Family, 1913."

"Damn," she said. "Before the first war and before—"

"Long, long before your father was born, over twenty years, in fact ..." Will twisted and craned his neck to see the photo from the seat opposite. "... by the end of the war most of these would be dead. But I expect your grandfather's there. Edmund. Trouble is, we can't tell which one of them he is."

She restored the frame as best she could and turned it over to look at it again. The first visual record she'd ever seen of her family. Embattled by mixed feelings, she strained to find any sign of the curse that had beset them all. But of course, she could see none.

Emma brought the photograph up to her eyes to get a closer look at the patriarch and his wife, her great-grandparents. He with beard and moustache, she with hands on knees, back straight, surrounded by a horde of sullen youths ranging from ten to maybe, twenty-five years old, though it was hard to approximate their ages. They all had the same stiff demeanour and slicked, side-parted hair. She shivered. What would life with them have been like?

"I know it wasn't form to smile in these old photographs," Emma said, jabbing at the picture, "but she looks as if she's about to scream."

"Alexandra Blaxton. I think I remember something about her developing a taste for what they used to call tincture of opium. No wonder. Apart from having to live with George, that monster, she bore witness to the family's decline, and the death of most of her sons. War, flu, bankruptcy—even suicide—dogged them till eventually the fire finished them off, ending the Blackstone line forever." He added, grimly, "Or so we thought."

Unable to tear her eyes away from the photograph, Emma fell into a long, silent reverie. Eventually, Will broke it. "How did it go with Westen?"

"Oh, that. Not too bad, actually." She restored the picture to its former glory and placed it on the table. "Things got really difficult in the cottage. Did you know about the little present he left me on the door?"

"I'm afraid so," nodded Will. "I didn't want to point it out at the time, you were upset enough." He took a pull from his glass. "Did he leave anything else?"

"You could say that." Emma told him about the note and the other 'presents' he'd left her, on the sofa and the bed. "I … don't think I'll be able to go back for a while. Not until—"

"Say no more. I'll book a deep clean. Also, I'll completely understand if you feel you want to live somewhere else. Why not have a chat with the estate agents? I wonder if Michael's still there?" He gave a little chuckle. "Have to say, it's a weird job for someone like him. He always looks so miserable."

Emma couldn't help but smile. Despite the trials of the morning, she really did feel a lot more relaxed.

More seriously, Will continued, "Until you make a decision, you're welcome to stay at the vicarage for as long as you need to."

"Thanks, I'll take you up on the offer but, long-term, and after all this is over, I do have a decision to make about where my future lies. I may want to go back to the city, but I haven't made up my mind yet." She gestured to the photo. "I hate them but can't deny them. They feel part of me now. I'm not sure I can go back."

Then, half-changing the subject, she said, "The police think I'm in danger from him. They don't know the half of it, do they?"

"Too right. And you won't have been able to give them the full story."

"Can you imagine Westen's face if I had? Obviously I had to keep mum about all of that. Gabby's right, though, she said it wouldn't be long before my ex made his next move, and so it has proved. I expect she knows about his visit to Clearview. Westen thinks they'll find him soon, but I can't see it, somehow. And if they did, God knows what'll happen next."

The more she thought about it, the deeper those familiar fingers of dread crept into her heart. Will must have sensed the change in her mood as he suddenly grabbed two menus from the placeholder on their table and gave her one of them.

"Okay, time to eat. I'm paying."

## ❧ 26 ❧
# CAUGHT

Despite their situation, Emma and Will found their stay at the Flammark Arms surprisingly convivial. They ate a great meal, drank a glass or two and mended the ills of the world by the light of the open fire. But they couldn't stay in the pub forever.

"Time to head back," said Will. "I need to make some calls, follow up on this morning's funeral."

"I think I might go and see Josie," Emma replied. "The police will have got back to her about Jim's crash." She had another reason for going. Maybe a quiet word with Connie might reveal some extra information about the old Chaytor line.

Since Connie's estate wasn't far, Will thought it'd be a good idea to walk off some of their lunch and said he'd go with her before heading back. The freezing December afternoon made Emma hunch into her parka, as they made their way as carefully as the icy pavement would allow.

Emma was enjoying being outside. Returning to the vicarage felt too much like a capitulation and she was glad to put it off for a while. She'd spent the last year being cowed by events, and though even greater danger loomed, her fears for the future were not overwhelming. She was fed up with being frightened.

Will said, "You're drawn to them, aren't you?"

"What do you mean?"

"The Chaters. I know you've developed a friendship with Josie, after that terrible Evensong service, but it's more than that now, isn't it? You're related."

Emma had been holding onto Will's arm as they walked. She squeezed it in acknowledgement. He spoke true. Apart from herself, the Blackstone line had died out. The Chaters, though only a remnant of it, were all the family she had in the world.

As they rounded the corner, Emma saw Donna Stirling bundling herself into her car. Perfect timing, she must only just have given Josie the lowdown on the accident investigation.

"Thanks for walking me, Will. I'll be okay now," Emma said, seeing the detective beckon her and open the passenger door. "That's Donna, the detective that interviewed me this morning. It looks like she wants a word."

"Right. I'll see you back at mine then. Don't forget … take a taxi back. No risks!"

She waved him away before turning back to Donna. A few seconds later she was clambering into the passenger seat, slamming the door shut against the biting wind.

"Emma!" Donna greeted her with a smile. "Are you feeling a little better? You certainly look less pale."

"Yes, much. I'd like to thank you for this morning. You were … brilliant … at the station."

"No problem. The Force is a lot more sensitive in these matters than it used to be. Did you have a good lunch? The Guv mentioned he'd taken you to the Arms."

"I did. Had a drink and a meal with Will. First time I've

been—such a great place. We had a long chat and I think I'm much clearer about things now."

"Good. I expect you've come to talk to Josie. Have you got a few minutes first?"

Emma nodded.

Donna held Emma's gaze then put a hand on her arm. "We've picked him up. Wasn't hard to find. He's at the station now, with the Guv."

Emma gasped and turned in her seat, hardly able to believe her ears. "So soon? The break-in was only last night. I-I can't believe it!" Emma's heart rate rocketed, and she grasped the internal door handle. "Shit. Sorry, Donna, I'm all over the place. One minute it's all going to be okay, the next ..."

"I know. Take a minute." The detective waited for Emma's adrenaline rush to subside. Then she said, "He's fucking with us. It goes with the territory, I'm afraid. It's what they do." She added, "Bit of a charmer, isn't he?"

"Charmer?"

"Don't worry. He doesn't fool us. We've come across his sort before. Looks as if butter wouldn't melt, but we know better, don't we?" Donna held her eye, as if to reassure her that not for a minute had they been taken in. "He's admitted everything. Says he didn't know what came over him at the cottage. Then talked about how you broke his heart and that he'd only gone there to ask you to go back. After that, complete blank. Apparently. Oh, and he's sorry. Said he knows you're both over now."

Emma still couldn't believe it, couldn't work out his game plan. As if he'd wanted to be caught. Was he playing with the police, too?

"He looks as if he's been in an accident, though. Cuts and grazes everywhere. I don't suppose you know anything about that?"

"No. Nothing. I haven't seen him for nearly three months. I don't know what he's been up to, apart from, well, you know ..."

"He wants to see you."

Emma offered a fragile smile. "That's not going to happen."

"Don't worry, we told him it's out of the question. If we get the aggravated burglary charge through, that will mean jail time, Emma. It's probably not much of a recompense for what he put you through, but his life won't be the same if we get a conviction. He'll be a felon. Meantime, we're going for remand. That'll take him off the streets until the court case."

"Where is he now?"

"We could have bailed him. The charge is borderline, but the Guv was adamant." Donna looked at her watch. "He's being taken to Oakmarsh as we speak. It's a secure facility about fifty miles away."

Emma let out a long sigh. "Donna, I don't know what to say. I never wanted it to come to this."

"Nobody ever does, Emma. Nobody ever does."

After she left the policewoman's car, Emma was too churned to see Josie straight away, decided to walk round the estate first. There couldn't be any danger now, since he was in custody. Could there?

She mulled over what Donna had told her and at one point almost laughed out loud. Didn't know what came over him, indeed. Wants to see her again. She bet he did!

Seely Tor loomed, as it did over the whole village, an ominous backdrop to her roiling thoughts. What was he playing at? It couldn't possibly be over with. Why had he let himself get caught? Something wasn't right. He had an agenda; she could sense it, could feel him playing and manipulating her like he'd always done.

Still the burning question nagged at her. How far was he acting under his own volition? If Gabby was to be believed, the creature on the way to Oakmarsh Remand Centre wasn't 'him' at all. Somewhere underneath, the spirit of the man she once thought of marrying might be literally fighting for his life.

It was a conundrum she had neither the desire, the energy nor the ability to fathom. She needed all the mental capacity she possessed to survive the next move. Was she meant to use some of it to bloody save him too?

Unable to unthink that thought, she churned and worried all the way back to Connie's. Ultimately, nothing could be done about any of it, except to wait and see what unfolded.

By the end of her walk Emma felt more wrung-out than at the beginning. As she rounded the corner to once more view the Chaters' house, she prayed Josie hadn't been too upset by Donna's visit. Whether Jim was still alive or not, neither option would be good news, and Emma was fast losing her capacity to offer support and encouragement.

She knocked on Connie's door, expecting a plump and smiling face to answer it. Instead, a large, semi-giant of a man appeared, his grey mop of hair dishevelled, as if he'd just got out of bed.

"Oh. Hi. My name's Emma. Emma Blake. Is Josie, or Connie, in?"

Connie bustled into view behind the man and swatted him away from the door with the tea towel she carried. Her copious apron, covered in flour—and a delicious smell exuding from the kitchen—suggested a baking session was in progress.

"Oh, Sam, get away from the door. You'll catch your death. This is Emma, Josie's friend." Connie smiled at her before resuming a harried frown. To Sam, she said, "Don't let her stand on the doorstep, where's your manners?"

Emma was hustled inside and introduced. "Emma, this is Sam, my hubby."

"Very pleased to meet you, Emma," he said, his voice deep and gruff. "I've heard a lot about you."

"And I heard you've been taken with the bug that's going round," she said, managing to sideline her worries, curious to meet a victim of the lassitude for the first time.

"The doc said it's a bug. Bloomin' odd, though. One minute, right as rain, the next, can't lift my head from the pillow. Today's the best day I've had in weeks. Still feel shattered, though. Good job I'm retired, don't know what I'd do if I still had to bring the pennies in."

"That's enough of that, Sam. Emma, would you like a cup of tea? Piece of cake?" Connie's voice lowered. "We've just had a visit from the police. No news yet about Abby, but they seem to be taking things a lot more seriously, thanks to you."

She lowered her voice even further, almost mouthing the words. "A woman detective's just told Josie that Jim's definitely gone. They got all the tests back from the pa ... paf ..."

"The pathologist?" asked Emma.

"That's right. She's not as upset as I thought she'd be, just a bit shocked. She'll be pleased to see you." Connie nodded to the living room door. "Just go in."

Then she turned to Sam. "And you, you can come and help me in the kitchen. Seeing as you're having such a good day."

Emma went into the cosy living room. Little had changed since her last visit. Josie sat in front of the gas fire, gazing out of the window. After greeting her, Emma sat down saying gently, "Hi, Josie. I've heard the news about Jim."

Josie shook her head slowly. "I don't know what to think, Emma. I was sure it was him."

"I know."

"It was Jim, in the shadows, strangling her. In a way, I'm glad he's dead, 'cos it means he couldn't have killed her. But I still don't know what to make of it all."

Emma remembered what Gabby had said. *It was playing with you.* Not words she felt appropriate to repeat to Josie.

"Did the police say anything about Abigail? Still no sign of her?"

"No," said Josie, eyes welling up. "It's been seven months now, she's been gone. *Seven months*, Emma. I wish I knew what's happened to her. One way or the other."

Connie and Sam came in. The room seemed crowded and Emma felt dwarfed by the man who'd plonked down next to her on the sofa. Still, Josie looked comforted by the company. The conversation stayed light and relatively easy as they took tea and cake, before Emma found her moment.

"I've been doing a bit of research into Flammark and your family name came up. It's very old isn't it? Used to be spelled differently though."

Sam answered, wiping crumbs off his chin with a giant hand. "That's right. Used to be a 'y' in it."

"Oh, Emma, dear. Don't get him started. He could tell you tales …" Almost in contradiction to her words, Connie nodded. As if encouraging him to talk.

"She's right. We come … from a line of bad'uns."

Sam had seemed fine until this point. Now his speech began to slur, as if his words wouldn't form properly.

"You seem to have turned out okay," Emma joshed. This sounded promising.

"Huh, I'm one of the l...ucky ones," said Sam, Emma could see real struggle now. "Things get … passed on."

Sam looked at his wife, his face wiped of all energy. "She'll tell you. I'm sorry, I've got to go. I … need my bed."

"All right, Sam," Connie sighed, "You go. Best not to overdo it, I suppose."

Sam lumbered up and his wife couldn't have looked more disappointed. She must have thought he'd been getting over it. By some enormous effort he reached the door and turned around. He said, "Back in the day, they hated us Chaters. In and out of prison, we were. Some were really nasty pieces of work."

And with that he was gone, leaving an awkward silence behind him.

"Sorry, Emma. I'm sure you didn't come here to listen to all that," said Connie, to the sound of creaking stairs taking Sam back to his bed.

Emma shook her head. "No, not at all. Poor Sam. The sickness has hit him hard, hasn't it?" After Connie nodded in agreement she continued, trying for a chuckle, "He certainly doesn't come over as a 'bad'un.'"

"Tch. No. Good as gold, is my Sam. Always has been."

Emma didn't know how to ask her next question. "Connie, did Jim …"

Connie was a wily one. She seemed to know straight away what Emma was getting at. "Jim was a good man." She looked at Josie. "He had a temper, didn't he love? But we brought him up right and he knew how to control it."

Which, Emma thought, he tried to do right up to the very end.

After her third cup she made leaving noises. Although only about half-four, it had grown dark. A strong moon lit up the freezing rime on the skeleton tree outside the living room window.

She said her goodbyes, wishing Josie well, and they made a date for another coffee in the village. Connie offered to ring for a taxi, but Emma broke her promise to Will and refused. It'd been a long day. The Chater's living room was really hot, and what with the meal at the pub and now the cake, she felt restless and muggy. It would take at least an hour to get to the vicarage, but the long walk would go far in allowing her to process events. Besides, she had nothing to fear for now. He'd been caught.

As she crossed High Street, deserted despite it only being early evening, her eye was caught by a large, flickering light, high on Seely Tor. Must be some sort of bonfire. Who'd be up there in this temperature? The wind whipped around her legs, penetrating her jeans, letting the cold in. She should have called a taxi after all.

Emma looked over her shoulder, her shivers not entirely down to the biting wind. Unable to shake a feeling of being watched, she quickened her step best she could, despite the risk of slipping.

Something wasn't right. Breath coming in short little gasps, she looked over her shoulder. Once. Twice. Certain she was being followed, she tried to walk even faster, frustrated that the ice on the pavement wouldn't let her.

She fought against the impulse to run. It was only her imagination getting the better of her. He'd been arrested and was on his way to prison right now. But the logic didn't work and the instinct to bolt became harder to suppress. Still not giving way to it, she walked on, but soon all Emma's efforts to contain herself came to nothing, as she heard behind her the creeping growl of a car.

Following.

The primal urge to flee won out, and despite the cold, wind and slippery path, Emma ran for her life.

Freezing air caught in her throat as she battled with the exertion, not seeming to make any headway on the icy pavement. Still running, she heard the engine die and risked looking over her shoulder yet again. The headlights were full on and she couldn't see a bloody thing. Consumed with blind panic, she tried to sprint.

No good.

Sliding everywhere, her upper limbs frantically wind-milling, she finally lost her balance and fell.

Right into the arms of Jamie Westen

## ❧ 27 ❧

## BECOMING

H e heaves in great gulps of air, cracks his neck one way, then the other. Stretches.

Stares down at the shattered handcuffs at his feet, then across to the two dead men in the car.

*Hot, hot. So hot it burns.*

*He takes off his jacket and his shirt. Shoes. Socks.*

*Ice crystals form on cold sweat. They animate his skin, melting at the next pulse of heat, before dancing once more.*

*HE IS MAGNIFICENT.*

*Where?*

*He tilts his head, listens to the voice inside it.*

*Turns to face the empty road. Stretches again and circles one shoulder, then the other.*

*He walks, runs, sprints. His bare feet, hardly touching the icy ground, move lightning fast—so quick the human eye can't see them.*

*Back.*

## ✣ 28 ✣

## A SECOND ESCAPE

Westen had no time for this. Emma kicked and swore and fought him, and it fucking hurt. When the screaming started, he'd no choice but to put a hand over her mouth and shut her up, whisper-shouting lest she roused the entire village. "Shhh … Emma, it's all right. It's me, Westen."

She didn't seem to hear him and didn't give way. Managing to free an arm, she formed a fist and lamped him right between the eyes. Never imagining for one minute he'd have to apply full-on police restraint to a woman of Emma's size, he nevertheless did that very thing and bundled them both into the back of his car.

Confined by the small space and the pressure of his arms, Emma grew still. He waited for the first sign of recognition.

When it came, he said, "I'm sorry, Emma. I didn't expect to have to do that." Relaxing his hold slightly, not letting go completely—just in case—he released a hand to gingerly check his face. "Have to say—respect. You give as good as you get."

"Well I don't appreciate being bloody followed. What the

hell are you doing here, Westen?" Then she looked down at his arm. "Am I under arrest?"

Easing his grip some more, he said, "No. I won't charge you with assaulting a police officer under the present circumstances. I didn't mean to frighten you ..."

"I suppose you didn't mean to grab me, either?"

"I came to find you. Donna said you were at the Chaters' but you'd left. I've been trawling the streets. When I got out of the car, you were already falling—" Waste of fucking time explaining, instead he cut right to it. "He's escaped, Emma. Gone."

He felt a judder go through her and knew the cold hadn't caused it. "I'm sorry. I'm taking you to the vicarage. Donna's called ahead and she's waiting for us there. Turner knows what's happened. We've all got a lot to talk about."

Still Emma didn't speak, and she fell limp in his grasp, all fight gone. The hunted look in her eyes as they glinted in the streetlight would haunt him for ever. He wished he had something useful to say, something that would mitigate the brutality of his news—and certainly the way he delivered it— but he could think of nothing. Instead, letting out a steadying breath he gently disentangled himself and got out of the car.

Back in the driver's seat he turned the ignition but left the engine to idle. Though in a desperate hurry to get her back, something about this woman gave him pause, compelled him to reach out and support her. He sensed her vulnerablilty, of course, but that wasn't the reason. She ... endured. He liked that, respected it. Didn't want to let her down.

He twisted round, arm over the car seat. How he managed a reassuring smile, he had no idea. Things were bad, and she didn't know the half of it.

"Try to keep calm, Emma. Trust me, we'll sort it."

As if suddenly energised, Emma rounded on him. "Sort it?

How the bloody hell are you going to 'sort it'? You've already let him escape and he's only been in custody for what, a few hours?"

She slapped an exasperated hand on the back of his seat. "Bloody hell, Westen."

He held her furious gaze for a nano-second before his smile slipped. Then he turned around and putting the car in gear, drove on.

The gritters hadn't been out. Ice on the roads meant it took a full fifteen minutes for him to deliver his passenger to the vicarage. Emma flung herself out of the car and stormed in. She stopped for a few moments to exchange words with Turner, who'd been waiting at the door for them. When Westen saw angry gestures coming his way, he sighed and rolled his eyes, ready to embrace the whirlwind.

Turner greeted him with a subdued, "Inspector, come in. We're in the library." Taking Westen's coat, he caught sight of his face, raised his eyebrows. "Good God, man!" he exclaimed. "What happened to you? How many were there?"

"She happened to me, Turner. Where's your bathroom?"

"Up the stairs, turn right, end of the corridor. Can I get … ?"

"No, you can't."

"Oh-kay, then." Turner's amused tone annoyed Westen. And was that a smirk on his fucking face? "There's ointment in the medicine cabinet. Help yourself."

Upstairs, Westen surveyed the damage. Had she actually broken his nose? It hurt like hell. The skin had split on the bridge, and purple bruises had begun to spread beneath his eyes. Blood spattered the front of his coat. He looked like a crime scene.

After cleaning up as best he could, which included the very careful attachment of a plaster, he found the library. Donna got up when he entered. Emma sat tightly curled and shut-off in an armchair by the fire. Even from where he stood, he could sense waves of anger coming his way.

He looked at his DC and jerked his head towards the door. After she'd left the room, taking off his driving gloves, Westen moved towards Emma, and crouched to warm his hands, levelling the height between them. Though known for his sensitivity, even he knew to tread carefully. She'd been through a lot, and it wasn't over yet. Softening his features, he said, "I don't yet know all the circumstances of the escape, Emma. I'm off to the scene as soon as I've finished here, but I can't go until I'm sure we have you adequately protected."

She threw him a long, hostile stare. But she couldn't keep it up for long. Out of the blue, she broke the tension and laughed—albeit with the slightest tinge of hysteria. "Did *I* do that?"

He nodded.

"Just deserts, then." She sighed and looked at the empty armchair opposite. "Sit down, Westen. Bad situation."

He didn't want to sit down. He wanted to be with Burrows; find out what happened to his men. But he acquiesced since nothing would be achieved unless he took his time. Christ, his head ached. He could have kissed the fucking vicar when he came in with some bottled water and aspirin, Donna also in tow.

"Now, Inspector," said Will, handing over the painkillers. "Tell us what happened."

Westen opened the water bottle and glugged down the pills, told them how the car carrying the prisoner had neither radioed-in nor arrived at Oakmarsh, and that he'd sent his sergeant to follow the route. He found the vehicle. What

Westen didn't tell them was both the driver and his partner were dead, nor did he mention the car had apparently stopped at the exact spot where Jim Chater had crashed.

"There's no sign of the prisoner. No tracks, no footprints, nothing. Emma, has your ex ever shown any sign of mental instability? Illness?"

"No. He was always in absolute control of himself." She shot an uncertain look at Will before asking. "Why?"

"Apart from broken handcuffs—we're trying to work out how that was done—he's left his shirt, shoes and, strangely, socks next to the car. It's fifteen degrees below out there. He couldn't last more than half an hour without getting hyperthermia, yet no one's seen anything and, so far, there's no trace of a body."

Turner returned Emma's look. It annoyed Westen. Like the night he'd been called out to Clearview, he couldn't shake the sense that the priest, and now Emma, were keeping something from him.

"To be honest, Inspector," said Turner, "I'm not surprised you haven't heard anything. There will be no witnesses. The village is sick."

"Come again?"

"It may be some sort of … virus. Flu-like symptoms, lots of tiredness, that sort of thing. It started a few weeks before Emma arrived. Two, three people a week at first. Robbie—Dr. Mason, our GP—thinks most households are affected one way or another. Shops are closed and people are staying inside."

He glanced at Donna. "Why didn't I know that? Have the health authorities been alerted?"

Emma said, "It seems to be confined to the village. Robbie's made the proper notifications. There are no recorded cases outside of Flammark."

Westen shrugged and let it go. He didn't want to get sidetracked. "Our main priority, apart from recapturing that bastard, is to protect Emma. That's who he's after. I'm not going to sugar-coat it." Westen locked his eyes on her. "He's a serious threat. Do you understand? You cannot go back to that cottage on your own. There's a safehouse in Ledbridge. Get your things, Donna will take you."

"No."

He'd been afraid of this. "What do you mean, no?"

"I've had enough. Enough of running, enough of being terrified. Time to draw a line in the sand."

Fucking stubborn woman. She must know the danger she was in—Christ, probably better than anyone. He had no time for this. With two of his own down and a manhunt about to start, he needed to be out the door. This wasn't something he could leave to Burrows.

Yet still he tried. "You do realise if you stay here, you'll be putting Turner in danger too?"

"Don't consider me," Will interjected, bowing his head slightly and raising the palm of his hand. "If Emma wants to stay here, we should let her."

Incredulously, Westen gazed at him, hardly believing his ears. Surely he could have relied on a vicar to give him some support. Emma was his friend, wasn't she? Why wouldn't he want all the stops pulled out to protect her?

Emma asked, "Can't you put someone here, instead of us having to waste your resources in Ledbridge?"

Westen took no pleasure in taking his turn to say, "No."

"Why not?" she said. "Look … he's dangerous, I get that. Believe me, I do. But you're dead right. It's me he's after and if I'm not at the cottage, he'll assume I'm here. Then you can catch him. If you hole me up at some dive or other, God knows how long it'll take you to find him."

Chewing the inside of his cheek, Westen couldn't deny her logic. Nor could Donna, who tentatively ventured,

"Makes sense, Guv. The letter he left at the cottage tells us he thinks something's going on between Emma and Will. He's bound to come here if she doesn't go home."

He took a moment to consider it. "No. Too much of a risk." He put down the pill-bottle he'd been nursing and made to go. "Emma, you need to leave with Donna. Now."

"No. I'm not going. My place is here, with Will."

The way those two looked at each other, as if they were conspiring, made Westen's hackles rise. What the fuck were they keeping from him? But he kept his irritation at bay for now; he'd get nowhere by losing his temper. Anyway, he didn't have the time to argue.

"Have it your own way," he grunted. "I can't force you, but remember, you're staying here against police advice and you're making my job a lot harder. Donna, I want you to stay with them. I presume that's okay with the both of you?" He held Emma's eyes a moment longer than was comfortable, before looking away.

She 'd won.

On seeing Emma and Will's enthusiasm for the new plan, addressing Donna, he said, "Be on high alert. Keep your two-way on at all times and use it if anything, and I mean anything, doesn't look or sound right. I'll get someone to relieve you tomorrow."

He made one last appeal for Emma to see sense. "Are you positive I can't change your mind?"

"Yes, Inspector. This is where I belong. If he is coming for me, can you honestly tell me there'd be a quicker way of catching him?"

On that he had to admit defeat. Again.

"Bait?" he said.

"No," replied Emma. "Trap."

∾

Westen departed the house. He fired up his car but left it idling a short while. Ice crystals had formed on the windscreen again, even though he couldn't have been in the vicarage for more than fifteen minutes. So anxious to get away, he'd not bothered putting his gloves on and his hands —not to mention his nose—ached with cold, despite only walking fifteen yards or so to the car. The temperature had taken another dive. The dashboard thermometer registered twenty degrees below.

Once the windscreen had cleared a bit, he left the vicarage and headed out to meet Burrows. He noticed grit on the road. Finally! He managed some speed and arrived at the roadblock about twenty minutes later.

Three police cars, blue lights flashing, were parked at odd angles. A fourth, ominously dark with all its doors open, sat in the middle of the left-hand lane. As he neared, a single uniformed copper, standing several feet before the accident tape, waved him down.

Weston clambered out and joined Burrows, who was just finishing on his phone. Pocketing it, he turned to his boss. A concerned expression spread over his face. "Blimey, Guv, what happened to… ?"

"Save it, Pete. I'm not in the mood." He lifted the tape and strode over to the darkened vehicle. "Where are we up to?"

"It's a weird one, Guv, that's for sure."

"Explain."

"Car seems to have stopped stone dead. Like with an EMP, though that would be a ridiculous in Flammark." As they neared the lonely vehicle, Westen had a déjà vu moment. Burrows had called it right. The car rested only a few feet away from the site of the Chater's crash, only yards in front of the Sandmarsh sign.

Westen shook his head. "An EMP? Fucking stupid. Dodgy alternator, more like."

Burrows pressed his lips together and raised his eyebrows, slowly nodding as he acknowledged the possibility. "Could be, Guv." Then he said, "Peterson was driving. He and Wright are both dead. Savage can't even make an educated guess at CoD. No injuries, no marks, nothing."

"When will he be able to call it?"

"They've only just taken away the bodies. He'll do the PM first thing. Doesn't normally manage it this quick, but he's stumped and wants to get on with it."

"What else?"

Burrows held up an evidence bag full of steel fragments.

"Fucking hell, are these his handcuffs?"

"They *were*. They're shattered. Savage has the clothes he discarded. Christ knows how he did this to the cuffs. Maybe the lab will throw some light on it."

"Any ideas what we're dealing with?"

Burrows shrugged, "Not a clue. Some sort of psycho, that's for sure. Who'd ditch their clothes in this weather?" As if to demonstrate, he blew hot breath into the air which condensed into almost pure white mist in front of them.

"Still no sign?"

"Nada. Completely in the wind."

"Where are we with the search?"

"As you ordered. APB, and two extra teams are joining us from Ledbridge, Tony's co-ordinating the house-to-house in Flammark as we speak. It's gonna mean a lot of upset people."

"Fuck that. He's got to be found. My gut tells me that's where he headed and it's not his intention to pop in and see Emma Blake for a little tea and chat, either. She's holed up in the vicarage and has refused a safehouse, awkward bloody woman. Donna's with her now but will need relieving tomorrow. Get Tony onto that too. We'll need a guard rota."

"Will do, Guv."

Westen stamped his feet. "Fuck it's cold!"

"We're twenty-two below, now. Nearly a record."

Westen took one more walk around the scene with Burrows, his jaw working up a storm, a restless thought churning in his brain, looking for a connection.

"What's this bug that's going round in Flammark?"

"Guv?"

"Something Turner said. A virus, bit like the flu but not the flu. Makes them tired, keeps them in bed. Apparently, it's been going around for months. What's the traffic been like?"

"Guv? Slow. Uniform haven't had any problems setting up a diversion and turning people back."

"See? It's what, just after six? A road-block would have caused mayhem."

"And you think it's this flu thing?" said Burrows, chin on his chest, eyebrows raised, looking askance at Westen.

"Possibly."

"Well, I've never heard of it."

"Yes, you have."

"Guv?"

"Didn't you say Holly lived in Flammark, and that he'd come down with something. It brought his retirement forward?"

"Yes, but—"

Westen put his hand to his thumping head and shook it. It was beyond even him to either argue or fathom what he was getting at. "Ignore me. I can't fucking think straight. It can't have anything to do with what happened here."

# 29

# UNDER SIEGE

W ill let in Donna's replacement, Tony Stamford, at around half seven and set him up, together with his impressively chunky police-issue laptop, on a window table in the library. The detective asked Will to show him round the vicarage so he could get a better idea of its stress points. After some shaking of doors and window locks, he accepted an offer of tea and toast and, an eye to the drive outside, began to work on the files he brought with him.

Will joined Emma, who'd been in the kitchen making breakfast. "Donna's gone and I've just let Tony in. He's had a look around. Not a chatty sort. Seems too interested in his laptop. But he managed to communicate he wants feeding, so I'll sort it."

"Isn't he supposed to be on 'high alert'?"

Will shrugged. "Well, he looks out of the window a lot and he said he'll be doing regular rounds of the place. Failing sitting in the hall with a shotgun across his lap, I don't suppose there's much else he can do. Even Donna dozed off in front of the library fire last night."

"You checked?" laughed Emma.

"I did," replied Will, sorting out a tray for Stamford and popping more bread in the toaster. "One has to look after one's women, you know."

Emma was just about to sit down at the kitchen table when she jumped at a light tap at the kitchen's back door. She was on her way to answer it when Will said, "Hang on, hang on. Not so fast. Let me see who it is first."

But there was no need. It was Gabby, and she had come in before he'd had chance to unlock the door. His expression puzzled Emma, until it dawned on her that this was the first time Will had knowingly engaged with the face of an angel.

Nonsensically, he stuttered, "G-Gabby, you're here!"

"Shh..." Emma said. "Keep your voice down. We don't need Tony in on this."

"Are you both all right?" Gabby said, almost whispering. "It's started."

"We know," said Emma, quietly. "Westen wanted us to go to a safehouse and he took some persuading to let us stay."

"Hah," Gabby snorted. "It's your decision. They can't force you, though I'm glad they're looking out for you. I gather there's another one of them in the library?"

"Yes. Will was just on the way to give him his breakfast."

He didn't move.

"Weren't you Will?" Emma grinned as he gave a start.

"Erm, yes. Yes, I was, wasn't I?" Will answered. Reluctantly, he picked up the tray, and tearing his eyes away from Gabby, disappeared into the hallway.

"How are you bearing up?" she said, taking a seat opposite Emma.

"You know about what he did at Clearview?"

"Yes, and that he got himself caught, then escaped. We saw most of it."

"Saw?" Then it dawned on her. "Were you and Michael on Seely Tor last night, by any chance?"

"That's where we are most nights, actually. We can watch much better up there."

"What, physically? I thought you people could just … well, see everything." She closed her eyes and lifted her fingers to her temples, circling her head in what she imagined was a scrying motion.

"I told you, Emma," Gabby let out a quiet chuckle, just like her old self might. "We're not the heavy mob. Not … omnipotent."

Emma still couldn't quite get over these kitchen conversations. Talking about finding heaven in ordinary!

She turned to find Will standing by the door, still unable to stop angel-gazing.

"Oh, do sit down, William," Gabby smiled. "Stop fussing."

They gathered around the table and Emma filled him in about the lights she saw on Seely Tor yesterday. "It's Michael and Gabby's base. Apparently it helps them keep an eye on everybody."

"Great! You'll know he escaped and where he is now. Spill, Gabby, and I'll tell Tony."

"You'll do no such thing," said Gabby. "And if it could only be that simple. We saw the police car cut out and stop, and then him running away from it, but that's all."

"Oh, that's just great," said Will. "What good is that?"

Emma looked at Gabby and raised knowing eyebrows. "That's what I said to her, only I think I used more … choice words."

Gabby ignored them and pressed on. "He's getting more powerful. He's going to find it easier to shut me and Michael out. I came to tell you we're nearing his endgame. Be on your guard. We'll do what we can to help but, as I keep on saying, we daren't interfere. You have to work this out for yourself. There's been enough … spillage."

Will started, "But, how are we—" before they heard footsteps coming through from the library.

"I've got to go, William. What you have to remember is, *we* are relying on *you*. Not the other way round."

Tony arrived as the back door closed.

"The Inspector's been on the two-way, checking all's well. We've got a task force knocking on doors and the dogs are out. The Guv'll be over just after lunch."

The two friends nodded back at him and he left for his next round of checks. Then, stomach suddenly lurching, Emma said, "Oh God, I forgot. I need to talk to Robbie. I have to tell him I won't be in on Monday."

"Em, hate to break it to you but you won't be going in at all. Not until they've caught him. Do you want me to ring? I'll tell him what's what, if you like."

"No. Thanks, but I should be the one to let him know." She thought for a moment, before saying, "Can you invite him over? If something's going to happen, I doubt it'll be during the day. I'd prefer to talk to him face to face, not that I'm sure what to say."

"Okay." Will got out his mobile and tapped the call. It went straight to voicemail. "I'll try him later. It's Saturday. He's probably in his shed."

"In this cold?" Emma replied. "I doubt it."

She cupped her chin in her hands. "What do I do now? It's not even half-eight. I'll go up the wall if I can't keep busy."

"I have just the thing." He left the kitchen and returned five minutes later carrying a large cardboard box which he dropped with a thump on the table.

"What's this?"

"Christmas in a box! This'll take your mind off things, at least for a few hours."

"Again, what is it?"

"Christmas cards. HQ delivered them last week, a thousand of them. A lot of churches send them out with a generic festive message, but I like the personal touch and sign every bloody one of them. Takes me ages. If you could print the labels and bung them on the envelopes, that'd be a big help."

"Okay," she sighed. "I suppose that sounds like a plan."

"Great! Let's get stuck in."

Will retrieved his laptop and set it up on the kitchen table together with a portable printer. He brought up his parishioner database and showed her how to merge it with a labelling program.

"Goodness!" Emma said, opening the box. She peered in at the massive quantity of cards and envelopes. "You do this on your own, every Christmas?"

"Yup."

She soon found her way around the software. Will made a drink for them, including Tony, tried Robbie again—to no avail—and eventually they settled into a routine.

"While we're on the subject of Christmas," Will said, "I say you spend the day itself here. I can invite Robbie. It'll be quite the party."

"You could ask Gabby and Michael. Now that would make for interesting company!"

"We could put them to work in the kitchen. Do something magical with the turkey! Tell you what, they'll be more use to us there than they bloody well are here," said Will with a half-smile. Then he continued, "I'm serious, Em. Love her though I do, Gabby just seems to parachute in, give us the benefit of her opinion, then piss off again. It's annoying."

The ludicrousness of the situation hit them simultaneously, and both burst out laughing. One way to relieve the stress!

"Well, she may be annoying," said Emma, the mirth fading. "And I have to admit, I got very angry with her when I got back from the cathedral. But if I know anything about this curse business, it's that it messes with your head. Maybe she shouldn't have interfered in the cycle, but if she hadn't Jim would have killed his daughter. I suppose Gabby's walking her own tightrope." She grabbed a few envelopes. "I wonder happened to Abby. *Did* she run away?"

They whiled away the hour in chit-chat and speculation, trying to keep positive. But the enormity of their situation never strayed far from their minds, and their mood began to darken. Eventually, Will said, "I've been thinking about the sickness."

"What about it?"

"You said it acts as a precursor, some sort of warning. As I remember, a few people started to come down with it just after Abby disappeared. It's so long ago now, I can't really get the timeline straight in my mind. I wonder whether it had anything to do with the cops being so recalcitrant. It always upset me. It was as if Abby didn't deserve their attention. I don't know what I'm saying, really. Just trying to make sense of it all, I suppose."

"Can you remember the name of the inspector in charge back then? Westen took over from him. He told me as much when I went in with Josie that day."

"Holbrooke, I think. I have a card here somewhere." He took a wallet from a trouser pocket and slid out something dog-eared. "Yeah, DI Stephen Holbrooke."

"You carry on," said Emma. "Maybe give Robbie another call. I'm just going to have a little chat with our detective constable."

She got a mug and poured yet more coffee for Stamford

and took it into the library. Ten minutes later she returned, a look of triumph on her face.

"He's from Flammark."

"Come again? I've rung Robbie again, by the way. No joy."

Emma nodded impatiently. "Holbrooke. He lives on the edge of the village."

"Don't tell me, you seduced Tony with your red-headed charm."

"Too right, I did, and not, I may add, with very much difficulty. Apparently, I'm something of a legend since word got around about how his boss ended up with that shiner!" Emma chortled. "Anyway, long story short, Holbrooke retired at the end of August. Apparently after a dose of flu he couldn't shake off."

"A dose of flu?" Will gasped. "Bloody hell, Em."

"You were right. If Holbrooke is a Flammark man, he would've been under the curse's influence. This goes back a long time, what, six, seven months? Holbrooke might even have been patient zero!"

Her brief ebullience soured. All the pieces were starting to come together and she could see the malignity of the Blackstone curse in each one. It was all-encompassing, suffocating. She fingered the scrollwork around her blackbird pendant—the *Blackstone* pendant. She couldn't shake the idea of being slowly hemmed in, as if she was in a tiny room with the walls closing in.

They both jumped at a loud rap on the front door. "I'll go," said Will. "It might be Robbie. I've left him enough messages."

A few minutes later, raised voices came from the library. She heard the fear in Will's voice as he shouted, "What do you mean, dead?"

Then, "Turner, keep your voice down. We don't want to alarm her unnecessarily."

At that point Emma had made it to the library door. "Alarm me about what, Inspector?"

Westen chewed his lip. It looked to her he was deciding just how much to reveal.

"Go on," she said. "Tell me. I need to know."

Hesitating, he replied, "I didn't want to add to your worries yesterday. When he escaped, he left two of my men dead."

She leant against the doorframe for support. "Jesus, Westen. I'm so sorry."

"We don't know cause of death yet. We don't know how he killed them or come to that *if* he killed them. I'm trying to keep an open mind till I get the results of the post-mortem."

Will glanced at Emma. Agitated.

She began, "Westen—"

His phone rang.

"Savage, finally … No, tell me now …"

After a quick-fire exchange he swiped off his mobile. "No point in keeping it from you. Both men had massive heart attacks. Given the circumstances, our pathologist thinks they were probably simultaneous." He took a breath, barely concealing his anger. Addressing Stamford, he continued, "I don't know what he did to them, or how he fucking did it, but by Christ I'll get him."

"I'm sorry, Westen," Emma said again. She couldn't think of anything else to say except, "This is all my fault."

"*Your* fault!" Westen shook his head angrily at her. "No. This is down to him. I wish you'd see sense. Can't you see how dangerous he's become? I'm really not happy about you staying here. He's a fucking maniac. Please Emma, come with me now."

Emma looked at Will's now terrified expression. She shivered, knowing it matched her own. The walls had advanced another notch. She wanted to leave with Westen but knew she couldn't. She had to remain where she was, and wait for —what did Gabby call it? The endgame.

The house phone rang, breaking the terrible silence.

"That has to be Robbie," said Will. " I'm sorry, Inspector, I have to take it." Will marched out of the room, face full of shock, full of dread.

Emma expected Westen to start up again, try once more to get her to leave with him. It surprised her that he didn't, and that unnerved her more. Last night he'd been confident they'd find him; today, not so much. Not after the circumstances of the escape and the death of his colleagues. The bait scenario was his worst and only option.

She asked, "Do you have any idea where he might be?"

"We've a theory, but it's a poor one," Westen said. "We're working on an assumption that he may have had help, and that someone is sheltering him, though God knows why. We can't make the connection. Our approach until now, has been that this is an extreme, though straightforward, case of stalking. We don't think that anymore."

He gathered himself, ready to leave.

"We think we know who might be harbouring him, but don't have anywhere near enough evidence to justify a warrant. To be honest, I'm just working on a hunch. Stamford's trying to firm it up now, trawling phone and bank records in the hope we find something. Meantime, I'm on my way to knock on a door, play it by ear. Hopefully, I'll have something concrete to report later."

"Thank you for telling me all this, Westen. I know you lot like to keep things close to your chest."

"We do, but sometimes it's best to share information. It can reduce the fear factor. You aren't keeping anything from us, are you?"

Will came in, saving Emma from having to answer. What could she have told him? She could tell him about Jim and

Abigail, the sickness and the Blackstone curse, but that would go down like a lead balloon.

She said to Will, "Is Robbie on his way?"

"That wasn't him, just the church warden asking whether I want to cancel the carol service. With the sickness, he thinks no one will turn up."

"I'll be off." Westen turned to his DC "We want those records analysed ASAP Tony. Phone me the minute you come up with anything. Donna'll be here at about five."

With that, he bade Will and Emma goodbye, and, refusing to be seen out, left as abruptly as he came in.

# 30

# CARNAGE

**W**ell, that went well," said Westen, as he threw himself into the idling car where Burrows sat waiting.

"No luck, Guv? She dig in?"

"Yup. But if I'm honest, she's right. As it currently stands, having Emma Blake staying put is the best hope we have of catching him." He rubbed his hands together and shivered. "Christ, Pete, it's not getting any warmer, is it?"

He sat back, letting the car's warmth defrost him. "I can't fault the logic. Though I hate putting civilians at risk, I don't see we've much choice except to go along with her. We've got to catch this bastard quick and easy. The longer he's out, the more desperate he's going to be. But it bothers me that we don't really know what we're dealing with. I'm going to double the protection."

"Agreed, Guv. The way he got loose—those handcuffs— don't mind telling you, it's put the wind up all of us."

"Let's get to Holbrooke's. See what he has to say for himself."

Burrows started driving, wiping condensation off the

windscreen with the back of his hand. Icy roads forced him to keep it steady, the ten-minute journey taking more than twenty as the wheels of passing cars threw up road salt and grime, splattering and sticking to the windscreen. He tried using the wipers to clear it off, but the temperature even froze the screenwash.

Despite nature itself seeming to conspire against them, they eventually found the turn and swung onto the narrow, winding lane that led to Holbrooke's place. Five minutes later, the road ended at a sign: *No Entry Private Property*. Behind it stood a huge set of wrought iron gates, wide open. Westen told his sergeant not to enter but to stop side on.

Burrows parked but kept the car running. With all manner of crap still on the windscreen, Westen had to power down his window to get a better view of the place. On cases like this, experience taught him to take stock, watch for signs of unusual activity before going in.

Holly had done well for himself. Before them lay a huge barn conversion, all birch cladding and glass. A grand design.

Everything seemed quiet, no movement inside, window blinds tight shut.

"You sure about this, Guv?" asked Burrows, craning his neck, trying to peer out of Westen's open window.

Westen shrugged. "I'm certain he downplayed Abigail Chater's disappearance. I've never been happy about her father's crash, either. It's beyond me how the van made that ninety-degree turn. The only people that could have thrown light on it were the accident investigators and we both know the cobblers Holly made them write. So, yes. I think he has questions to answer."

"I'm not seeing how he could be connected to the Blake woman, though."

"Me neither. And we've absolutely no grounds on which to question him, let alone get a warrant. I just can't shake the feeling that he's involved. Now we've another incident in exactly the same spot as the Chater crash. We've got to see if Holly knows anything."

After a long minute, Burrows said, "What do you think, Guv? Shall we go in?"

"Can't see a car, but it might be in the garage. Those blinds look bloody odd; all down, lunchtime, no glimmer of light. He could be away, of course." Westen exhaled then pressed his lips together. He made his decision. "Take us in, Pete. Have a look around, see what you can sniff out. I'll stay in the car and wait for Tony's call. He may have found something that'll give us an angle and get us in—if they're not away, that is."

After a quick manoeuvre Burrows drove through the gates and parked in front of the house. He turned off the ignition, left the keys dangling and climbed out, turning up his collar against the freezing wind. Westen watched him head for the large, detached garage and heard his feet crunch on the gravel drive. He tried its door. Nothing. Still in view, Burrows moved around to its side, shielding his eyes to reduce the reflection, and peered in its window. He turned to face their vehicle, shook his head and mouthed, 'No car.'

Westen's phone chirped. "Stamford. What've you got for me?"

He listened to the urgent tones of his DC as the sergeant reached the house and walk around the back. With the blinds down there was no point looking through the windows. Suddenly, his face darkened at Stamford's words, and a split second after he'd finished, Westen swiped off the conversation and bolted out of the car. He sprinted the few yards to the house and banged on the front door. Shouting for Burrows, he kicked and shouldered at it before the sergeant, having legged it to the front, shouted, "Hang on, Guv. Round the back. Kitchen door's easier. Glass."

Westen rushed around the back with him. Burrows wrenched a stone statuette from the patio's water-feature and smashed it into the glass three, maybe four times, before the double-glazed pane gave way. Seconds later, Burrows had knocked out the broken shards round the edge of the pane, leant over and turned the key from the inside. They were in.

The stench hit them first. Sickening, sweet, metallic ... and something else. Something like ozone. Empty food packets, remnants of strewn vegetables and half-open cans lay scattered on the kitchen floor. Doors hung off cupboards, the shelves inside stripped bare. The door to a huge larder fridge hung open, its contents either spilled or decimated; and everywhere—on the table, the counter-tops, in the sink—were bottles and bottles of water, wine, mixers and empty cans of beer.

The horrific scene told the two men that worse—much worse—was to come. The imperative to check the Holbrookes were safe rendered waiting for back-up completely out of the question. It took only a few seconds to exchange looks and agree a silent strategy. Westen signalled for Burrows to go upstairs, he'd take the bottom floor. He whispered, "Check it's clear first, no matter what you find."

His sergeant gone, Western edged slowly forward, out of the kitchen and through a large archway that led to the living room. Try as he might, he couldn't manage it quietly, his feet cracking over fragments of glass, remnants of smashed furniture and other detritus. He rubbed his neck against his collar. Hairs were rising on the nape.

The metallic smell intensified. Westen stopped dead in his tracks. Mouth filled with saliva, he swallowed once, twice. Then, his gorge under control, he completed his sweep and shouted, "Clear!"

He returned to Holly's enormous living room and peered at the bloody carnage at his feet. Hearing the tone of

Burrows' strangled echo, "Clear!", Westen didn't doubt for one minute, that his sergeant was witnessing a similar scene upstairs.

Staring up at him lay the body of Stephen Holbrooke; naked, riven with cuts and stab wounds. He lay spread-eagled, amidst all of his blood, each hand and foot pinned by a steak knife, rammed impossibly deep into the boards of the hardwood floor.

Westen squatted next to Holly's body, resisting an over-whelming urge to close his dead colleague's eyes. The policeman in him tried to take it all in objectively, see the truth, do the best job he could for one of his own, but the stench nearly did for him. Burying his nose in the crook of his arm, he noticed a small pistol. It lay only inches away from the outstretched bloody fingers of the dead man's hand.

The poor bugger must have fought like crazy to reach it.

After a few moments, he noticed the quiet. He tore himself away and ran upstairs. "Burrows … Pete … what've you got?"

As naked as her husband, Mrs. Holbrooke lay likewise spread-eagled but on a blood-soaked bed. Her hands and feet were tied to its posts with pieces of torn sheet. Her face would have been unrecognisable to anyone who knew her and Westen hoped, but did not believe, that she had died before the bastard had taken away her eyes, her breasts and eviscerated her bowels.

The two men stood in silence. Twenty-five years of combined experience in the Force had not prepared either man for what they beheld. Burrows turned his drip-white face to Westen.

"How did you know?"

Westen, himself struggling for composure, replied, "Tony's call came through. He'd been going through their phone records. They showed five 999 attempts came from here between two and three o'clock this morning. He checked dispatch. None of them were received at our end."

"Jesus."

"Call it in, Pete. Call it in."

Anger. Sheer, uncontrollable, fucking anger.

Westen wrenched open his car door and got in. He stared out of the grimy windscreen, shaking with rage. He'd no time to indulge it, but he sure as hell would keep it with him until he caught the sick bastard. The how and why of it could wait. He had to turn to the living, and to one person in particular. Emma Blake. The Holbrookes hadn't been the focus of the madman's anger, but she was. After seeing what he'd done to them, Christ alone knew what he had in store for her.

He wouldn't stop at Emma, either. Turner and one or both of his DCs were in the firing line too. The vicarage had lost all sanctuary status. He couldn't give a flying fuck what she wanted. He was getting them out.

Now.

He called Stamford on the two-way but all he got was an earful of static. Tried to raise him on his mobile. It rang but he didn't pick up. Then he called Turner, mobile and landline. The same. He rang Emma.

Nothing.

He peered at his phone as if it had gone mad. Full signal. He tried Stamford again. Fucking nothing. In vain, he called the station.

He looked over at Burrows, who was staggering out of the house, stupidly shaking his phone. Westen waved him over. "Is your's fucked too?"

Joining him at the car, Burrows half-cried, half-shouted, "It's ringing, Guv, but no one's picking up. Must have been

the same last night, when Holly—or maybe Mrs. Holbrooke
—called triple nine."

Westen had got to his tether end. "What the fuck's wrong
with this place? Why can't we get through to anyone?"

Burrows stood pale-faced and stricken, the white mist of
his short breaths clouding his face.

"Right, I'm off," said Westen. "I've got to get to the
vicarage. Warn them. Get them out!" He pointed at Burrows'
phone. "Keep at it, Pete, keep ringing the station. Tell them to
send me an Armed Response Unit. Now!"

Fuck, fuck, fuck.

He turned the ignition, and, resting his arm on the back
of his seat, twisted round to make a one-handed reverse. His
wheels spun on the gravel, getting fucking nowhere. He
eased up on the accelerator enough for them to gain traction
and get him into the road. But the temperature had plummeted yet more, and he struggled to maintain contact on the
icy lane that had never seen a gritter in its life. Peering
through the grimy gaps in the windscreen he fought the
wheel, but his temper got the better of both of them. Not
more than two hundred yards from Holbrooke's he skidded
into a deep ditch, the sideways collision forcing the bonnet of
the car to spring open. It stopped, listing to one side, its two
offside wheels off the ground, spinning uselessly.

In utter, utter frustration, he punched the steering wheel
with the side of his fists. No time. No time! He thought
about the bodies behind him in the house and his mind
lurched to Emma and the others.

Westen couldn't bear it. But he had no choice.

He could do nothing but climb sideways out of the car
and jump out, then slip and slide his way back to Holly's, to
wait with Burrows for back-up.

## 31

# PREPARATIONS

*SING A SONG OF CHRISTMAS, A POCKET FULL OF LIES …*

*He hums the tune between gulps of water that leak from his mouth and drip from his chin. Liquid gleams on his naked torso as he lights the fire. He is burning already but she mustn't get cold.*

*He places candles on her windowsills, prepares the bindings and sets them aside.*

*The knives are on a shelf.*

*He laughs to imagine the terror on her face. Yearns to hear her pleas …*

*… and her thank-yous.*

*Picking up the sharpest blade, he finds a space on his flesh to take its edge.*

*In an orgasm of exquisite pain, he stands in the centre of the room, arms outstretched, blood dripping from the knife in his hand, savouring the agony, catching his breath in half sobs.*

*The cut that burned him fuels his thirst.*

*Throwing the knife down, he runs to her kitchen, turns on the tap.*

*Drinks and drinks and drinks.*

*Ravenous hunger haunts him too. He wrenches open the cupboards but neither fruit nor cheese, the raw meat in her fridge or the cans he bites through, can satisfy it.*

*He breaks a block of butter and stuffs half in his mouth but before he can manage the other, his thirst roars back and he drops it to guzzle the tap.*

*Fuck, will he ever be able to leave it?*

*He has to, for an even greater impulse calls him.*

*He tears the plastic off a pack of bottled water, grabs one and tears off its top. It is finished before he finds his discarded knife. He puts out his tongue and caresses the side of the blade with it. He is cut and the blood comes so thick he can suck it down in gobfulls. Then, hardly able to wait for her to come to him, he starts to sing again, spitting red.*

*WHEN HER THIGHS ARE OPEN, THE BIRD BEGINS TO SING*

*ISN'T THAT A DAINTY DISH TO SET BEFORE THE KING …*

*He chuckles at his song, laughs at his cleverness—he can't stop! He grasps the knife and trips along to the other room, swaying to the music of his soul, screaming with laughter as he anticipates her howls when she sees what he's done …*

*To the good doctor.*

## ❧ 32 ❧

## FOG

**D**onna arrived at the vicarage door at five, sharp. Emma was about to let her in when Tony burst out of the library and beat her to it.

"Give us a minute," he said, before gently grabbing his colleague's arm and pulling her into the library. He shut the door tight behind them.

"What's that all about?" Will said, as he joined Emma in the hall.

"God knows. Whatever it is, it doesn't sound good."

Unashamed hovering outside the door didn't yield any further information but after a tense five minutes the detectives came out. Tony gave them a quick nod and left.

"We have a developing situation, I'm afraid," said Donna, as she turned to the anxious pair, "which means none of us can stay here. Under any circumstances."

Emma asked, "What situation? What's going on?"

"To be honest, I'm not a hundred percent sure. The two-ways aren't working, and Tony can't get through to the Guv, Sergeant Burrows or the station. There's been no contact with them since just after they arrived at Inspector

Holbrooke's. He managed a quick call then, but after that, nothing."

Holbrooke's! So, Westen had been thinking along the same lines she had. Emma raised her eyebrows and gave Will an I-told-you-so look.

Donna continued, talking quickly now. "Apparently, they've been trying to get through to us. He's had two missed calls from the Guv. I've checked my phone, it's completely dead. We don't know what's gone down or whether there's a link to our situation. Tony's outside now, checking if anyone's about. We'll leave in convoy, then he'll split off to find the Inspector Westen. If the Guv's still there, he'll be able to tell him I've taken you both to the station. We can work out next steps later." Donna chewed her lip before continuing. "Before we go, can I ask you to check your phones first? See if either of you have been left any messages?"

Will slid his mobile out of a pocket. Dead. Emma retrieved hers and reported the same. "But that's not unusual," he said. "Our signal often goes down. We think it's something to do with the mast."

Ignoring him, Donna checked the landline. It seemed okay, and there were no messages on the answer-machine.

"Will's been the only person to use that," Emma said. "He's been trying to get through to Robbie Mason, the doctor, but hasn't been able to raise him. There's only been one other call, but nothing since the Inspector left."

"Right. Find something warm to put on. Don't waste time getting anything else. We're leaving. Right now."

Emma and Will looked at each other again. This was it. She remembered the conversation with Gabby about the night of Jim Chater's accident; that he'd died trying to escape the curse, desperate to leave Flammark in order to keep Abby safe. Though Donna might insist they go, she knew they wouldn't be allowed to.

Those walls just slid closer.

Tony came back to give the all-clear and the two detectives got into a huddle to work out the logistics, until Emma interrupted.

"We aren't coming with you." She knew she'd be courting Donna's anger but that couldn't be helped. "We have to stay here."

Donna swung round. "No. No, sorry. I'm under orders; anything suspicious and we're out of here. I think not being able to contact my boss counts as suspicious, don't you? Not that I want to worry you, but—"

Emma held fast. "We aren't coming, Donna."

Tony's turn. "Look. Not to put too fine a point on all this, if we can't get in touch with the Inspector, we're isolated. This chap's resourceful and he's obviously had help. We can't guarantee your safety. DC Stirling's right. You need to come now and be quick about it. To make matters worse, there's a pea-souper outside and we'll have to go slow as it is. I don't like the look of it."

Donna opened the front door to check it out. Creeping wisps of fog wrapped around her leg as she peered out. She wrinkled her nose. "That came down quick! Jesus, I've only been here a few minutes and I can't even see my car. It smells weird too, like someone's dug up a body." She turned back at Emma and Will. Tried to josh them along. "Come on, folks, this is stupid. We have to go."

By some instinct, Emma's hand reached out to find Will's and together they stood, shaking their heads, steadfastly sticking to their hidden agenda.

Donna seemed to know a brick wall when she saw one. Pursing her lips, she made a sudden decision. "Tony, someone needs to find out what's happening. Go. Get to

Holbrooke's and find out what Westen wanted. Tell him I'm staying here with these two … idiots."

"No!" said Emma, only now realising the consequences of her decision to stay. Shit. It was plain obvious Donna wasn't prepared to leave them. Emma searched Will's face. He wasn't happy either. Almost pleading, she said, "Donna, you can't stay. It's all right, really. Go. Please."

The policewoman ignored her. "On your way, Tony. Find Westen and get back-up. Keep trying the two-way."

"But—"

"I have seniority. You need to do as I say. Go. Now."

Stamford ran back into the library and grabbed his laptop before returning to the hall. It seemed he couldn't resist one last try, saying accusatively, "You do realise it's not only *your* lives at risk?"

The sharpness of his tone took Emma aback. Was she being stupid? Irresponsible? Probably. But the line had been drawn and she would not cross it. She could not be held responsible for Donna's decision to stay. She stood firm.

With an exasperated grunt, Stamford left the building.

"Well," Donna said, putting down her bag, "I hope you two are satisfied."

As they listened to the sound of Tony's car leaving, they faced each other in silence.

"I thought you had more sense, Emma." Disappointment had crept into the detective's voice. "After everything he's put you through."

Emma had no reply to this. All she could do was take Donna's disapproval.

They stood in awful suspension, fear and apprehension descending as thick and heavy as the fog outside.

Then came tapping from the kitchen.

It broke the impasse. Through gritted teeth, Donna said, "Stay here!" and moved to investigate the noise.

But she was overtaken by Will. "It's okay, I know who it is."

Less than a minute later, he brought Gabby through. Donna gave both of them a hostile stare as he tried an introduction. "This is ... my friend and parishioner, Gabby—"

"I don't care who she is. What's she doing here? I've enough on my plate without having to protect her too."

"It's really, really nice to meet you," said Gabby. Emma narrowed her eyes, shaking her head. Gabby was being disingenuous. All smiles, as if they were going on a picnic, she continued, "I see things have started to develop. Are we ready for the off, then?"

"Off? Are we not staying here?" said Will. He began to gabble. "Surely it's s-safer here. At least there's more places to hide. Plenty of nooks and crannies. We could—"

"No, William. I can protect you better in the church. Surely you must see that."

"I'm sorry, but who are you, again?" asked Donna, frowning incredulously. She looked as if she was going to lose it. Big time.

"I'm just a friend, dear. Don't worry about it."

"But—"

Gabby raised her palm and Donna immediately shut up. The policewoman put her hand to her throat. She tried to make words but couldn't—not even a croak. All she succeeded in doing was to lift angry and astonished eyes to the other two. Emma was horrified. "Did you really have to do that?"

"Yes, Emma, I did." Gabby's tone became firmer, brooking no argument. "We can't afford the energy it'll take to look after Donna. She won't understand and we need to keep our focus on what really matters."

The policewoman's face had reddened with fury clearly struggling to both comprehend the situation and to speak.

Gabby laid a hand on her shoulder. "Gently does it. Everything is as it should be. Calm yourself."

Donna visibly relaxed and she smiled at them all. Beatifically.

Still Emma objected. "I don't like this, Gabby, I don't like it at all."

"Nor do I," agreed Will, "but I can see Gabby's point. There's nothing to be gained by going over it all again, particularly to someone who won't understand."

Emma, neither happy nor convinced, nevertheless dragged her gaze away from Donna's beaming face. "Explain again, Gabby, why the church? If it's as protected as you say, then what's the point? If it's shielding us from him, he'll be shielded from us. It won't get us anywhere!"

"You won't be staying long," replied Gabby, refusing to be drawn. "It's only so we can prepare in safety."

Looking at the grubby old mac Gabby always wore, Will said, "Well, it had better not be for long. You don't feel the cold as we do. It's freezing in the church and we wouldn't last five minutes. Believe me, I know."

"Don't worry, you'll be perfectly comfortable. The heating's back on."

Will stood aghast. "You've fixed the boiler—"

"And the lights. Now, get your coats, it's still freezing outside. You'll need scarves too, so bring one for our friend here." Knowing it was impossible to argue, they both did as she asked. Donna hadn't taken her coat off, so she stayed, exchanging witless smiles with Gabby. Emma thought about taking her bag but decided it would be an encumbrance. However, there was one thing in it she couldn't bear to be parted from, so she rummaged into it and thrust the little black casket into her pocket before casting the bag aside.

"Ready?" asked Gabby.

All three nodded and followed her out, Emma leading the grinning detective by the hand.

The fog was indeed a pea-souper. And Donna had been right about the foul smell. Were it not for Gabby a few steps ahead, clearing swathes of mist as she walked, they wouldn't have been able to see their hands in front of their faces.

"This is his doing, isn't it?" asked Emma, as they closed in on the church, coughing at the fog that stank in her throat.

"Yes," Gabby replied, grimly. "He's closed everything down. Nothing is clear, even to Michael and his powers are greater than mine."

They could feel the heating as soon as Will unlocked the church's studded oak door.

"Lock it behind you, William," said Gabby.

Despite the familiar atmosphere, Emma could take no comfort from it. Gabby hadn't led them here so they could feel better. It felt more like a way-station; she and Will, semi-willing lambs to the slaughter.

She tried to swallow down her fear, wishing she could share Gabby's faith in her. What use was she really going to be? All she'd ever managed to do was run away. The prospect of confronting him again, after all these months, made her want to run out of the church, fire up the jeep and drive on forever.

Then she thought about Jim, and realised she was never going to be allowed to leave.

They moved into the nave, candlelights on its windowsills once more reflecting against the glass. But the scene did not resemble the Evensong debacle. Electric light had also been pressed into service, bathing them in a gentle glow, going some way to soothing their embattled nerves.

Suddenly, Emma sensed Will stiffen. He was staring fixedly ahead. Following his gaze, she could see something move just inside the chancel and as she peered into its shadows, she could just make out the outline of a figure.

"No. It can't be." Will peered at it and in astonishment turned to Gabby.

A small, dark-haired young woman slowly came before them. She wore a black coat over a long skirt. Emma, hardly able to believe her eyes, gulped in recognition of the waving apparition that had haunted her ever since she arrived.

But Will knew her as someone else and his shout filled the church.

"Abigail!"

## ❧ 33 ❧

# RETURNING

As Westen left the car, the fog descended like a sack. Under its pall, stinking fingers of dank, suffocating mist penetrated his clothes, got into his lungs and messed with his head, making the few hundred yards back to Holbrooke's seem like miles.

He kept to the left edge of the icy road, arms outstretched at whatever angle would keep him upright. After too fucking long, the 'No Entry' sign loomed out of the murk. He scrambled towards where he knew the wrought iron entrance gates must be and soon felt the gravel of Holly's drive underfoot. He shouted to Burrows but his words didn't carry, so swallowed were they by the heavy atmosphere. He edged further up the drive towards the front door, coming upon his freezing sergeant waiting on the doorstep.

"What the f—" shouted Burrows.

"It's only me, Pete. Tell me you got through to dispatch."

"Jesus, Guv, you frightened me to death!" Burrows held out his phone, as if he'd been clutching it for dear life since Westen left. "No luck contacting anyone. Battery's nearly dead too. How come you're back so soon?"

"Nothing? Shit." Westen stamped his feet and wrapped his arms around himself. "I pranged the car. It's in a ditch down the road. Took me fucking ages to get back. This fog!"

"I know. W-weird. Reeks too." Burrows' voice chattered. "Came down just like that. It's bloody p-perishing. I thought of going inside but didn't want to contaminate the crime scene."

"We'll be dead of hyperthermia if we don't." Westen stopped talking, felt close to losing function. Panic could do that to a man. He tried taking some breaths to calm down but coughed as the fog caught the back of his throat. "Fuck this."

He pushed open the front door and swiped the light switch with his gloved hand. This entrance led straight into the living area, Holbrooke's ravaged only a few feet away. But Westen wasn't up for a second look just then, the stench offered more than enough reminder of what lay ahead for the forensic teams when—if—they ever sodding well arrived.

They picked their way to the kitchen, careful to disturb as little as possible, and upended some barstools. They sat in silence for a few moments, letting the central heating, its settings conveniently left untouched, warm them up. Westen's jaw worked.

"You got through to no one?"

Burrows shook his head and Westen slammed his fist on the kitchen worktop. "Fuck. It's not only the Blake woman and Turner I'm worried about. It's our two."

"I've been thinking the same thing, Guv, but Donna and Tony aren't wet behind the ears."

"That may be so, but have you ever come across anything like this?" He waved in the vague direction of the front room. "I haven't and I'm fucking sure they haven't either. Try the phone again."

Burrows slid out his phone and made for the speed-dial

when it chirped out a triple bleep. "Battery, Guv. I'm out."

Westen felt in his pockets for his. "Fuck, fuck, fucking hell! I've left mine the car, with my two-way."

"I wouldn't worry about that, Guv. The radios are useless. All you get is an earful of static."

Engulfed in impotent rage, Westen sat, silently fuming until Burrows cocked his head, got up and moved through the hall to open the front door.

"Guv!"

Westen got up and all but ran to his side.

"It's a car!" exclaimed the sergeant. "Thank God!"

Heart in his mouth, Westen heard the sound of an engine grinding its way through the fog. Its lights dimly swept across them as the car entered the drive. "It's the SOCOs!" he shouted, flooded with the relief of wishful thinking.

"No, Guv. Looks like Stamford!"

Sure enough, a few moments later, the young DC clambered out of the vehicle and straightened, putting his hands on his hips to stretch his back.

"Where's Donna? Where're the others?" shouted Westen.

Stamford said nothing until he reached the door. Then his inspector started on him. "Where are they all, Tony? Tell me you didn't fucking leave them!"

To Stamford's great credit, he made a good fist of keeping eye contact with his boss. "We tried to get Turner and the Blake woman to come with us, Guv, but both of them refused point blank."

"What the fuck? Why aren't you with them?"

"We knew you've been trying to get through and guessed something was up. Comms were also down at the vicarage, and Donna was bothered *you* might need back up too. She couldn't leave Turner and Blake exposed, so she pulled seniority. Told me to keep trying to call for support and check on the situation here, before going back. I knew you had a problem when I passed your car on the road. Have to say, I'm relieved you're still here, to be honest, Guv. I need to get back. He could get up to anything in this fog and we wouldn't see him coming."

"My fucking point exactly! Which is why you should have stayed put." Westen spoke with his teeth gritted, a pulse working at his temple. He clenched and unclenched his fists looking ready to punch something—or someone. Burrows intervened.

"Difficult call for Donna, Guv. I think she did the right thing."

Westen hissed, "We'll have to see if events agree with you, sergeant."

They took Stamford into the house and through to the kitchen, bypassing Holly's body, which couldn't be seen from the door. The last thing Westen had time for was a debrief.

"Christ almighty, sir," said the young detective, "what the hell went down here?" Then he wrinkled his nose and realisation dawned all on its own.

"Hell's about right. Burrows'll talk you through it," Westen said. "I need your car. You stay here, *I'm* going back."

The young detective reached into his pocket and gave him the keys. "No problem, Guv. Petrol's a bit on the low side, though. Half an hour in low gear did it. There should be enough to get you back to the church, though."

Westen grabbed the keys. "Has your phone still got battery?"

"It's low, but I'll look around. Holly's bound to have something I can cobble together to charge it. I've got my laptop too." He patted a bulge under his parka. "I'll see if I can tap into the wifi. Maybe send an email. Leave it with me."

"Good." Westen nodded as he moved out of the kitchen. "Find whatever tech you can, but with minimum disturbance.

I want the scene as intact as possible. Keep trying the station and get Armed Response out to the vicarage."

He turned to Burrows. "We need forensics on this ASAP. Do not leave until they get here. I don't know when I'll be back." He glanced through into the living room, lowered his voice so Stamford couldn't hear, "... and let the lad down lightly about Holbrooke."

Burrows nodded. "Understood. You go, Guv. We know what to do."

Westen, on his way out of the front door, paused. He looked over his shoulder and saw the two men he left in close discussion. Unobserved, he quickly side-stepped into the living area, once more to behold Holbrooke's poor ravaged body. But he didn't linger over it, instead he bent over and snatched up the little pistol at its side. He quickly hefted it— it felt fully loaded but he could check that later. He quietly pocketed it before once more entering the freezing fog. With Holly's porch light just about able to guide him, he found Stamford's car. To his complete relief, it started first time and he was away.

Westen had learnt his lesson. Slowly and carefully, his face pressed almost to the window, he set out once again down the slippery lane, never budging from second gear. After a while, he passed his own vehicle, thought for a second, then stopped. Keeping the engine idling, he got out and wrenched open the passenger door of the abandoned car. He hadn't expected the phone to have remained where he left it, but there it was, having withstood the angle of the car's final resting position by dint of the well in the seat.

Thanking the gods of Flammark that Stamford's Honda still chugged away as he returned, he heaved himself in, got into gear and moved slowly forward; in the ice, in the fog, until he reached the junction and made the turn.

Back to the vicarage.

## 🦎 34 🦎

## THREE DAUGHTERS

All but one of the tiny throng stared dumbstruck as Abigail moved further into the churchlight. *Comeliness* did not go far enough to describe the young woman's beauty. Her long dark hair fell almost to her waist, in straight, uneven layers and braids of beaded threads. It framed a heart-shaped face within which large, kohl-rimmed eyes glittered with reflections from the candle flames. Lockets and charms hung about her neck and long, silver-black earrings shimmered and danced as she looked from face to face. Her dark, lipstick-smile betrayed obvious relish at the impact her entrance was making. She'd certainly dressed for the moment; a theatre of faded purple skirts, layered to her ankles, wrapped inside a heavy black overcoat.

Gabby walked up to her and, taking her hand, led her to face Emma.

"I think it is time you two met properly. Emma Blake, this is Abigail Chater."

Abigail held out her hand. Hardly breathing, Emma lifted her own but couldn't follow through. Instead, she reached beyond it, and, unable to help herself, touched the front of

Abby's coat. Was she even real? She caught her scent. Patchouli. Despite herself, the whiff of naff teenage goth culture made her smile in the realisation that not only did Abigail exist as a fully corporeal being, she was just a kid.

Emma eventually took the proffered hand and the tension eased. Will broke the silence. "Gabby. What did you do?"

"Sit down, all of you." They moved the chairs into a rough circle and did as she said, for there was no doubt who was in charge. Donna was still smiling, but Emma sensed hesitation in her movements. Gabby's charm had begun to wear off.

As it clearly had with Will.

"I thought your interfering days were over, Gabby," he said. "You do realise Josie has been out of her bloody mind with worry?"

"I know, I know. But we thought the curse had died in the flames with Jim. When the lassitude started a full two years after he died, well, we had no idea what would unfold for her. As far as we knew, there weren't any Blackstone men left to fall prey to the curse. Then Michael suspected the very thing we had been sent here to avoid, had happened; that we—I— had unleashed the evil to roam farther afield. Since Jim had died protecting his daughter, the very least we could do was to follow suit."

She squeezed Abigail's hand and jutted out her chin. "You can't know how hard it is … seeing someone you care for become a living sacrifice. We're designed never, ever to get involved. I failed. Badly."

Will's gaze didn't soften. "Believe it or not, Gabby, I'm quite used to the idea of living sacrifices." He shuffled in his seat. "As a theory, anyway. And I have to say, from my point of view, I don't see it's been so very hard for you at all. You're more than willing to let events take their course." He nodded towards Emma. "No matter who might get hurt."

Uninterested in Gabby's reply—not that they got one—

and still unable to let go of what she'd done to Donna, Emma turned to Abigail. "Where have you been living? Have you been in Flammark all this time?"

*Emmmah…*

Emma started. She shivered as she heard the familiar tone in her head, appalled that in the middle of all this, memories of his voice chose this moment to come and haunt her. Her pendant was buried deep under her jacket and scarf, so she fingered the carvings around the Blackstone casket instead, so very, very glad she brought it.

Abigail's eyes darted towards the window for a second, before answering. "They put me under protection, and I've been living in Gabby's cottage ever since."

"What? All this time and you've been living practically next door?"

"And a right small place it is too, isn't it, Gab?" Abigail remonstrated. "Bored out of my skull, I've been, I can tell you."

Gabby chuckled. "That day I came round with the flowers, Emma, and you told me you'd seen a woman with a long skirt and black overcoat, I thought Abby had done a runner. I had to go back and check."

"Frightened me to death when she came back," said Abigail. "Asked if I'd broken curfew to play silly buggers down the church. Hadn't, of course. Don't know what all that was about."

"So, what had I really seen?" asked Emma.

"You can't stay close to someone like me and not be touched by some of our … abilities. Abby has … sensitivities. It seems we may have amplified them. She must have made some kind of psychic connection with you." Gabby shrugged, with her unique calm. "It was a sign of your importance. When you as well as Josie were treated to the manifestation in the church, that clinched it."

"You keep on saying 'we,'" said Will. "Where is he? Where's Michael?"

"Where I left him, on Seely Tor. Like I told you, it's where we can see you all best."

"Except he—my ex—has brought down the fog, hasn't he?" said Emma.

"Yes."

"Well, that shouldn't make much difference to you," huffed Will. "Can't you people 'see' everything?"

Gabby sighed. "You've been watching too many films, William. And this is no ordinary fog. You must know that."

Out of the blue, Donna piped up. "It's really thick. It'll take Tony an age to get to Inspector Holbrooke's."

"Ah, yes," said Gabby. "I'm not sure what exactly happened there, but we believe things went very badly for him and poor Edna."

"What do you mean?" asked Donna. The smile had left her face. It had taken on a sort of puzzlement as if she was back in the game but not quite fathoming out the rules.

"I'm sure the inspector will tell you the details, dear, he's no doubt on his way." To the others, Gabby continued, "Edna's mother used to work under George Blaxton at the old hall, before the fire." Gabby shook her head in grim reminiscence. "Literally. When she fell in the family way her parents tried to cover it up. Terrible business, and Edna's never been quite right in the head."

*Emmmah, you're not listening to me.*

A crushing sensation gripped Emma's stomach. What the hell? She froze, grinding her fingers against the box in her pocket, listening intently. Not an echo of the past, not a bloody echo at all! Amazing what denial can do. Somehow, he'd entered her head, *in the present moment*. On high alert, finally getting it, she took shallow breaths, on the one hand trying to focus on what Gabby had to say, on the other, waiting; silently waiting for the terrible disembodied voice to whisper in her ear again.

She felt Abigail's eyes on her and realised that, somehow, she'd heard it too; one of her 'sensitivities?'

Emma struggled to get the words out of her dry mouth. "He's close, isn't he?"

Nodding, Abigail moved to the triptych window and without possibly being able to see anything, stared into the grim darkness, towards the cottage. "He's in Clearview, Gab."

Gabby stood up. "It's time."

"Hang on," said Donna. "You can't … *you can't* be contemplating going there on your own? I don't know why I'm here or what I missed—did you slip me a bloody mickey?" Donna was on her feet fuming, glaring at Gabby, confusion written all over her face. Screwing up her eyes in an obvious attempt to garner some coherence, she said, "I'm sure Tony's got hold of Westen by now. We're staying here … Why are we here? Why—"

"It's all right, Donna," Gabby said briskly. "We know what we're doing." She turned to the others. "Everything is aligned now. We have got to put this thing to rest once and for all. Flammark has had enough."

"What the fuck are you talking about?" exclaimed Donna. "What do you mean *aligned*?"

Will stood up too. With surprising forcefulness, he said, "Donna, we're really sorry you've been caught up in all this. We'll try and explain later but for now we have to concentrate on what to do next, and for some of us, waiting here is not an option."

Donna ran to the back of the church aiming for the door. But Will, sensing her intention, was quicker. He overtook her and got stopped her from running the bolt.

She narrowed her eyes at him, clearly trying to work out

her options. Will, holding her gaze, did not back down until she looked away.

"I'm sorry, Donna, leaving is not an option just yet. Trust me."

"Trust you lot? Fucking never!" Fuming, frustrated, she broke the stand-off and strode back to the others but kept apart and leant against a wall, still eyeing the door.

Will followed. Half-looking towards the thwarted detective—keeping tabs—he turned the rest of his attention to Gabby. "It's all very well me saying all that to Donna, but we don't have the semblance of a plan, do we? And if we did, you wouldn't be part of it, would you?"

"Correct," replied Gabby. "We're going to need all our energy to stop the curse leaving the village. If the worst happens, that is."

Will's turn to be frustrated. "You people. You think nothing of putting us in harm's way, do you?"

"Look what happened last time we interfered; at what Emma had to go through before she came here. Had we let the curse have its way the first time," Gabby threw an expression of compassionate regret at Abigail, "it might have died a natural death instead of finding a new host. We have to make sure it never finds another."

"I still don't see how?" Emma's brow furrowed as she racked her brains. "How can we possibly know what to do?"

"I can't tell you because we don't know. What we can say, is that everything, *everything* that's happened in the past few months, points to you. We're trusting you to put this together for us. We're sure you have everything you need." She nodded at Emma's pocket. "That box you're fingering, for example. No one has ever opened it, yet we know it opens. When the time comes, we're confident you'll know what to do. You've used one before that looks just like it, to lock away those memories."

"Yes, but that wasn't real. Just a coping mechanism for my mind to—"

"Metaphor is a powerful thing, Emma, and it took incredible resolve to use it. A very, very clever thing indeed. It can't be a coincidence the box in your pocket matches the box in your head. If you can lock him away once, you can do it again, but for real this time. And forever. That's where you have to trust us. We're sure we're right."

*Emmmah, I'm waiting for you.*

Abby turned from the window. Emma put her hands over her ears to blot him out. But he was inside her, grating her nerves, penetrating her senses. Gabby could go to hell. That voice—his voice—was all that mattered. Terror gripped her. Whatever he'd put her through before, could only be a fraction of what he intended to do next.

She should run.

*Emmmah, I have your doctor.*

"No!" On her knees, Emma keened, looking about wildly, as if the voice would embody itself somewhere in the church. As her outburst reverberated, the others gaped. Abby ran over and knelt down, put an arm around her. "Gab!" she cried, "He's got Doc Mason."

Gabby's face suddenly drained. She put her fingers on the bridge of her nose, bowing her head in concentration. Her expression darkened, as whatever mental power she had just drawn upon, confirmed that Abigail spoke true. He had her friend.

Then Gabby emitted a long, ear-splitting wail.

When it was over, the atmosphere suddenly changed. Struggling for breath, Emma put her hand to her throat. It felt as if the air was being sucked out of the church. She swallowed hard against the crushing sensation in her ears. They were about to implode! Gabby's distress filled the room, crowded them out, made them moan and cower, their hands raised to protect themselves against the storm of primitive energy.

Emma could see Will attempting to reach her, clawing at the backs of the chairs hand over hand as if trying to push through an invisible hurricane, trying to breathe and keep upright as he moved. Donna lay curled on the floor, her mouth opening and closing like a beached fish. Abigail stood flat against the window, static blasting strands of her black hair wildly into the glass. Her large eyes looked up and up and up, filled with awe, glittering with excitement.

Emma followed her gaze. The massive figure of Not-Gabby towered above them, her friendly, chubby face transformed into something harder, chiselled: asexual. Her mouth, once a home for friendly smiles, stretched into a cavernous hollow, forcing Emma to squeeze her head between her hands, protecting her ears against the next scream.

Instead she heard a simple shout.

"GABRIEL!"

At the sound of this new voice, the air rushed back. Donna, gulping, sat up. Will snatched away his dog-collar and unbuttoned the top of his shirt. Abigail remained standing, her chest heaving, eyes still wide and dancing bright.

Gabby had come back to them. No longer terrible and awesome, she stood small, shamefaced and stricken, her head bowed before another presence that had come upon them, despite the bolt on the locked oaken door.

Michael.

Were those tears in Gabby's eyes as she turned to him? "It's got Robbie. How could we not have known?"

As if carrying the weight of the world, Michael, grave and stony-faced, spoke again. "Do not say you were not warned. Did I not tell you to keep your distance from these people?"

Turning age-old eyes upon them, he continued, "You must

forgive her. Aeons of time have not been able to quell her passion for humans."

He moved to the back of the church.

"We cannot put this off any longer. It is time to go, time to play your part. Once you leave, we will isolate the village so that if you fail, the evil cannot escape."

"If *we* fail? Hang on," said Will. "Are you just going to abandon us? Have we to work everything out completely by ourselves?"

"Yes," said Michael with devastating dispassion. "If you fail to stop the evil, we will need all our energy to contain it. But …" he turned to Emma, "you *can* do this. You have the means."

Emma stared at him aghast, feeling the blood drain away from her face. Jesus, they really were going to do this. But something in Michael's stony eyes stirred her. Reassurance? No, that wasn't it. *Conviction.* He really believed she would prevail.

Hardly able to drag her eyes away from the angel, Emma cried out at Will. "He's right. We've run out of time and I think Robbie's been harmed. It's me he wants. We have to go. Now!"

"You can't be seri—" said Donna

She fell silent as Michael turned ancient his eyes upon her. "The inspector is on his way. You need to stay here and prepare your report. Do you understand?"

Donna nodded, as if taking instruction from a superior—which, in a way, she was. Full of purpose, taking a pen and notebook out of a pocket, the young detective sat down and started to write.

Emma, turning to leave with Will, discovered Abigail next to them. To Gabby she said, "Is Abby coming with us? I thought you wanted to protect her?"

Gabby smiled at both women as she said, "Always. But

you complement each other, which doubles your power. Two daughters in the same Blackstone cycle. It's unprecedented."

"I've been wanting payback over Dad for two years," Abigail said. "You'll have to tie me down to stop me coming with you."

The three walked towards the door and Will pulled back the bolt, lifted the heavy latch and opened it. Foetid vapour poured in like vomit.

Shrouded in mist and fear, they paused on the threshold.

"You sure about this?" asked Will.

"It's what I'm here for," Emma said. "Apparently."

Then the three of them, scarves lifted to their faces, left the church and entered the fog.

## 🦋 35 🦋

## A MAN POSSESSED

Walking into the unnatural murk, though flanked by her friends, Emma had never felt so alone; as if she had been placed into some foul, sensory-deprivation tank, filled with a suffocating, earthy miasma that reeked like the grave.

Her teeth chattered as tendrils of icy fog penetrated her coat and threatened to invade the soft skin beneath. Caught in their stinking grasp, they propelled her onwards.

"Can you feel it?" Emma said.

"Yes," Will replied, his voice muffled beneath his woollen scarf. "It's pushing us forward."

"I don't like it, Emma," said Abigail. "It's like it wants to be inside me."

"Try not to think about it. Concentrate on where we're going. Push it out."

"You sound like you're speaking from experience."

"I am," came Emma's grim reply.

They walked in silence for about twenty yards before Emma spoke again. "We still don't have a plan."

"No we don't," agreed Will. "Maybe that's a good thing. If

we don't know what we're doing, then he—it—won't know either."

"That's a load of bloody rubbish and you know it," said Emma.

Too soon, they were standing at the open gate to the cottage. To their utter surprise, at the fence-line, the fog lifted. With a questioning jerk of his head, Will took two steps back. Black mist immediately encompassed him, disappearing him from sight.

He returned to stand next to them. "He's well and truly isolated us, hasn't he?"

The cottage blazed with electricity, every light and lamp pressed into service to animate and excite the building, as if it couldn't wait for them to go inside. Random rays, escaping through the blinds in both front rooms, illuminated the path before them, leading their gaze to the torn and straggled remnants of blue and white crime-scene tape, which garlanded the front door. Without thinking, they reached out and held each other's hands.

Like children in the dark.

"I hope Robbie's all right," Emma said.

"I'm sure he is," Will replied. "It's not Robbie he wants. It's you. Jesus, Em, I can't believe I'm saying this!"

Emma thought hard about what Michael had said. *You have the means.*

She said, "I've got an idea."

"Thank God for that!" said Will.

"We need to find out if there's anything left."

"Left?" asked Abigail. "What do you mean?"

"Something Gabby said. If the curse possessed him, it could only have been a subtle influence at first; it wouldn't have taken him over completely. If it had, I'd never have fallen for him so I think its influence was gradual. I may be kidding myself, but I have to believe there was love there at one time so if there's anything left of the man I first met, I have to find it. Maybe I can get him to fight it from the inside."

"And while you're at it," Will joined in, "if you can keep him distracted, maybe we can find a way to make sure Robbie's okay and get him out."

Emma nodded and squeezed their hands. Will and Abigail squeezed back. If nothing else, it was a start.

"Will, I want you to promise me something," breathed Emma. "Let me do the talking and keep away from him. Remember Sebastian Gerard and the others. If you interfere, it'll—" Emma swallowed away the words 'kill you'. If she spoke them out loud, they may happen.

"It means all of us great harm, Em."

They broke their clasp as the front door cracked on its broken hinges and opened, seemingly of its own volition. Emma's stomach heaved and then settled. The thought of seeing him again terrified her, and her hands shook now they weren't holding someone else's.

Together they walked up the path. The door, still slowly opening, revealed her light-blasted living room in increments. She craned her neck, dreading—yet needing—to see him again, not from any feeling of desire—God no—but rather, from a kind of perverse curiosity at what the curse had done to him. Did he even look the same?

As they moved inexorably forward, she felt the weight of her friends' presence. At least she wouldn't be facing him alone.

They crossed the threshold and were in. The broken door slammed tight shut behind them as they entered.

Into chaos.

Defiled, lay her beautiful living-room sanctuary. Randomly displaced furniture sat amidst a floor crowded with trash. Books and ornaments, thrust from their shelves, lay torn and broken. Ripped cushions spewed out their stuffing on the sofa, her lovely mis-matched chair thrown on its side next to it. Surrounded by a litter of empty water bottles, food detritus and other rubbish, there he stood.

Him.

Yet not him.

Emma said nothing. Let no expression manifest itself. She did not want him to witness any visible evidence of her horror, even though there must be, since she sensed all blood had drained from her face.

She'd expected to see blonde, boyish good looks; had anticipated the acid glare of cold blue eyes, and his speciality: the cruel half-smile, which signalled the start of a twisted game. Emma swallowed down nausea, fought the urge to retch, for this was, and was not, the man she knew. All his meticulous refinement stripped away, he could not have looked more monstrous.

Naked to the waist. Multiple cuts and slashes covered his emaciated torso so densely she could see little virgin flesh. Glistening with sweat, it gleamed and shimmered in the roaring firelight.

Though not quite as brightly as the scalpel in his hand.

Gripes of pain squeezed her stomach. Still yet she held her bile. Fighting the impulse to be sick, she found enough saliva to swallow away the acrid bitterness rising in the back of her throat and forced herself to stare unblinking at a face distorted with possession and pain.

The flesh wounds, presumably self-inflicted, had obliterated every inch of his former charm. One eye seeped pus, the other remained intact. It fixed on them—on her—with a lascivious malevolence so intense she knew it could—and eventually would—impel her to do whatever it wanted.

His lips curled as they formed a rictus grin, and spit drooled down his chin. Then he moved, proudly lifting up his arms, waving them around the room as if to show off some act of good housekeeping.

He swayed. Humming something familiar, he puffed out his pathetically skeletal chest in a grim gesture of triumph.

He had completely lost his mind.

But she had to find it.

Despite the bitterness returning in her throat, the familiar thrumming in her ears—dry-mouth—she fought for equilibrium, finding calm by fingering the box in her pocket. She had to be able to talk; needed to sound in control.

"Hello, Ben."

The rictus wavered, just for an instant.

The voice that came forth bore no resemblance to anything she recognised. It must have hurt, for his vocal chords sounded scratched beyond endurance. A trail of blood started from the corner of his mouth, drying in the fire's raging heat, as out rasped:

*"Emmmah …"*

The pool of terror was great inside her and it swelled as he hissed her name. But desperate moans coming from the next room quelled it long enough for her to remember their plan. She sensed the others edge towards her study door.

"It's good to see you, Ben. I'm glad you found me."

*"Emmmah …. It's good to see you. Finally."*

"I'd hoped we could talk. I'm sorry I left the way I did. It was … cruel."

The skin round his lips curled and a mirthless cackle came out.

*"Cruel. CRUEL! You do not know the meaning of the word. But we will teach you."*

We! Good. Plural meant separate.

Still she made no visible movement, her fingers continuing their frantic trace of the casket's surface, keeping her calm, helping her think.

"Ben," she said, speaking louder as if to reach more deeply into him. "Do you remember the night we first met?"

The eye flickered, the rictus faltered; her friends took a sideways step.

"Remember going home together? How we held hands while I walked barefoot?"

*"Shut up, bitch! We know what you're trying to do."*

Emma paused, but not before she'd seen some inward perturbation begin within him. For a moment, the eye lost its intensity as mini convulsions pulsed within his torso.

Will and Abigail moved another step nearer to the study door.

"Do you remember, Ben? The moonlight, talking for hours?"

She followed the upwards line of fleshy waves and could have wept with tragic relief at hearing the scratchy remnants of Ben's authentic voice. "Emma ... Emma ... "

The creature jabbed the scalpel into his ear and twisted. Revolted, calling out, she stepped back, barely able to comprehend the abomination of blood gushing down his neck. She baulked at the quivering reaction deep in his midriff and worse, lower down, at the obvious arousal the blade had caused.

Pain. The creature was using it to control the man inside. A distillation of the sadism that had subjugated Blackstone women for centuries. Had Ben truly understood his actions had not been his own? Had he ever fought against them? A familiar rage surged up. If they survived this, she would ask him.

Slowly, the rictus smile returned wider than ever. With a wet squelch, the creature yanked the scalpel from his ear and the torso convulsed again, before all movement stopped and the eye closed for the few seconds it took for it to savour the second wave of pain.

Moans from the other room came louder now. Abigail and Will were almost at the door when, having heard them too, the creature opened his eye and jerked his head towards them, turning up the corners of his mouth.

Tapping a temple, he hissed, *"You can't get to him. I have the key. In here."*

He leered at them and caught sight of Abby. *"Ahhhh. Ab-i-gail."* Licking his lips, he said, *"I missed you the first time, when I was in your father. Now you'll have to wait."*

Will took a step forward then stopped dead, unable to move, rapt in the gaze of the eye. *"And the priest. So glad you brought the priest. I haven't played with one of those for a very long time."*

Moaning became wailing.

Shaking his head in mock sympathy, the creature wheezed, *"He's in a bad way, a very bad way. When he saw me, he felt cut to the bone."*

"Give him to us, you bastard," Abigail cried, fists to her side. "He's done you no harm."

His laugh came as little more than catches in the back of his throat.

*"What do I get in exchange?"*

He began to dance and sway, his eyes back on Emma.

*"THE WIFE IS IN THE PARLOUR, TAKING OFF HER CLOTHES, READY FOR A BLACKSTONE MAN TO PECK OFF HER NOSE."*

Jesus, what was this shit? Suppressing the urge to panic, Emma groped for words and found, "But you're not a proper Blackstone, now, are you?"

It stopped. It rasped, *"That doesn't matter. I'm free of them."*

"Then why are we here? Why couldn't you do your thing back home, where Ben and I lived?"

The swaying stopped.

"You needed to bring us to Flammark—didn't he, Ben?—

because this is your family seat, where you belong. Like it or not, it's where all your power lies. You're doomed to stay."

*"I can go wherever I like. I've proved that now."*

"Have you?" Emma persisted, driving the logic home, hoping Ben could hear. "Does it feel right, possessing a body not of our line?"

*"Enough! Enough talking. It's time I taught you the lesson I should have made him give you long ago."*

He started humming that tune again. Over anything else thus far, this creeped her out the most. With the bloody scalpel still in one hand, he unzipped and freed his cock with the other.

And swaggered.

This she had seen before and it held no fascination. Instead she stared at his new weapon, the blade, because it made Emma remember something. It offered a chink of light, a way to defeat him.

But how to go about it?

Stealing a glance backwards, amid the insane warbling, she mouthed 'distract him.'

Abigail nodded. Took a step forward. Undoing the top button of her frock, she took another step. Will cried, "No! Abby, don't!"

But she held her arm out behind her, palm down, signalling him to stop.

The creature took his eye off Emma and licked again his sore, cracked lips, as Abigail sashayed towards him. The hand of her outstretched arm now signalled Will to get to Robbie's door, as she popped another button.

The eye ogled and the rictus gleamed, and a grating, obscene, ravenous groan rose from deep within the creature's throat as he leered at the girl.

With the creature enthralled, his eye elsewhere, Will

found he could move again. He reached the door to Emma's study and slowly turned the handle.

The peeling lips parted, and drool dripped as the cock rose, fit to burst.

Will slipped out of the room.

Abigail had a problem. Having come to a stop no more than two yards from the creature, she'd started to tremble, her teasing hubris all played out. She looked uncertainly at Emma as the moment of no return arrived. The cock-tease of all cock-teases could only end in one way: she'd have to touch the fucker.

Not on Emma's watch. While Abigail still held the creature's fascination, Emma tore away and sprinted into the study. It took all her self-discipline to ignore the sight of Will kneeling over Robbie's prone figure on the Chesterfield, frantically scanning the room for something else.

His medical bag.

She heard a loud smack and a wail from the living room. She hadn't expected that and prayed the creature hadn't hurt Abby too much, but she had to press on. Emma got to the desk, grabbed the bag and flew into the kitchen with it. But he was too quick for her. She could smell the stench of his rancid breath as his torn fingers swung her round. Will, leaving Robbie's side, ran up behind him and threw an arm around the monster's neck and by some miracle managed to yank him off her.

Emma barely had any time. Will would soon be overpowered. If she didn't get what she was looking for then it would be game over. Desperate, she scrabbled through the doctor's old leather bag and fumbled past his scalpel set—one missing —looking for what she knew he always carried with him. Like at Josie's.

She'd got to them just as the struggle behind her ended in a harrowing cry from Will.

Emma whirled round, the objects she'd found held fast behind her back. Will had been cut. He lay on the floor, a pool of blood gathering under his shoulder. She wanted to call out, to ask him if he was okay, but she'd run out of time. The monster, blade in hand dripping with Will's blood, rose from his prostrate figure and lunged towards her, his foul, inflamed, tumescent penis leading the way. Giving it not one jot of thought, she kicked the thing with all the rage and revulsion and pent-up fury she'd been nursing for a year.

Enjoy that, you motherfucker.

She knew he would and banked on his need to savour the agony of her kick, praying there'd be enough time to pierce the tiny tranquilizer bottle with the syringe. If she could kill the pain, he would lose his control over Ben and ...

Too soon. Too soon. He'd made his recovery and swayed towards her. She couldn't tell how much of the liquid she'd drawn, or whether it would be anywhere near enough to down a man possessed.

With a roar that echoed and grated around the kitchen, the creature flung the scalpel away and went for her, pinned her arms by her side as his stinking mouth panted out its foul air. As she lifted her face away, she could see Abigail rush through the door, one eye swollen and partially closed, the other scanning wildly, fixing upon a cast iron wok. Holding the very end of its wooden handle with both hands, she managed to lift the thing high above her head, leaping forward to crash it down onto his.

Nothing.

He didn't fall, he didn't react—praise the Lord, he didn't sing. But he did let go of Emma and stared at her with his eye...

... which wavered, and looked down, at the fragile syringe she'd stuck firmly between his shrunken pecs.

Like a rabid dog, he hung and swung and salivated. He

didn't react as Emma sidestepped and ran around him to join Abby and get back to Will. Her friend had managed to sit up, but looked pale and shocked as he nursed his bleeding shoulder.

Robbie lay unconscious and silent.

"Will!" screamed Emma, "Can you get up?"

"I'll be okay. He got me with the damned scalpel. Hurts like bloody hell."

"Will you be able to help Abigail get Robbie out?"

He winced. "I can try. What about you?"

"I have to stay. It's not over yet."

"But—"

"There's no time to argue. Get out."

"He'll have to manage Robbie on his own," said Abby. "I'm staying."

Will looked from one woman to the other. "I can't leave you two alone with that monster. But I can't leave Robbie, either." He winced. The pain must have been excruciating. "He looks bad, really bad."

"Will," Emma said, "Go." She turned to Abby. "You should leave with him. I want you to leave with him."

"You remember what Gabby told us?" said Abigail. "Two daughters? You need me, Emma. We're getting somewhere, but it's not over yet. Not by a long chalk."

Hastily, they huddled around Robbie. He'd regained some consciousness and was making deep-throated, agonised moans of pain as he tried to lift his hands to his stomach. They quickly opened his shirt and saw the flesh beneath had been scored with deep gashes. He'd lost a lot of blood. They had to get him out now. He had no time for them to waste.

Emma looked at Will's shoulder and almost sobbed in frustration, "You won't be able to carry him. You're much too injured."

Will admitted defeat. "I know. I can barely lift my arm."

"It's all right," said Abigail. "Gabby and Michael will help. We just need to get the men out of the house. They'll sort it from there."

Emma grabbed Robbie under his arms. Abby took his legs. Between them, the two women heaved him off the Chesterfield and grappled with his dead-weight. Scarce, fresh blood seeped out from his clotting wounds. Emma shouted, "Come on!"

As they half-dragged, half-hauled him out, Emma bit back her panic, hearing more groans, loud and hideous, coming from the kitchen.

"We're out of time, Abby. We've got to move faster!"

Will wrenched open the front door with the hand of his good arm and tried to help but got in the way. "Leave us to it, Will. Go and get the throw. You know the one I mean. It'll be near the sofa."

The women heaved and grunted as they persevered with Robbie, out of the cottage and down the path until, finally succumbing to his weight, they dropped him as gently as they could. Not gently enough. The pain had pierced him into full consciousness and he shouted as he hugged his stomach.

"He'll be all right. Me too," said Will, staggering down the path with the throw, handing it to Abigail. "Gabby'll know what's happened. She won't let Robbie die."

Sounds of smashing furniture came from the house and Emma knew she had to go back. Now. But, by God, was she torn. Relief almost overwhelmed her as the mist parted and a corridor of clear darkness appeared. Will had been right, the men were going to be okay.

She had no time to linger to see who would appear from the mist. The groans from inside were amplifying into roars. Now or never, she and Abby had to go back.

To finish the job.

## 36

# TRICK OF THE BOX

The two women ran back into the cottage. Shivering with shock, cold and exertion, they pressed their backs to either side of the study's kitchen door, chests heaving.

Tentatively, Emma peered round.

At some stage, the creature must have fallen for he was in the process of clambering up, his back towards her. All Emma's instincts told her to run and get away from this place, but they had come too far. Though all her fear and dread crawled back, she had to finish him.

Emma signalled Abigail to stay put while she entered the kitchen alone. Fragments of smashed chairs littered the floor, and wooden splinters cracked underfoot as she stepped onto the terracotta tiles. He swung round to face her. His lips curled in suppressed fury and he grabbed at the syringe, still within his breast. He yanked it out and threw it at her. Missing by an inch, it clattered to the ground.

Never taking his eye off her, he moved over to the sink and plastered his lips round the tap as he turned on the water. She watched as he guzzled, sucking in his cheeks with great long pulls to quench his desperate thirst.

The tranquiliser had worked, and they'd got Robbie out. But she was out of ideas.

Too soon he finished drinking. Wiping the back of his hand across his cracked and bloody lips he rasped, *"You've decided to stay. Excellent choice."*

He made a sudden move away from the sink and before she knew it, just like the bad old days, he grabbed her hair, twisted it in his fist. He pulled her by it through the other door into the living room. Emma held onto his bony hand, in a pathetic attempt to mitigate the pain in her scalp, desperately pedalling the carpet with her feet.

Useless.

He threw her on the floor in front of the fire. Her forehead met the bricked hearth with a crack, and she felt numb and sick. Vaguely she heard Abby's shout as she'd followed them in from the kitchen.

"You bloody bastard," she said, to the sound of his screechy laughter. She ran to Emma and gently pulled her into a seated position. "Are you okay, Em?"

Emma nodded, placing her fingers on her head, tracing the start of a very large lump.

Then he stretched out his arm to an alcove shelf and picked up something neither of them had noticed before.

A tray of kitchen knives, and two sets of handcuffs.

He put the tray down on the coffee table and picked up a set of restraints. Striding over to Abigail, the monster kicked her in the stomach. As she doubled over, he snapped a handcuff over her wrist. She tried her best to fight and kick but to no avail. A few moments later, both hands were cuffed behind her back and he was holding her from behind.

Emma, still numb, screamed as she saw the creature put his hand inside Abby's dress and cup and pinch the breasts within. "Get away from her! Leave her alone! Keep your fingers to yourself."

Expressions of revulsion and disgust flooded the young woman's face, a vein in her neck pulsing as she craned with all her might away from him.

He pressed himself into Abby, then pressed again, an arm around her neck. A narrow man undulating against a small, curvy woman. This was the exhibition she and Josie had been treated to in the church, in the shadows. Not a flashback at all. A foretelling.

After more dry thrusts, he threw the girl on the sofa. *"Later,"* he said. *"I have a better woman to do."*

He tore off the remnants of his clothes and strutted naked in front of Emma.

Her heart and head thumped. "Ben," she managed, "Ben! Don't let him do this. Please!" Emma could see the tumult inside the creature's gut build again, stronger this time. He picked up one of the knives and found more space in his flesh with which to subdue the man inside. She waited for the torpor to come, like the drugged-fuelled surrender only junkies can embrace.

But nothing happened.

He applied the knife again.

Nothing.

The drug had not worn off.

Looking completely nonplussed, the creature took the blade a third time. Still nothing. The convulsions in his torso intensified. The ravaged, naked figure quivered before her with such intensity it became little more than a blur. Some sort of battle raged in him; a supreme struggle taking place between the spirit of the man and the spirit that possessed him.

Ben was taking his shot.

What then? She couldn't let the evil escape. If Ben

succeeded in ejecting it, Gabby and Michael were right. Where would it go, who would it infect next? Her fingers once more tracing the carved line of the on the box in her pocket, Emma racked her brain for what to do. She looked at Abigail. Despite obvious pain, the girl had managed to spit out the cushion stuffing she'd been thrown onto and heave herself up. But she could offer no help. She was pressing the corners of her mouth down and shaking her head in a haven't-a-clue expression.

Then something.

Emma stopped fiddling with the box. She forced her fingers to slow down and trace its carvings more methodically, back and forth, back and forth, until her brain finally clinched what her physical memory was telling it.

In a flash she knew what to do. She'd found the trick of the box.

She peered at the warring figure by the fire. Like the watcher of a wrestling match, she screamed, "Come on, Ben!" as the quivering and bending and shaking continued. On it went as Emma took out the stone casket whilst shouting desperate encouragements to the man she'd grown to hate.

She grabbed her blackbird pendant and snatched it off her neck. Throwing Abby a triumphant look, she placed the pendant inside the carving at the top of the box. The setting fitted it perfectly and she heard a click and a little whirr. Triumphantly, she balanced it on the palm of her hand with not a clue about what magic it might contain. She just knew it would work.

It didn't.

"What the … ? I-I don't understand." Emma almost burst with the failure of it. Incredulously she stared at the casket, still held aloft, willing the damned thing to open. Crushed with defeat, she tore her eyes away from the stubborn object and towards the creature. Sure enough, Ben's efforts were dwindling.

"Emma!" exclaimed Abby. "Look! Can't you see? On the side!"

Emma looked at the box again. There *was* something different about it! Suddenly she saw. A keyhole. The pendant had opened a keyhole. But where was the key?

Crying with frustration—what the hell else did she have to do?—she drew her eyes back to Ben's waning efforts as the last remaining chance to free him—and them—was slipping away.

"Emma!" Abby shouted again. "Round my neck!"

She was jutting out her chest, her eyes full of a strange agony. "It's the tiny one, next to the locket."

Amidst the plethora of chains and charms hung a miniature key, all by itself, glinting against Abby's throat. Silver.

Without ceremony, just as she'd done with her pendant, Emma reached over and tore the charm away from Abby's neck, shoved it in the keyhole.

It turned.

A mechanism slid into motion. Slowly the lid rose to reveal a model of a tiny blackbird, rotating on tiny claws and out of its little orange beak came the bell-like tinkle of a once beloved nursery rhyme: "*Sing a song of…*"

The creature froze.

Emma heard a sound coming from the kitchen but that wasn't what made him pause. He'd stopped to listen to the song of the bird. He cocked his crazed head, listening to it with his one good ear, as if enthralled, the fight forgotten. Ben took his chance as with one huge convulsion, something cycloned out of his body in a growling onrush of foetid air.

The force of the invisible parasite whirled around the room, again and again. Emma could feel it, could see it, as fire-smoke and dust-mites were sucked into an ever-compressing entity, affording it both form and petty substance. Before long, as a miniscule, wheeling ball, it hovered for an interminable moment above her, before breaking shape and disgorging itself into the tiny black stone box.

Where else could it possibly belong?

Emma snapped shut the casket and turned the key. The mechanism slickly clicked again and both her pendant and the silver key popped out, the hole from whence it came, vanished.

In the silence that followed, she held it, her mouth open, palm outstretched, staring in utter disbelief. She could barely take the measure of what had just happened, nor properly grasp the impossible magnitude of the thing she held in her hand.

She put it back in her pocket. There were more pressing matters.

Naked and exposed, damaged and devastated by wound upon wound, Ben had collapsed. Though the rictus had gone, his face no longer distorted with possession, it was clear the terrible damage and disfigurement he sustained would be permanent. He stared around with one good eye, as if seeing the room for the first time, then gazed down at his violated nakedness, shaking his head in obvious disgust and disbelief.

Painstakingly he moved an arm and shrieked out in a pain no drug could diminish as he managed to reach his blood-soaked ear. Then he caught sight of Emma, herself trying to deal with the terrible pain coming from her cracked head. Agonised, using the arm of the sofa Abby sat on to drag himself up, Ben somehow managed to get onto his red and blistered feet. Though his emaciated legs could hardly support him, he stood and croaked, "Emma ... Emma."

"Sh...shush, Ben." Emma nearly went to him—should have gone to him—but she held back. She couldn't do it.

Only a minute ago—a year ago—he was a monstrous thing, wanting to do unspeakable things to her.

He tried a pathetic smile. Despite the extent of his horrendous injuries, she thought she could see the man behind them, the one she'd first fallen in love with, before the bad times. He started to move towards her, his anguished limping moving her to tears. "Emma, I am so, so—"

The sound of a single shot seared the air, and Ben collapsed onto her. He weighed almost nothing. Not knowing how or why he fell, torn between horror and terrible sadness, Emma held him and found she could not let go.

Until Westen put his gun in his pocket and threw him off her.

"Fucking piece of shit."

# 37

## THE END

Emma was glad Will had got his wish. There they all were, festive and replete, gathered around the Christmas table in the vicarage kitchen.

Robbie had wanted to make the dinner himself and have everyone over to his, but a slow recovery from two deep scalpel wounds—the one in his chest in particular—prevented him from doing anything more than directing operations in Will's kitchen. He'd been glad to get out of the hospital—doctors making the worst of patients—and had managed reasonably well at home. After the meal he insisted on making a toast. "To have given me the gift of your splendid company on this day and, between you all, saving my life." Not that he remembered much about it. The police went along with telling him there'd been a jealous madman on the loose, who had something to do with Emma, and that, being someone she was fond of, he'd been abducted and made to suffer at her expense.

Not a word of a lie.

Emma could not have been more thankful and relieved when he pulled through. Having this bear of a man next to her, on this day, pulling pathetically on a cracker, nearly broke her heart all over again.

Abigail sat opposite, looking … well, stunning. Her purple paper hat could have been made for her, had it not come out of another cracker. Given the scale of everyone's injuries, she'd done most of the heavy lifting in the kitchen. How she managed to persuade Josie and her grandparents to let her spend Christmas Day with her friends, Emma had no idea. She knew they still found it hard to forgive her for running away and not getting in touch with them. But they'd been prepared to accept that she'd never really got over the death of her father and needed to 'find herself' in a commune that had opened in Sandmarsh. She'd planted the idea that she'd fallen foul of one of the members—a boy. It proved to be a blessing in disguise since the black eye he'd given her had been the tipping point that brought her back home. Sam had wanted to go and 'sort the lad out,' but his granddaughter had told him the place had closed. Projects such as these never last for long.

Like Robbie, Will too had been poorly. A surgical sling still strapped his left arm to his body. The physio said it would be a long while before the ligament would heal, but it didn't stop him using the hand on his good arm to baste the turkey and turn Abigail's nut roast. He also helped her avoid the worst of Robbie's culinary diktats by pressing onto the good doctor shedloads of single malt.

Emma hadn't been sure she would be able to make it back in time for Christmas. She'd sustained a concussion but spent only a single night in hospital, resting up later in the vicarage. The past two weeks had been terrible. She'd arranged for Ben to be taken back to the city and became the lone attendee at his funeral in the chapel of a crematorium. Decorated in the impersonal style of seventies anodyne, the place nevertheless felt strangely appropriate, since she never knew who Ben really was. She'd raked through his immaculately organised filing system and couldn't find a single person to notify. There was a copy of a will, however, solicitor's letter attached, both confirming his parents had long ago passed away. She must have been the only person he had in the world.

So many emotions to reconcile. When she'd left Ben all those months ago, she'd wished him dead. That night at the cottage, seeing what evil had befallen him, Emma had genuinely wanted him to live, wanted him to … what? Repent? Possibly. But in her heart, she knew he was doomed. His wounds were too great, his body and mind too broken.

Had he ever loved her? Ever been *capable* of love? His final unfinished sentence came to her yet again, and she wondered for the millionth time what he'd been about to say. Some kind of apology, perhaps? She desperately wanted to think so. Despite the present company, she welled up, semi-pursed her lips and blew out a sigh. Her last sight of Ben would haunt her forever and her yearning to understand the truth of it would never go away.

Then there was Westen. She knew he had not killed Ben for mercy's sake, but Emma still wanted him to be sorry for killing him, for calling him shit. After he dragged Ben's body off her, she'd screamed at him, beat his chest as he took her in his arms and held her and held her and held her until she finally quieted and the blue lights flashed outside.

And this was why he too was present. Last in the party, and possibly the most incongruous. After Donna had got over the baffling influence of 'who-the-fuck-does-she-think-she-is' Gabby, she and Emma had become firm friends. It was Donna who had told her the detective would probably be spending Christmas alone.

And that she couldn't have.

After the meal they all withdrew to the library and sat

around the large open fire to mull over their tall tale. Not that the full extent of the dark force Emma had vanquished that night could be revealed to everyone.

"What I can't understand," said Will, "is how Inspector Holbrooke became involved. I know there was something to do with his wife."

"I can't tell you everything about what we discovered that day. 'You wouldn't want to hear it anyway," said Westen. "Suffice it to say, it hit us all very hard. Holly—Inspector Holbrooke—and his wife both suffered terribly. But following up, we found Mrs. Holbrooke had suffered from bi-polar disorder. Long-term, apparently. According to her psychiatrist, after finding her wandering down their lane, ranting about bastards and blackbirds, her husband felt it time to give up his badge and take her on a cruise."

"Aye, that'll do it," said Robbie. "Bi-polar, when it's bad, can be a curse."

"I remember someone mentioning that Edna Holbrooke had a connection with the old Blackstone family." said Will. "Rumours that she was George Blackstone's illegitimate daughter and that her mother had been a maid there."

Westen shrugged. "I don't know about that, but she was definitely unwell. She wrote the anonymous letters, you know. We found more half-written, addressed to various good citizens of Flammark. We think Holly had suppressed elements of the original investigation, having recognised the handwriting." Glancing at Will, he said, "We also think she was responsible for the desecration."

"Gawd," said Will. "I was sure that was a man. Just … the mechanics of it, you know."

"It's not that hard to work around. She'd have brought a bottle, probably."

The gallows humour managed to lift their mood. It was getting unseasonably sombre

"We still don't have a clue on why your ex descended on them, Emma," said Westen. "I don't suppose we'll ever know."

She shrugged. That's exactly the way she wanted it to stay.

"Time for a refill!" Will proffered more of the single malt, careful not to spill even a drop in the light of Robbie's eagle eye on it. Being effectively one-handed, he used a second trip to fill Abigail's glass with the elderflower cordial she'd brought.

"You've never been tempted to imbibe, I see," said Robbie.

"No. It's the devil's work," Abby replied, with a mock Scottish lilt, grinning. Then, tapping her finger to her temple she said, "It dulls the senses."

"Aye, you're not wrong," he replied with a grin, "that's why I like it."

Emma sat back, letting the warmth off both the fire and the company of friends envelop her. She had been undecided whether to stay in the village, but looking around now, on this Christmas Day, she finally made up her mind. She'd sell her family home. Josiah would understand. She couldn't go back and live with the awful memories, and anyway, there was nothing there for her anymore. Flammark was quite safe now. Safe enough for her to return—the sole survivor of the Blackstone family proper— knowing the curse to be gone forever. She liked to think Josiah would want her to come back to her roots; to where she truly belonged. There was a synergy to it, especially as she'd found a new family in her distant cousins, the Chaters.

And she had friends. Donna, Will—and Robbie, of course —and from the corner of her eye she glanced at Westen sitting next to her. He'd been looking at her too and held her gaze for a few seconds before awkwardly averting his eyes.

Her thoughts turned to Gabby and Michael. Absent, but in no way forgotten. They seemed to have disappeared from the face of the earth. After she and Will had been discharged from hospital, they had all met up and the two 'co-workers' had taken the box off Emma's hands. Michael said they knew of a place 'from whence the evil inside would never return,' and reassured Will that it would reside nowhere near the parish it had blighted for centuries. The friends had no real understanding of the magic within the little casket or why Abigail had been in possession of its key. But when Michael reminded them, in that austere and dispassionate way of his, that Abigail's father had been the village locksmith and it was therefore only natural that she should have been attracted to the little silver object at a Flammark flea market, the symmetry made them smile. Abby in particular, would always hold the key closest to her heart, in remembrance of the father who had made the ultimate sacrifice for her.

"Now for presents!" Will's voice shook Emma out of her reverie, and she put her glass down.

"But we exchanged ours earlier!" exclaimed Abigail. "When we first arrived."

"I know. But these came yesterday with specific instructions not to open them until we were all together. I think this is the right moment."

Westen said, "Well, there won't be one for me. Not that I'm bothered, you understand, just—"

"Don't you worry about that," said Will, palm up, head bowed. "Just enjoy the moment. And you never know, the Spirit of Christmas might have left even you something."

Westen rolled his eyes and grinned. Looked at Emma again. She had never seen him so relaxed, even though the perpetual stress-knot he wore still hovered between his eyes.

The huge tree glistened with fairy lights and tinsel. Underneath, rested a small pile of perfectly wrapped parcels.

Contrary to Westen's assessment of the situation, there seemed to be something for everyone, and each waited for the other to open theirs, so all could share the admiration and wonder.

Will went first. He picked up a small but heavy package and opened it to find an ancient copy of the Book of Common Prayer. The fly leaf contained a bookplate declaring it to be the property of one Sebastian Gerard. His predecessor had written the name in his own hand, in the same secretary script as the intercession that had first got them involved in the terrible Blackstone saga.

"Oh. My. God. This is wonderful. I'll be able to add it to my collection." He looked around at the others but knew only Emma would really understand.

Setting it aside, he rummaged under the tree and retrieved a parcel with Robbie's name on it.

The doctor teared up when he'd finished opening it. A model bus, just like the ones he used to ride on during those trips he took with Gabby as he struggled to cope with the death of Joanie, his wife. He smiled and frowned in equal measure. "I know who this is from! She's left us, you know. Gabby has family further north and has decided they need her more than we do. Maybe all these presents came from her?"

Abby beamed as Will passed her what looked like a square box, wrapped in 'tree-of-life' paper. She gently opened it and found within a beautifully mounted crystal ball. "Yes, of course they're from Gabby!" she exclaimed. "She knew I'd been after one of these for ages!" She held up the bluish-clear glass. "Ooh, it's proper quartz."

Emma's present did not fill her with similar joy. It was a replica of the carved black stone box with which she captured the spirit of the same name. Her first reaction was to throw it in the fire, but Will, obviously sensing her ambivalence, rested his good hand on her arm and gave it a little squeeze. "Open it. There's bound to be something inside."

She looked at him, then surveyed the box, hoping she wasn't going to have to invoke the power of bloody Greyskull to open it. She needn't have worried. To her great relief it opened easily and without the appearance of a singing bird. Inside lay a cross of St. Jude, which she immediately took out and clasped around her neck. It replaced Josiah's pendant. She'd tried to wear it again, when the dust had settled, but the trauma had been too great, and every time she felt it or caught sight of it in the mirror it reminded her of Ben.

Only one present remained. No one was left without, so it could only be meant for one person. Uncertain and uncharacteristically flustered, with some hesitation Westen took the tiny parcel from Will and unwrapped it for all to see. His eyes opened wide in disbelief, then, obviously astonished, he grinned as he picked up a rather fetching keyring, from which dangled …

… a fucking zebra.

## ACKNOWLEDGMENTS

My first thanks must go to my husband, Malcolm, steadfast and encouraging as always. To Beth for all her graphic expertise, and Lucy for pushing me (very hard) to dig deeper into the narrative.

Thanks also to Dan and Andrew who gave me invaluable input and saw me right through to the end. Good luck with your books!

Finally a grateful shout-out needs to go to Alexander Sinn, whose amazing photo became the inspiration and starting point for my book cover.

# DEAR READER ...

Thank you so much for reading "When Angels Fear." I do hope you enjoyed it as much as I loved writing it!

Ready for the next story in the Flammark Series?

ANIMUS is out now. Search Amazon (or click here for Book 2)

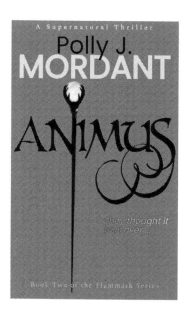

For Flammark gossip, giveaways and other stories - click here to sign up for my newsletter. (If you are reading the print version, you can sign up by visiting my Facebook page or my website: https://pjmordant.co.uk).

And if you're looking for more Flammark weirdness, I

have a Friends of Flammark Facebook group. Either search (or click here to join.)

Thank you again for reading. If you have a few minutes to share your thoughts with others by leaving a review, I'd be chuffed to bits! You can also follow me on any of the platforms below.

Happy reading!

facebook.com/pjmordant
twitter.com/pjmordant
instagram.com/pjmordant

Printed in Great Britain
by Amazon